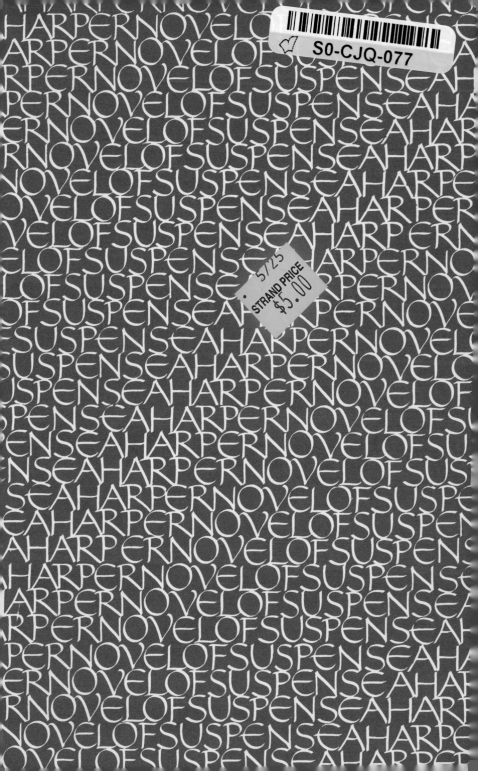

ANGLE OF ATTACK

A JOAN KAHN BOOK

BOOKS BY REX BURNS

Fiction

ANGLE OF ATTACK
SPEAK FOR THE DEAD
THE FARNSWORTH SCORE
THE ALVAREZ JOURNAL

Nonfiction

SUCCESS IN AMERICA: THE YEOMAN DREAM
    AND THE INDUSTRIAL REVOLUTION

Angle of ATTACK

by REX BURNS

1817

HARPER & ROW, PUBLISHERS
New York, Hagerstown,
San Francisco, London

A HARPER NOVEL OF SUSPENSE

FIRST EDITION

Designer: Eve Kirch

Copyeditor: Marjorie Horvitz

Library of Congress Cataloging in Publication Data

Burns, Rex.
  Angle of attack.
  "A Joan Kahn book."
  I. Title.
PZ4.B96835An 1979 [PS3552.U7325] 813'.5'4
ISBN 0-06-010523-2   79-1699

---

79 80 81 82 83 10 9 8 7 6 5 4 3 2 1

To
George Arthur Sweitzer

one

It came like a whiff of sewer gas on a cold night: "Do you remember that Marco Scorvelli thing? The guy that got aced nine months, maybe a year ago?"

Homicide Detective Gabriel Wager set his beer down and peered at Tony-O through the dim lights of the Frontier Bar and Grill. The lines across the old man's face always made it hard to tell whether he was ready to smile or ready to frown. "We never got a thing on that one," said Wager.

"Everybody in Denver knows that. But maybe I heard a little something."

Wager raised his empty glass and held up two fingers. Rosie, rushed by the Sunday-afternoon crowd, bustled past with a row of dirty dishes on her sweating arm and nodded an answer.

"You want to tell me, Tony?"

That was the way the testy old man liked it: first you asked him if he wanted to, then he always said "Yes," then you let him give it at his own speed. If you tried to push him, he'd tell you to go to hell.

"Yeah. But it ain't much."

Something where there was nothing was always much; Wager split the beer remaining in his bottle between their glasses. Marco Scorvelli had been found in his front yard by a milkman on his morning delivery. A shotgun blast hit him at the navel and angled upward to unzip his belly and spread his intestines over his new raw silk sports coat. The sawed-off shotgun, clean of prints, was left lying like a message squarely across the sidewalk; somehow Scorvelli lived long enough to crawl fifteen feet toward the front door before dying. Neither Scorvelli's widow nor the neighbors in the surrounding split-levels reported hearing a thing. Except for the carcass of a justly suspect member of a local crime family, there was nothing to build a case on.

Rosie came back with two bottles of Coors and Tony-O waited until the head on his refill settled back below the glass's rim before speaking.

"What I heard was the hit didn't come from outside. It was made to look that way—the shotgun on the sidewalk and all."

The shooting had taken place before Wager joined homicide, but the news of anything involving one of the Scorvellis went through every division of the police department faster than a list of new promotions. At the time, there was little doubt it was a gang killing; but oddly, nothing ever came after it—none of the muted, vicious squabbles over territory, none of the bloody advertisements of revenge or triumph. Marco Scorvelli had been killed for a reason, but that, like everything else in the case, remained hidden. "We figured that if it was local, it would have been followed by a little more action. We figured it was a revenge hit for something Scorvelli did in Vegas or Chicago," said Wager.

2

Tony-O shrugged. "I'm only telling you what I heard, Wager. If you heard something better, then you tell me."

Gabe let the old man have a minute or two to cool off, but Tony-O didn't continue. "Can I ask you where you got it?"

"Sure. You can ask." Tony-O's tone said he might or might not answer. He studied the long neck of his beer glass, rubbing a wrinkled thumb up and down its smooth curve and watching the strings of bubbles rise like points of light from the bottom. The old man had become the neighborhood *jefe* about the time Wager reached nine or ten years old, and his air of power and mystery used to awe Wager and the other kids who ran up and down streets and alleys that had since disappeared into freeway interchanges, industrial parks, and a new university campus. For a long time after he grew out of short pants, Wager had felt uncomfortable calling him Tony-O instead of Mr. Ojala. But that was the way the *jefe* wanted it, so that was the way it was—to adults he was Tony-O, to children he was Mr. Ojala, only because children should develop respect for their elders. If a family in the old neighborhood had trouble with city hall, they talked to Tony-O and he would call someone; if a son or brother or father was picked up by the police, Tony-O could tell the worried women what the charges and bail were—and, more importantly, how badly the accused was tangled in the mysteries of the legal web. When election time came around, Tony-O rode in the same convertible as the alderman; and whenever the mayor marched down Larimer Street, Tony-O was just one pace behind him all the way from Seventeenth to Ninth Street. If the election was going to be a close one, he even walked beside the mayor. For those who had the money, he could arrange purchases that the Anglos officially frowned on but unofficially sold—a little marijuana for the nerves, a safe corner to have a cockfight for some excitement at fiesta time. There were rumors that he could do other things, too, through connections from the old Prohibition days; and if a man wanted to lay some of his paycheck on the horses or the Lotería Nacional, Tony-O could fix him up for a small percentage. Wager remembered him best from the war, when, if the price was right, he was good for whatever the black market was handling; and if a family had a son or husband in the service, they'd find a few extra ration coupons in the mail at Easter or Natividad, free. Tony-O was the neighborhood *jefe,* and he looked after his people.

In the early 1950s, Tony-O was arrested for murder. But even with a change of city administration and a new look at all the people still voting from the cemetery, Tony-O had a few strings left to pull—and he used up the last ones to get the charge reduced to manslaughter. He came out of the penitentiary at Cañon City four years later, just as Pfc. Gabriel Wager came out of boot camp headed for Korea, and the only thing the ex-*jefe* had left was a tavern and its parking lot. Soon that, too, was gone like the whole Auraria neighborhood, because in those four years Tony-O's contacts dried up, and big money had come to buy and develop the twenty or so blocks that the new city planners labeled slums. After the forced sale of his property, and with social security, the old man got by. And people still talked to him who would not talk to Wager because he had turned cop.

Tony-O talked to Wager because he liked him, cop or not, and not just for the old days; he liked him because Wager had once looked out for his son, and that made Wager a lifelong friend. "Besides," the old man once told him with a dip of the wrinkled eyelid that drooped at the corner like a sad smile, "I had lots of cops for friends when I was *jefe.*"

The old man looked up from watching the strings of bubbles wind through his beer. "You finished butting in?"

Wager sighed. "I'm listening, Tony-O."

4

"What I heard was, his own brother was behind it—Dominick. That's why nothing blew up when Marco was killed. Everything went straight to Dominick and there wasn't no waves, not even a ripple."

"I heard that Dominick put out a big reward."

"What else could he do? Hell, he'd never have to pay it off, would he?" Tony-O took a long drink and pinched the moisture from the deep creases at his mouth's corners. "I also heard a name for you." He took another drink.

Talking with Tony-O was a lot like a slow checker game; every sentence was studied from all sides before it came out. Wager sipped and waited.

"Frank Covino."

"What's his connection?" asked Wager.

"I don't know. I just heard the name. Like I said, *no vale mucho.*"

When Wager reported for duty Monday morning, he began thumbing through the "Cases Current" drawer for Marco Scorvelli's file. His partner found him ears deep in the diagrams of the scene, the police reports from the morning of June 4, the autopsy reports of the following day, and the glossy 5″ × 7″ photographs of a figure whose nattiness was lost in the sprawl of death.

"Don't tell me it's slow enough for a little recreational reading?" said Maxwell T. Axton—inevitably called "Max the Ax," a nickname that pained him. ("I don't like hurting people. Civilians hear that name, and right away they start thinking police brutality. In my heart, I'm a pacifist; a cop's job is to prevent violence, not make it happen. So just call me Max. O.K., Gabe?") He stood six four and, in his mid thirties, was just beginning to struggle to stay as thin as a tree trunk. He was one of the few blue-eyed Anglos Wager had known whose gaze could seem deeply sad and concerned, and never more so than when he was quietly talking a murderer into confessing.

"Max, do you remember Marco Scorvelli? Whose case is it?"

"Sure—everybody remembers Marco. We all worked on that one. It was before you got here, when the cases weren't assigned to individuals but were carried over from shift to shift. I guess it's never been assigned to anybody. What the hell was there to assign?"

Wager told him.

"Frank Covino?" Max's fingernails scratched under his square chin. Wager had occasionally wondered if Axton's gentleness came from being big enough to worry about accidentally stepping on others. Just as his, Wager's, occasional mild abrasiveness came because he was short, and short cops were always called on to make up in deeds what they lacked in appearance. Max's large head wagged thoughtfully. "It doesn't ring a bell. Have you looked through the contact cards?"

"Not yet."

"Be back in a minute."

He was, broad hands empty. "Nothing under Frank Covino. There's a Gerald Edward Covino, currently on vacation in Cañon City, but no mention of a Frank, and no aliases."

Wager folded the yellow manila cover over the thick pile of papers and photographs. Maybe he could get Tony-O to tell him a little more, maybe not. Probably not. They'd just have to keep their ears open, ask around, talk to fellow detectives and street cops and see if the name brought some nods. As always, there was the easy way to get information, and then there was the usual way. He dropped the file back into the "Current" drawer, where all the unsolved cases sat waiting for the time when something might break. Some had been waiting there for years.

The Homicide Division was on duty all hours, every day. When, as now, there were no murders or no weapons fired, the shift was to patrol likely trouble spots around the city. The first tour every morning for the day shift, just after the 8 A.M. traffic cleared, was past the trashy clutter of Spanish-named bars that made up Little Juarez, and then through its neighboring Asian section, clustered at the front of the pale-tan tower of retirement apartments and fancy restaurants called Sakura Square. Inside the unmarked police sedan, the air was still stale with the breath of the preceding crews and of the hundreds of tours before that one; Wager rolled his window down halfway to let the cold air of early spring blow out the odor. In the glaring sunshine of a cloudless morning, and with the smog driven out by the westerlies of the last few days, even the tired brick walls along Larimer Street looked bright and warm and stood etched against the hard blue sky. It reminded Wager of one of those paintings his ex-wife had showed him: blank streets lined with aging buildings and vacant pavement, but full of a brittle light that made the colors solid and sharp. What was that painter's name? Hooper? Hopper? For some reason, his ex-wife had thought the paintings said something about him.

He swung the car around the sterile concrete of the Sakura Square tower and down across the bumpy railroad tracks toward Union Station, cruising slowly beneath the grimy viaducts and along the unused and weedy rear doorways of warehouses and office buildings whose windows were painted over and blank. It was an area undecided whether to live or not, and it was here, especially on Sunday and Monday mornings, that the day shift would find the dead winos.

"Is that one?" Max pointed at a pair of legs lying toes down in the tall grass beneath the rotting timbers of a loading dock. Wager turned through the crackle of splintered bottles to park, and they got out, deliberately, two men beginning another long day and a bit reluctant to have it start so soon and in such a way.

Even before they poked through the screen of weeds to peer beneath the shelf of weathered wood, they could smell the sour bile and feces from the figure.

"Watch your shoes."

"Yeah." Wager hauled at the grime-slick coat and rolled the man's dark, seamed face from the stringy mud of his own vomit. A bubble of saliva broke in a large gap between his rotting teeth and his eyelid lifted once to show the yellow of an eyeball.

"Dead?"

"No. Crawled under here to sleep it off."

"It's nice to see civic pride."

Wager used to be able to haul the drunks down to the station and lock them up for a day or two so they'd get a couple of good meals and a free delousing. Now a new city ordinance had given the winos their rights, and the cops were ordered to let them lie in their filth like the free citizens they were. He and Max went back to the cruiser, and Wager guided the car down one of the littered alleys that ran behind a row of weary flophouses, whose tilting, paintless back porches and rusted fire escapes held shapes that watched them in cautious silence. Near the alley's end, their radio popped: "Any homicide detective."

Wager answered, "X-85. Go ahead." "X" was the Detective Bureau designation; the 80 series meant the Homicide Division.

"Go to blue channel," said the dispatcher.

"Ten-four." He switched to the frequency that was secure from the police band scanners sitting in news rooms all over the city.

The dispatcher was waiting for his acknowledgment. "You

8

got a body in the 2700 block of Denargo Street. Officers on the scene; Code Two."

Code Two: siren and lights at officer's discretion. "We're on our way."

Wager didn't bother with running hot; traffic was light and the victim wouldn't be going anywhere. Denargo was one of the nearby streets close to the South Platte River, and he reached it beneath the bridges and viaducts over the river's rubbish-filled flood plain. The street occasionally lost its outline in loading aprons and the snarl of bumpy railroad tracks, but half a block ahead, they saw the blue-and-white unit marking the site. Two uniformed officers had separated a pair of witnesses and were taking notes when Wager and Axton pulled up.

"Jesus, it didn't take you guys long."

Wager recognized the black corporal talking to the older of the two civilians. "We were just around the corner. What do you have for us, John?"

"This here's Mr. Walker. He called in the report about ten minutes ago. We haven't really gotten started yet."

Wager nodded good morning to a lanky man whose hair was combed straight back in oily flat grooves above his ears. "Why don't you answer Officer Blainey's questions, Mr. Walker, while I take a look at it?"

"Sure. But listen, I got a load of perishables to move. How long's this gonna take?"

"It won't be too long, Mr. Walker."

"It's over there, Gabe. Between the buildings." Blainey's Bic pen bobbed at a narrow gap between the long windowless walls of the brick warehouses.

"Identification?"

"Don't know. We didn't move a thing. And Mr. Walker here says he and his buddy just took one look and called us. We ain't seen nobody else around."

"Well, I sure wasn't going to touch him. A guy with a hole like that in the top of his head . . ."

"You did the right thing, Mr. Walker." Wager motioned to Axton. He left off talking to the other officer, a young kid Wager didn't know, who frowned earnestly when he talked.

Careful where they put their feet in the pebbly soil, Wager and Axton stood at the alley between the chipped bricks of the close walls and stared into the narrow canyon which was about half as wide as a doorway. This body, too, lay toes down on the packed dirt and the sprouting clumps of grass between the walls. But unlike the drunk, there was no need to see if he was breathing; as Walker had said, a hole that size in his head left no doubt. The hard, blue-green glints of flies moved busily at the ragged edge of the slightly bloody hole with its eruption of gray brain. It was the kind of wound blown by a large-caliber dumdum or a shotgun. Wager keyed the GE radio pack on his belt and called for the lab people and the medical examiner.

"Looks like he's still got his wallet." Axton pointed to the bulge that had worn the rear pocket of the denim trousers pale in a square shape.

"See if you can reach it," said Wager. "My arms are too short."

Axton braced himself against the painted brick and stretched out to tug the wallet from the tight pocket. It was rubbed shiny and held the curve of the man's buttocks, and was cold to the touch.

"Money's here—twenty-eight bucks."

"Who is he?"

Axton flipped through small plastic windows that had two or three smiling pictures and various cards. In the front panel, he found the driver's license. Then he looked at Wager and blinked. "Frank Covino."

10

two

"The medical examiner guesses he was killed in that location sometime Sunday night; apparently, he wasn't moved after he was shot." Fred Baird, the lab technician on the day shift, took off his gold-rimmed glasses and blew at something clinging to the lens. He, Wager, and Axton sat around one of three desks in the small cubicle that was the single office for all the homicide detectives. They were supposed to have moved to a new police and justice building a year ago; but the date had shifted more often than a politician's word, and all three crews were still jammed into the same space. Each of the desks had a glass top. Under them were lists of telephone numbers, codes for quick reference, names and addresses that meant something to one of the three people who shared the desk; on top of this one were spread the color photographs taken that morning by Baird. They still held a slightly acid odor, and their shiny finish was tacky under Wager's thumb. "One shot was fired," Baird went on. "At close range; probably a contact wound because it's smoothly marginated and has a lot of powder residue as well as localized discoloration of the skeletal muscle. The intake of carbon monoxide causes that," he explained. "The area of penetration is centered approximately nine millimeters behind the point of the chin and five millimeters to the left of a mid-sagittal line. The path of penetration angles upward into the brain at approximately sixty degrees from a transverse plane to emerge at the top of the right parietal, effecting subtotal decapitation with an orifice of approximately six to ten centimeters."

"Good God," said Max. "That rolls trippingly off the tongue."

"Baird, why can't you just tell us what the hell happened?"

The lab tech glanced with surprise from Axton to Wager. "I did! That's the medical description."

"Then why don't you give us the civilian description, Fred?"

In the short silence, a twang of country-and-Western radio music rose above the steady clatter of office machines and police frequencies from the busy Records Section down the hall. "It won't be very goddamned scientific that way," Baird said with disgust.

"But it may be a hell of a lot clearer," answered Max.

Baird shrugged and put his glasses back on and blinked once or twice as if seeing the two detectives for the first time. "If that's what you want. Say this pencil's the path of the round." He held the yellow shaft just under the left side of his chin. "It entered here and took off the back of his tongue and soft palate . . ." He lowered the pencil. "That's part of the roof of your mouth."

"Come on, come on," said Wager.

"It went through the opening behind the nasal area and through the brain. The shot widened out in the brain and emerged near the top of the skull. Back here." His hand patted a spot on the top of his head near the little tonsure of thinning hair.

"The weapon used was a shotgun?" asked Wager.

"Double-aught buck. The doc found seven of the pellets inside the brain and we found a few more in the alley. This supports the idea that he was killed right there. The lividity and rigor fit, too, so it's pretty definite."

"A shotgun. That won't help much," said Max. "Smooth bores don't leave much identification."

"Not without the shell; that's right. We're still looking around for evidence, but don't keep your hopes up." Baird pushed the photographs apart to find those that gave the long-range views of the crime site. "We couldn't find any footprints or fingerprints that were worth a damn, except yours, Max. You left a beautiful set on this wall here."

"It's when I took his wallet."

"Whatever. There were no tire tracks that meant anything, either; there's too much vehicular traffic around the site during the day. So that's the sum of it—about five pounds of nothing. No leads at all. We did take samples of the environment. Bring us a suspect and we'll try to match his clothes to the environment."

"Sure," said Wager. "A suspect. We couldn't even find any eyewitnesses."

"You've been a great help, Fred."

"Always glad, Max." Baird stood. "Next time, pick a better corpse. I'll get the complete autopsy report up to you sometime tomorrow."

"Was the identification positive?" asked Wager.

"Right. Fingerprints match the driver's license application. It's Frank Arnold Covino. Got his address?"

Wager nodded and also stood. "Let's get that over with," he said to Max.

The Covino address was on Quivas Street, a gently rundown neighborhood that once had been Italian and was now becoming Hispanic. One or two Italian restaurants still remained, the biggest being a rambling wooden house with a giant neon sign: "Pagliacci's." Half a block farther was a Mexican restaurant, and graffiti covered the cracked stucco walls of the remaining stores: "Chicano Power," "Viva FALN," and "Libre Puerto Rico." Axton glanced at the sprayed slogans as they passed. "Did I tell you I'm taking bagpipe lessons?"

"What the hell for?"

"It's part of my heritage—I'm a Scot."

Wager looked to see if he was joking, but the large face remained placid. "You going to wear one of those little dresses?"

Axton winced. "It's not a dress, Wager. It's a kilt. And yes, I'm buying one. I had to order it from San Francisco."

"I hope you've got cute legs."

"There's nothing wrong with ethnic pride! I like to see it —there should be more of it. I like the variety we've got in this city. Hell, you Chicanos are always talking up your Mexican roots, so there's no reason why a Scot can't. Or an Eskimo, or a Greek."

"I'm Hispano."

"What's the difference?"

"Plenty."

"There; see? I didn't know that. If you took more interest in your cultural heritage, people would know the difference between Chicanos and Hispanos."

"I don't give a damn whether they do or not."

"Well, I'm as proud to be a Scot as somebody else is to be Chicano. Highland, too."

There was a big difference between being something and saying you were something, and it seemed to Wager that these days everybody was claiming identification with some group or another. Maybe they needed it—even Max. But not Wager; he had discovered a long time ago that he held within himself all that he would ever need, and it kind of surprised him that someone as big as Axton felt the need for more identity.

Finding the house number, Wager wordlessly slipped the car into a no-parking zone. In the nine or ten months he had been in homicide, he and Axton had gotten along better than Wager had expected. The big man was as steady as one of the mountains squatting on the western horizon, and Wager had begun to trust him. Axton put his trust in Wager, too. With time and care, it could turn out to be the kind of partnership every cop would like to have but too few did; though it would be all too easy to snuff out the understanding and trust necessary to it. That was something Wager wanted to keep in mind at times like this, when Axton struck him as a little bit weird. He turned off the car's motor. "You ready for it?"

"Nope," said Axton. "But what choice do we have?"

The old house was similar to the rest on the block, dark-red brick with a small front porch held up by square pillars of half brick and half white wood; a second floor was cramped under the sloping green roof, a low, flat dormer over the white trim of its window. The yard had fewer worn spots and more early crocuses along the foundation than did the ones on either side, and from somewhere around back came the thin crowing of a young rooster, a sound that Wager hadn't heard in a long time. The lady who answered their knock was in her fifties, short, thick-bodied; beneath the cropped gray hair, her eyes were red-rimmed.

"Yes?"

"Are you the mother or a relative of Frank Arnold Covino?"

"No. I'm a neighbor. Mrs. Covino's inside." She did not move from the doorway.

Wager showed his identification and badge. "We need to ask Mrs. Covino some questions about her son."

"It's a bad time."

"It's never a good time, ma'am," said Axton. "But the faster we can get our information, the better our chances are of finding the people that did it."

For a moment more, she didn't move; then, "Come in." She led them through the living room to a tiny formal parlor. On a shelf opposite the door was a small madonna with two red prayer candles at her feet. Three women sat on the maroon sofa; Mrs. Covino was apparently the one in the center. The thin light from the curtained window made the lines on her wide forehead and cheeks deeper, and her graying hair lay straight down her back, as it probably had since the telephone call early this morning. The pain in the room was so thick that Wager felt as if he were wading through a cold current, and like the crowing of the rooster, the feeling brought the distant memory of other parlors and other dead.

"They're policemen, Alice," said the woman with the short hair.

"Mrs. Covino? Can we talk to you?" asked Wager.

The woman nodded silently, tugging the collar of her robe closer to her neck.

"Do you have any idea who would want to do this?"

Mrs. Covino's broad face sagged and she pressed a wad of handkerchief under her nose to stifle the whining moan; it was a long two minutes before she could breathe evenly, her loud sighs gradually shuddering into long, labored breaths.

16

"Tell them," she said to no one. "Tell them he was a good boy. No trouble. Never."

One of the women on the sofa, younger than the others, stroked Mrs. Covino's hand and glared at Wager. "Haven't you people done enough to her through Gerry? Now you got to start on Frank, too?"

"Gracie . . ." Mrs. Covino sucked another deep breath loud and flat past her stuffy nose.

"Mrs. Covino's daughter," explained the woman with short hair. "Frank's sister."

"Detective Wager, miss."

"Detective Axton. We're sorry to have to be here, ma'am."

"Tell them we got some coffee, Gracie," said Mrs. Covino. "Get these gentlemen a cup of coffee."

"I'll do it, Grace. You stay here with your mother." The fourth woman, silent until now, rose and went into the kitchen.

"Can you tell us something about Frank, Mrs. Covino? Who some of his friends are? If he had any enemies? If there's someone who might know why it happened?"

"Why? I ask God in heaven why! There is no why! Tell them, Gracie—tell them he was a good boy and didn't have no enemies!"

"Alice . . ." The woman with short hair put an arm around Mrs. Covino's curved and shaking shoulders. She, too, glared at the detectives; in her case, Wager felt, not because they were cops but because they were men, and men—sons, lovers, husbands—were the cause of the grief of womankind.

"I'm all right." Mrs. Covino dabbed at her eyes. "Frankie was the youngest. First Gerry, then Gracie, then him— Frankie. He had lots of friends. Everybody liked Frankie. Tell them about Frankie going to college, Gracie. Tell them about how he was studying electricity."

The young woman nodded. "At Metropolitan College downtown. He was a work-study student."

"Did he have any other jobs, Miss Covino?"

"At Aztec Liquors, over on Federal."

"Tell them what Mr. Rosenbaum said, Gracie, about Frankie being such a good worker that he could own his own store someday. But he wanted to study electricity."

"Did he work days or nights?"

"Afternoons," said the young woman. "Sometimes nights or weekends, but Mama didn't like that. She was afraid he'd get hurt in a holdup."

"Cream or sugar?" The woman from the kitchen held a tray of guest china out to them.

"Neither, ma'am." Wager took the flowered, fragile cup; his finger did not quite go through the small handle. Beside him, he heard Axton rattling the china softly, trying to figure out a way to pick up the cup politely in his large fingers.

"Can you give us some names of his friends, ma'am?" asked Wager.

Mrs. Covino let her daughter name eight or ten while she nodded and said, more to herself than to Wager, "I forget all his friends. He had so many friends."

Wager listed names and some addresses in his little green notebook. There were three that the mother said were her son's best friends, so he penciled boxes around those.

"Did Frank happen to tell you where he was going last night?"

Again Mrs. Covino spoke to her daughter, as if otherwise she would not be able to speak at all. "To a movie with friends. He ate supper and he phoned one of his friends, didn't he, Gracie? And then he just went out the front door like any other time. . . . He said, 'Don't wait up, Mom,' and went out like always. And I didn't wait up—God forgive me. Maybe if I'd waited up . . ."

18

"Alice, it's not your fault."

They sipped their coffee and studied their shoes until the wet, muffled explosions stopped, and then Wager asked, "Do you know who he might have gone with? Which movie he went to?"

"No. It was on the phone. I didn't listen," she said weakly. "Oh, God, what could I do? What could I do?"

"Is there a photograph that we could have to show people?" Axton asked the daughter. "We'll copy it and get it right back to you, ma'am."

"There." Mrs. Covino's puffy eyes looked hungrily at the shelf of family pictures lined up against the dark wall near the madonna. "Gracie . . ."

The girl brought it quickly, not looking at the high school graduation face that smiled out through the glass; with tight lips, she thrust it at Wager.

"Did Frank have a car, ma'am?" he asked the girl.

She described it, the mother adding, "He loved that car. Always, he bought something for it. Maybe that's why! Maybe somebody wanted that car!"

"That could be, ma'am," said Wager. "We haven't found it yet." He tried to make the next question sound equally routine. "Did your son ever talk of knowing a Marco Scorvelli?"

"God, no! Tell him, Gracie—I know who that is, and tell him that Frankie never knew that kind of man!"

"My brother was good! Why do you want to say these things that aren't true? It's bad enough what you cops did to Gerry!"

Axton leaned slightly forward, the dark, thickly padded chair creaking under his weight. "Would that be Gerald Edward Covino, miss? The one in Cañon City?"

"What do you think?"

"Gracie, Gracie," said the mother wearily. "Not now; please, not today."

The young woman stood quickly. "You through with those cups?"

"Yes, ma'am." They set them gingerly on the tray and she left with the quick, stiff strides of anger.

Mrs. Covino closed her eyes and rocked to and fro, talking in a low voice to no one in particular. "Some of it was Gerry's fault. But not all. What can anybody do with kids? No father; you can't pick their friends for them; you can't be on them every minute of the day . . . Gerry wasn't a bad boy. He was so afraid when they sent him to the reformatory that time. 'Mama,' he said, 'Mama, I don't know if I'll make it.' But what could I do? They just took him. He was caught stealing a car—it was the first time, and he swore to me it wasn't even his idea. It was the ones he ran around with. But they weren't caught. They weren't the ones sent to the reformatory. Almost a year, and when he came out, he wasn't my Gerry any more. He wasn't anybody's anything any more." The tears started again, as much for the living dead as for the newly dead.

"Mama, they don't want to hear that." The daughter in the kitchen doorway, leaning against the frame with her arms crossed tightly on her chest. "They got their files and their records. They know all about Gerry in their files."

"We know he has a second conviction," Wager told her.

"Sure! He ain't Anglo, is he? That means guilty, right?" She glared at Wager, daring him to say no. "And don't you go trying to make Frankie out like that. If Gerry did something wrong, it was because he never had a chance. Nobody gave him a break. But Frankie wasn't that way. Now why don't you two just go on out of here!"

In their car, Wager pulled a very deep breath, then asked Max, "Well? What do you think?"

"I sometimes think this is a shitty job."

There was nothing new in that. "Miss Gracie feels the same way."

"Yeah," said Axton. "She and her people have inherited a lot of hatred. More than she knows how to get rid of."

"Maybe it's a crutch. She's as ugly as a goddam totem pole."

"For God's sake, Gabe—these people have a right to feel resentment! Anybody would."

"They have better things to resent than us. They can try resenting the sons of bitches that bring us down on them."

"Maybe it's not that easy. I mean, it's her own brother in the pen, and cops helped put him there. Now another brother's dead, and two cops come around making more implications. I'll bet if some kid from Cherry Hills or the Polo Grounds steals a car, he won't be sent to the reformatory. The judge will give him a tut-tut and a big bad frown. And a free ride home."

But Wager knew a lot of Hispanos who took everything that was thrown at them and never whined. They minded their own business, they worked hard, they moved up. And then they were envied and hated by people like Gracie, for whom hatred was life because they could not leave old hurts behind. "They should both be sent up," said Wager. "At least we got one of the little bastards."

Axton's head wagged from side to side. "And these are your own people!"

Wager almost replied. The angry words pushed against his clamped teeth to tell Axton that "his" people were cops and cops only. Not the criminals, not the civilians, not the goddamned activists who would rather see a cop than a hood lying in his own blood. But he did not say it. Fancy words and explanations and excuses were for the world's lawyers, not its cops; cops had to do their duty, not just talk about it. "Well, right now, *amigo,* one of 'my' people is in the morgue.

21

And I have a strong feeling that the rest of 'my' people either didn't tell all or didn't know all there was to tell us."

The large man squeaked some air between his teeth in a faint whistle. "Yeah. Kids sure as hell don't tell their parents everything. God knows, I didn't."

It could be that, Wager agreed. It wouldn't be the first time that a parent didn't know—or was willfully ignorant. It was Wager's theory that a lot of parents didn't have the guts to ask questions of their own kids. "Somebody has to go down to Cañon City and have a talk with Gerald."

Axton stretched and pushed his big frame against the seat. "You want to do that? I'll start on this list of friends."

"All right. You cover for me this afternoon. I'll go down after lunch." Wager turned the car across the Sixteenth Street viaduct toward headquarters, radioing a stolen car report on Frank Covino's missing vehicle.

He had read over the jacket on Gerald Edward Covino before making the three-hour drive to the state penitentiary in Cañon City. In addition to his adult record, Covino had a juvenile sheet, mostly petty theft. It culminated in a tour in the reformatory at Buena Vista for grand theft, auto; the last adult conviction was for breaking and entering a place of business. That was the tumble that put him behind the walls at Cañon City. There were half a dozen contact cards on him, too, which revealed him to be a suspect in various burglaries and even a couple of armed robberies. None of those ever got as far as the courts, though of course the cards didn't state why. But as Wager's grandfather used to say, when you step on a thorn long enough, you know something's there; to his sister, however, Gerald was just one more downtrodden victim of a racist capitalist materialist sexist society, and it was everybody's fault except his.

Wager steered the road-hot vehicle off Highway 50 to the

parking lot of the prison. As usual, the pale stone walls and the gnawed-at granite of the hillside behind them spoke of eternal rock and dust and heat. No trees, no grass, no shrubbery that could shelter an escaping inmate; blank walls that gave clear fields of fire from the towers, and were surrounded by acres of crushed gravel. People had been crushing that gravel for a lot of years here, and Wager was damned satisfied that he had swept some of that garbage off the streets and stuffed it behind these walls.

He showed his identification to the matron in the control center and filled out the request form, sliding it across the scratched and stained fiber tabletop to a turnkey.

"You want to sit over there, Sarge? I'll see if he's in."

It was a tired joke and Wager didn't smile back. He chose one of the sticky plastic couches of the reception area and waited to be called to an interview station. It was between visiting periods and the only other person in the room was a young black woman who smoked steadily and tried hard not to look worried. In about twenty minutes, the turnkey called him by name. "Station two, Sarge."

Gerald Covino was waiting when Wager entered the booth with its warning signs and bars and the thin plexiglass barrier forming the line between inside and out. Gerald was in his late twenties, Wager knew, but the face that looked guardedly at him over the inside telephone had that stiff prison quality that could have been anywhere between twenty-five and forty.

"I'm Detective Wager, Covino. Homicide Division, D.P.D. You heard about your brother?"

"What about him?"

So the sister who loved him so much had not bothered to telephone the news down yet. And the papers and television had not broadcast the name. "He was killed last night. Gang style."

"Frankie? You sure it was Frankie?"

Wager gazed through the plexiglass at the man's bulging eyes and probed for the seam between sincere shock and expert lying. With this one, it would be hard to tell.

"Do you have any idea why somebody might want your brother dead?"

Covino, still chewing on the news, shook his head. His straight black hair swept back above his ears into a ponytail on his neck, and a thin scar ran through his upper lip to make a light line across the dark flesh. The man's face slowly stiffened again into the prison mask.

"It's your brother, Covino. Somebody executed him. They used a shotgun on his head and left him like a scumbag in an alley. I'm not asking you to fink on any friends of yours; I'm asking you to give me something on whoever wasted your own brother."

When the man finally spoke into the telephone, it was to say, "I don't know, man. What do I know, stuck here in this fucking place?"

Sometimes inmates knew things as fast as the police—or faster. "Was Frank into anything?"

"Frankie was clean! He saw what happened to me, man; he didn't want nothing like this." Covino stared at the plastic top of the shelf for a long minute, and through the shadowed reflections in the plexiglass Wager saw the man's knuckles grow white around the telephone. "Mama," he said softly. "He was the baby. It's gonna kill Mama."

This one had done his share, too, Wager thought. "She's suffering," he agreed.

"You went and seen her?"

"I did."

"You told her that Frankie was mixed up in something?"

"I did not. I asked her if he was, and she said no."

"You didn't even have to ask her that! Anybody could of told you—he was clean!"

"Then who executed him? It wasn't an amateur hit, Covino. His car is missing, but his wallet, watch, and money were on him. We figure he parked his car somewhere and took a ride with somebody who knew exactly how to handle the job. Now come on—he was your goddamned brother!"

"I told you, Wager—I told you, I don't know! He was a kid—seven years younger than me. We didn't even go around with the same bunch of people. But he was no *chulo.*"

Wager turned back to fiddling with his pen and with the little green notebook that lay open on the tabletop, which was gummy with the nervous, oily sweat from countless other arms. "All right, Covino. Let me tell you what it looks like so far. If your brother was as clean as you say, then it looks like somebody might have been after you. Or wanted to tell you something." He glanced up. "Was anybody with you in that breaking and entering?"

"Maybe; maybe not."

"Did any of them ever think you might fink?"

The man's black eyes narrowed. "I don't fink. Nobody thinks that. Is that what you're after? You come down here giving me all this shit about my brother being dead, thinking I'll fink?"

"Frank is dead," said Wager. "It'll be on the news tonight. And what I'm after is a lead on who did it. Is anybody after you, Gerald?"

The scarred upper lip twisted into a sour grin. "If anybody wanted me, cop, they could get me in here. For one fucking carton of cigarettes. Look, Wager, I been inside ten months now. Four more, maybe six at most, and I'm up for parole. It's downhill on my time, man. I'm not gonna fink on anybody now. Why should I? And everybody knows it: Gerry

Covino's no fink. If somebody's trying to tell me something by offing Frankie, I swear I do not know who or what."

"Ever hear the name Scorvelli?"

A total blankness of expression. "Who hasn't?"

"I had a tip just before your brother was killed that he knew something about Marco Scorvelli getting wiped last year."

"Shit! Who handed you that shit, man?"

Wager half smiled. "Sure—I'll tell you! What do you know about it?"

"I know it's a bunch of crap. Somebody's crapping all over you. Frankie was straight—he didn't know Scorvelli or anybody like him."

"What about you?"

"What?"

"Did you ever know any of the Scorvellis?"

"No, man. We don't run in the same circles."

"Denver's a small town."

"Not that small. I heard the name is all. But they don't even know I breathe their air. The wops don't like us, you dig?"

Nothing. Wager tapped the ballpoint on the table. Maybe nothing would turn out to be something. Sometimes it worked that way. But more often, nothing was just that. "Covino, I'm sorry you lost your brother. I'd like to nail the ones that did it. Here." He wrote a telephone number on a leaf of his notebook and turned it so Covino could read it. "This is my number—memorize it. If you get any ideas or hear anything, use one of your telephone calls to help me get whoever killed your brother."

The hard black eyes never shifted from Wager's own. "I'll be keeping my ears open, don't worry about that. But I don't fink. Even on this."

26

three

The next morning, Wager reported in early, as always. Munn, who was alone on the graveyard shift this month, had that baggy-eyed look of someone who has suffered a long, slow night waiting for the sun to rise. And then didn't like what he saw. "How're you doing on that Covino shooting, Gabe?"

Wager looked through the papers in his box and glanced over the twenty-four-hour board for any messages. "Not a thing so far. Maybe Axton had better luck."

Munn stretched and drained his coffee cup and tried not to look too eager to leave. "Nothing happening last night. Dull as a goddam cucumber."

"Cucumber?"

"Ain't that the expression? Cucumbers always struck me as being pretty goddam dull. Next to zucchini."

Wager turned back to his handful of papers.

"God, I feel lousy," said Munn. "I think I'm coming down

with something." He snorted some phlegm down his sinuses and into his throat. Munn really didn't look healthy; dark skin puffed under his eyes, and beneath the stubble of morning whiskers, his cheeks were sallow. "Maybe I had too much coffee. I always drink too much coffee on this shift. Especially when it's so goddam quiet."

Wager looked at the electric clock high on the tan wall. The walls of the building were either anemic tan or sick green, and because the department had been scheduled to vacate a year or so past, they had not been painted in a long while; around the base, the color was leached out by the splash of mop water, and the morning light, cheerful coming through the window, lost its warmth on the dirt and scuff marks in the gray film. The clock said 7:45. "Why don't you take the rest of the day off?"

"You're a real jewel, Gabe."

He was glad to see Munn go. When the old shift hung around, there was always the feeling of intruding; and when Wager was on duty, he liked to think of it as his shift, and his only. Tossing the mail onto his desk, he took it in random order: a request for information on a suspect being held in Phoenix, a query from neighboring Jefferson County about the disposition of a case, the union telling him what great benefits they had won for officers in New York and asking why he didn't join the Colorado chapter now. It was the usual routine pile of papers, but down at the bottom was a memo from Chief Doyle: "You and Axton see me before leaving this morning." It was noted 0730; the Bulldog seemed to spend as much time here as Wager did.

He pulled the Frank Covino file and spread the photographs and the lab report and the offense report and the witness statements across the glass top of the desk. When Axton came in at precisely 8 A.M., Wager was staring at the pictures and at the jottings in his green notebook. But if Max

28

had asked him what he was thinking, Wager could not have put it into precise words; it was more subjective—more like absorption than thought.

Axton's first move was for a cup of coffee; his second, to ask about Wager's progress down in Cañon City.

"Gerald's tough," answered Wager. The Spanish word was *duro* and was more accurate, but Max wouldn't have understood it. "I tried to shake him into telling me something, but he wouldn't even squeak. It was his own brother, and still he wasn't about to talk to any cop."

"Sounds as if you like the guy."

"Hell, no." Though maybe he admired Covino's tenacity. It was always good to see someone under pressure who did not crack or give up; it restored Wager's faith in humanity. "But I have the feeling he's keeping secrets. Maybe he wants to even things up himself."

"Yeah, it wouldn't be the first time somebody tried that —you screwball Chicanos and your codes. Did he hint anything at all?"

"Not a word, and I don't think he will, to us." Wager gazed at the papers and photos on his desk. "Do you know who the arresting officer was on Gerald's bust?"

Axton shook his head. "It wasn't on his sheet."

Wager pushed the telephone button for Records and asked the same question of the police person who answered; in a few seconds she came back to say, "Detective Franconi; Burglary and Stickup Division."

Under the desk's glass top with its rings of dried coffee and rubbery threads of old eraser was the month's duty roster for all the detectives. It noted that Franconi was on the four-to-midnight shift, and Wager would have to talk with him then. Possibly the burglary detective had heard something about Gerald's brother. It was a very slender angle, but Wager would play them all; sometimes the angle you missed, no matter how unlikely, was the one that would pay off. "What about Frank's friends?" he asked Max.

"It took me all afternoon and half the night to locate eight of the people on that list—kids that age never stay in one spot more than ten minutes. But not a one of them knew of any reason why Frank would be killed. They all said he was a good kid, hard-working, a real boy scout."

"Were any of them with him Sunday night?"

"Not that I talked with, and they all had verifiable statements. There's five or six more, that I couldn't catch up with; maybe we'll have better luck today. I did go see the owner of that liquor store where Frank worked."

"Same story?" That was a dumb question. If it had been different, Axton would have told him.

"Just about. According to him, Frank was very reliable and got along real well with the customers—which, he said, is no easy thing over there." Axton sighed, the chair back ticking lightly as his torso rose and fell. "Gabe, I'm really beginning to dislike the bastards that killed this kid."

Wager knew what Axton meant. There was a correlation between the kind of victim and an attitude toward the killer. If the murder was the result of a family fight, Wager might feel a little sorry for the husband or wife who did it; if it happened between criminals, the only feeling he could recall was a tinge of satisfaction at getting two for the price of one. But the victim who didn't deserve it—the child, the waste of a decent, innocent person—that stirred Wager's anger; and so far Frank Covino seemed to be the kind of Hispano Wager liked to contrast to the loudmouths and whiners. But, Wager reminded himself, all the evidence wasn't in yet; what things are often turn out differently from how they seem, and the luxury of anger could wait for a certainty. He gathered the file together. "The Bulldog wants to see us."

Chief Doyle's thrusting lower teeth showed briefly when

30

he said good morning, and Wager and Axton took it as a friendly snarl. "If you gentlemen want some coffee, there it is." His office had its own machine and it was rumored that he ground the blend himself—by hand. It did not taste any different from the hot, metallic flavor that boiled out of the division pot, but the detectives always told Doyle how good it was. "Bring me up to date on this shooting."

Wager did, Max adding a point or two about Covino's acquaintances.

"Any chance it's a thrill killing?"

"There's the chance," said Wager. "But it doesn't have that feel about it." He listed the reasons why. "A shotgun's not a thrill killer's weapon, there were no signs of torture or a struggle, and the killer didn't walk around and look at the body when he apparently had a chance to. What it feels like is a professional hit."

"Mistaken identity?"

"That's a good possibility." Wager told him about his suspicions concerning Gerald Covino.

"But the brother gave you nothing solid?"

Wager wouldn't be sitting on his tail in the Bulldog's office if he had something solid; Doyle knew that. Wager did not bother to answer.

"Marco and Dominick Scorvelli . . . That's one very interesting wrinkle." Doyle's gaze roamed the wall over their heads. "How reliable is your source for that information, Wager?" Doyle still had lingering suspicions about Wager's Narcotics Division background, and they crept out every now and then in questions of judgment that he would not ask other experienced officers.

"He's been around a long time and a lot of people talk to him. When he gives me something, it's usually been good."

"How much do we pay him for it?"

Doyle was always worried about that. "I drink a few beers

with him now and then. He won't accept any money."

"Jesus," said Max. "The taxpayers could use more like him."

Doyle only grunted. Then he said, "Well, we're getting some media interest in this shooting—nothing heavy, but I'd like to wrap up the case as soon as possible. Why don't you drop by the Organized Crime Unit, Wager? You know those people over there; see if they'll tell you what they have going on Dominick Scorvelli. Maybe we can come at this thing from another direction."

Doyle had called the O.C.U. "those people" because they had their own budget and organization and liked to work without letting the regular units of D.P.D. know what they were doing. Security, they called it; arrogance was how most of D.P.D. saw it. But Doyle was right on two counts: it was worth a try since nothing else seemed any good; and since Wager had worked over there not too long ago, they might be a little more relaxed about giving information to him.

Outside the Bulldog's office, Max asked, "You want to split up? I'll take the remainder of this list of Covino's friends while you go visit the O.C.U.?"

They would cover more ground that way, but sometimes it was better, as his grandfather used to say, to run with slow strides. "If we're together we might come up with more." Besides, there was still so much missing—still so much that he couldn't squeeze between these ten fingers—that he was hungry to handle every fragment of the case. It was the same feeling as when he sat and stared at the photographs—the same need to absorb every detail he could.

As they left main headquarters by the rear corridor, a voice cut through the clatter of machinery from the building under construction next door. "Max! Max the Ax—wait up!" Police reporter Gargan, his familiar black turtleneck shirt showing through the open parka, jogged toward them from the new performing arts complex. "Max—can you give me something on this shooting?" The reporter ignored Wager and looked up at Max hopefully. "Anything at all?"

"Not yet, Gargan. The killer or killers didn't leave much information. We're just doing what we can with what we've got, and right now that's not a hell of a lot."

"Would you call it a gangland slaying?"

"Well, no . . . We can't really . . ."

"Do you think there's any possibility of another gang war starting? Like, maybe, the unsolved Scorvelli killing last year?"

"There's no link that we know of."

"I heard the victim might have been connected with Scorvelli's death."

"Who the hell told you that?" asked Wager.

Gargan finally looked at him, his lips stretched in the kind of smile that twisted the corners of his mouth down. "You did, Wager. When you tried to find out from Mrs. Covino if her kid was tied in with the Scorvellis. That really got to her, man—you really have a talent for doing that to people. You must have hair on the bottom of your feet." He turned back to Max. "All that poor old lady could talk about was how Frankie wasn't like his brother in Cañon City. You got to admit that it looks like a gang killing, Max, and you guys were the ones who brought up the Scorvelli name. What about it, now—is there anything to it?"

"It does look something like a gang killing, Gargan. But it could be that someone was just after his car; the street divisions haven't run across his car yet. Why don't you check back with us tomorrow? I hope we'll have something by then."

Gargan finished scribbling a few words in his notebook. "All right. It's 'possibly' a gang killing, and the Scorvelli name's been mentioned. That's all I'll say, Max, I swear. And thanks." He left without nodding good-bye to Wager.

Max watched the figure hurry away between the parked cars. "What's Gargan got against you, Gabe?"

"We had some fun and games a few months ago. I had him busted for drunk driving."

"You set him up?"

Wager shrugged. "He had it coming."

"That could have cost him his job!"

"That's what he tried to do to me. It was a fair fight."

Axton's thick eyebrows bobbed. "Still, you start using the law like that . . ."

"Sometimes the laws aren't enough," said Wager. "Besides, Gargan did break the law—after a small shove."

"You are one hard little bastard, Gabe."

Wager unlocked the cruiser's door and slid beneath the wheel, set his radio pack in the dash mount and reached to unlock the rider's door for Axton. "I sure don't feel bad about it."

"Well, you didn't make any lifetime friend out of him."

"Tough titty."

Their first stop was a Buy-Rite gas station on North Federal, just past the city-county line in an unincorporated corner of the sprawling suburbs. They were looking for one Terry Valdez; his name had a little box around it in Wager's notebook, indicating that he had been a close friend of Frank Covino's. "His mother said he worked from seven to three," Axton told Wager. They pulled onto one side of the concrete apron and the two detectives got out.

The station manager, from his desk near the cash register, watched them all the way into the small building. "You guys cops?"

"Are we wearing a sign?" asked Max.

"It's the way you walk. You walk like cops. Who're you after?"

34

"Do you have a Terry Valdez working here?" asked Wager.

"Yeah. He's in the service bay. What's he done?"

"Not a thing." Axton smiled. "We just want to ask him some questions about a friend of his."

"What friend? Is it something I should hear about?"

"Why should you?"

"I mean, he's only been with me three or four months. They told me I got to hire a minority, so I got this Valdez kid. If he's in trouble, I got a right to know about it, right? It's bad enough they tell me who to hire, but I sure as hell don't have to have a thief working for me."

"We're not after Valdez for anything, sir. We just want to ask him about one of his friends," said Axton.

"Well, birds of a feather, you know."

"Birds of a feather what?" asked Wager.

The manager looked at him closely and ran a pale tongue over his lower lip. "Nothing. He's out there. Being paid by the hour."

They went into the small service bay, the kind of unit that a few self-serve stations still have. "Terry Valdez?" called Wager.

"Down here." The grease-streaked legs of red overalls stuck from beneath the end of a '69 Ford. "Be with you in a minute."

They waited until the young man slid from under the car on his creeper, then showed their badges. "We'd like to ask you some questions about Frank Covino."

"Oh, God." The thin face with its soft, struggling mustache paled slightly. "That's awful. It's like you're walking down the street with your buddy and you turn to say something to him and he's gone. Just like that."

Axton asked gently, "You fellas were good friends?"

"Sure—all the way through school together. Grade

35

school, junior high, high school. Just a couple minutes ago I was thinking about giving him a call tonight to see what was going on. It was a habit—give old Frankie a call." Valdez scrubbed at his grimy hands with a wipe rag and looked at them closely. "Tonight's the rosary. That's what he's doing tonight."

"Do you have any idea who'd want to kill him?"

"Some fucking loco! If I knew, man, you people wouldn't have to be bothered!" His glance shifted to Wager, the dark eyes suddenly shot with a mixture of anger and pain. "He was my *compadre,* you know?"

"Did you see him at all the night before last?" asked Wager.

"Sunday night? No. I saw him Friday at school; we had a beer and then he went to his class and I went to mine."

"This is at the college?" asked Max.

"Yeah. I go to Community. I'm taking the automotive course. He's at Metro State in this electronics program. He wanted to work in the space business. He could have, too—he was smart, man."

"Did you see him after class on Friday?"

"No. He was on this work-study deal and had some stuff to do in some office. His old man was Italian—Covino—but his mother's Chicana. So he applied for this minority grant. What the hell—it's the same thing the *chicas* do who marry Anglos, you know? They keep their Chicano name so they can get the grants. Mrs. Martinez-Jones—like that."

"You have a grant?"

"No, I didn't want to be bothered. Too much paper work and crap. You should see the papers Frankie had to fill out —every cent his whole family made he had to put down."

"Did Frankie need the money badly?" asked Wager.

"Well, he qualified for the grant. But he wasn't hurting; he had this job over at the liquor store and his mother has

36

her pension from his old man's death. He was a miner. It was more that Frankie wanted it on his record. You know, for job applications and such. Frankie, he talked me into taking this job. I was going to work construction for more money, but Frankie says it would look better if I had a job in my field. Like an investment." The thin face smiled for the first time, a flash of white teeth beneath the struggling mustache. "That old man, he don't like it, but I'm as good as any he's got and a lot better than most around here."

"That's the station manager?"

"Yeah." The smile went as quickly as it had come. "Frankie was like that, always planning ahead. But not like a strainer—not like he was trying to jew somebody out of something; he just had good ideas about what to do."

"Do you know anything about his activities last weekend?"

Valdez shook his head. "We didn't have anything lined up. I had a date Saturday night, and he was working at the liquor store. I didn't even ask what he was doing after work." He studied the greasy wipe rag again. "Next thing I know is when I called up his house and Gracie told me what happened." Suddenly Valdez moaned and slammed the rag to the concrete deck. "Aw, crap! Why'd it have to be him?"

Wager nudged the lifeless cloth with his shoe. "That's one of the things we're after—why." And when they had that, who. "Was Frankie ever mixed up with the Scorvelli family?"

"Scorvelli?" The wide, dark eyes seemed genuinely shocked. "Frankie? Come on, man!"

"We heard he might be," said Wager.

"You heard wrong! He wasn't that way, man." Surprise gave way to anger. "He wasn't no *pollo*—he could look after himself; but I knew Frankie like my own family, and there was nothing like that he was into!"

"We're sure of that, Mr. Valdez," Axton soothed. "But we don't have much to go on, so we have to ask all sorts of questions."

"Yeah. O.K. But you talk to anybody—the priest, anybody. They'll all tell you the same: Frankie was a good man." Again Valdez's voice almost broke. "Good!"

Wager convinced Valdez to give them the names and addresses of a few more of Covino's acquaintances who might have seen him Sunday night, and then, still watched by the seated service manager, they swung back toward town among the midmorning traffic on Federal. Here, north of I-70, the four-lane street made long rises and falls across the sandy flats of lower Clear Creek valley. This time Axton drove and Wager stared in silence out the window. It was one of those light-filled spring days whose sun stung hot through the windshield. Only when you saw the roadside dust scud across the highway or felt the shudder of the car did you know how hard the wind was blowing off the iron-colored mountains. Wager watched the snapping pennants and blurred plastic windmills over the truck and camper sales lots, the passing furniture warehouses and cut-rate lumber stores, the plaster horses that touted Western gear; just beyond the cluttered line of sprawling one-story commercial buildings rose a fringe of cottonwood trees not yet ripped from the stream bed to make room for more asphalt. Their sharp lines of branches had grown slightly fuzzy with the pale green of early leaves. Wager gazed at the faint spring greenness and wondered why someone wanted to tear up those trees instead of build around them—wondered what was in some people that made them search for the tallest and cleanest, the noblest, just to disfigure and destroy it.

Axton broke the silence. "I get the idea we're going in circles. It all comes back to the same thing: he was a good kid and there was no reason for what happened." He eased up

38

on the gas, coasting until the distant traffic light changed and the column of waiting cars and trucks began to move; then he smoothly joined the line without wasting motion.

Axton was like that, Wager mused; he had the kind of forethought Valdez admired in Frank: looking ahead, planning the moves for the greatest economy of effort. Maybe that came from living in a body as big as Axton's: you learned to look ahead for low doorways or jutting furniture, you stayed at the edge of crowds, you sat with care on strange chairs. "Do you think Valdez was telling the truth?"

"Don't you?" Axton's question meant "What did I miss?"

"Yeah." Wager's fingers rapped the dash. "I guess I do." He knew he'd held a faint hope that Valdez would lie about something. If the kid had lied, their work would be a hell of a lot easier. But Valdez had not seemed to, and for a cop to have too much imagination was as bad as not having enough. Wager knew that this was one of those dangerous times when his hopes, guesses, and inventions were beginning to be churned by impatience, and he could feel himself pulling against the facts to create a pattern of motive and opportunity. But take it easy—*cachaza*. "The seed sprouts when it will," his mother would have said. "Chico, you'll end up with a fistful of farts," would be his father's warning. It all said the same thing: stick to the facts.

"You know the only link we have between Scorvelli and Covino is your informant's word. Maybe he was wrong, Gabe."

It could be. Information like that came in whispers and nudges and not in legal depositions. Every informant's words had to be salted a little, and some more than others; though Tony-O was the most reliable Wager had found in ten or so years of sifting information, the wrong word, the wrong interpretation, was always possible. "Right or wrong, it hasn't taken us anywhere. I think we should know more about the victim before we talk to the rest of the people on that list."

Axton eased into the left lane for the turn onto the I-70 freeway and the quickest route to the downtown campus. "Valdez said Covino filled out some work-study forms at the college."

Max was thinking Wager's thoughts again, which is what good partners did. "That's what I had in mind, too."

Wager was lost. The Auraria neighborhood that had been his home was gone, and in place of the rows of small brick houses there now sprawled two- and three-story buildings that looked vaguely like factories. He recognized the large block of blue tile and white brick that was the defunct Tivoli Brewery and, near it, the freshly painted yellow and gray plaster of old San Cajetano's bell towers, empty of everything except bird droppings. But these and the abandoned red stone synagogue were the only buildings left that he recognized—churches and breweries being prime targets for historic landmarks—and the very pattern of streets had changed, too. Some were gone completely beneath the new campus's grass and malls and buildings; others were blocked off by steel pipe and chains. The location was just half a dozen blocks from main headquarters, but since it had its own security force, the D.P.D. detectives had few calls to the area. Except for the bomb squad: several times a year they were alerted by anonymous threats to destroy that symbol of an evil society, the university. "Let's try the campus security office. It's supposed to be over on Seventh Street."

They were helped by a blue-uniformed sergeant whose brightly colored shoulder patch said "Auraria Campus Police." She had shoulder-length black hair and said "sir" at the end of every sentence.

"How'd you get in police work, Sergeant?" asked Max.

"I was a philosophy major, sir." That seemed to explain it for her; she showed them on the map where the Metro State student aid office was located and then aimed them out the door in the right direction. Past a building that looked as if it were made of flattened tin cans and was labeled the Learning Resources Center—Wager had always thought books were kept in a library—they rounded a corner to see the granite blocks of St. Elizabeth's church. Somewhere near here, beneath the Vibram soles of the students in jeans and down parkas who streamed in and out of that Learning Resources Center, was the spot where Wager had lived when he was a kid. Maybe he and Axton were even now walking over the old basement where his father and his mother's brothers made their wine every year, mashing the grapes in the smoothly worn wooden tub—never a metal washtub like some used—and sending Wager and his cousins scouting through the autumn streets for empty jugs and bottles, tinted glass only, because too much light wouldn't be good for the wine. Wager could still remember the heavy, dizzying smell trapped between the basement ceiling's joists, where drops of resin had long ago aged to amber beads and glinted in the motey light of the single basement bulb like the eyes of a hundred spiders. And he could still feel the cold, spongy glide of grapes popping beneath his treading feet; and he remembered, too, the dark-red stain halfway up his shins that wouldn't wash off but had to wear away while other kids at school, whose fathers didn't make their own, would ask him what kind of socks he was wearing. His father had always given one of the first bottles to Mr. Ojala; you could never tell when someone in the family might need Tony-O's help. That was—Jesus!—twenty-five, almost thirty years ago.

"Here we are, Gabe."

It was an office with thin, movable walls and unpainted

concrete beams and pillars. Wager had heard the design described as "functional modular," but that was just another name for cheap. He hoped the new justice center which they were to move into someday would not be as ugly. The dark-eyed girl in jeans who sat poking two fingers at an electric typewriter seemed surprised to see Wager and Axton, their ties and sports coats, the slacks and shiny shoes. "You need some help?"

Axton showed his badge. "We're trying to get some information about Frank Covino, miss. I understand he had a job here?"

"Oh, wasn't that terrible—he really was a nice guy."

"Did you know him?" Wager quickly asked.

"He was in and out of the office. I bet you want to talk to Mr. Dumovich."

"Who's Mr. Dumovich?"

She looked as if Wager ought to know. "He's the director. Just a minute."

It was half a minute. Her head came back through the doorway cut into the thin wall. "Come on in."

Mr. Dumovich was in his late thirties and trying to look younger, pale hair sprayed to lie straight to his collar. He didn't wear jeans; instead he had on washed khakis that reminded Wager of his own Marine Corps summer uniform. But Mr. Dumovich did wear the same kind of Vibram-soled hiking boots that all the students clumped around in, and as the man walked back to his desk, he rocked slightly fore and aft in the thick, unbending leather.

"Yes, Frank Covino was one of our students. But the only information we have would deal with his family's financial status and his academic standing. We don't look into a client's personal life."

"Can we see his file?" asked Wager.

Mr. Dumovich frowned. "I don't know about that. There

42

have been so many changes in the access rules, and the dean hasn't sent down a memo yet . . ."

"The man's dead," Wager said. "He's not going to complain about an invasion of privacy." If need be, they could get a duces tecum subpoena for the records. But that would take time and mean another trip.

"His relatives might! It's surprising how many people these days are after personal information of the most innocuous type. And I certainly don't want the college or this office to be embarrassed in any manner possible."

"Mr. Dumovich." Axton leaned toward the man like a falling, smiling tree. "Nobody wants to embarrass anybody. We're just asking for a little help in catching the boy's murderer. It would embarrass me if I didn't want to help catch a murderer."

"Well, of course I *want* to help! But the records access rules . . ." He fidgeted and looked from Axton's gentle smile to Wager's not so gentle one and finally said, "Oh, very well. But it must be entirely confidential, understand?"

Dumovich called to the girl laboring at the typewriter in the outer office and she brought the folder. Beneath a pile of pay receipts for the last year and a half, it held a computer printout labeled "BEOG-FFS" and a mimeographed form with the title "Application for Financial Aid." Max took one, Wager the other, and they began reading the several pages of each. Buried among the sections requesting information about the student's status, about his spouse if any, his parents if living, his residential history, his job history, current in-state status, evidence of taxes paid, was a section for Income and Expenses. Covino had listed his basic family income as $500 per month for three people; source, United Mine Workers survivors pension, social security, Black Lung Pension Supplement. He also listed as his own income his liquor store job at $2.35 an hour, and his sister's $1.75 an hour as a waitress. At the time of the initial application, almost a year and a half ago, he carried the minimum twelve credits of academic work and had a B average. Under the heading for Assets and Liabilities, he listed only a 1972 Chevrolet, value $1100.

"This is it?" asked Wager. It wasn't a hell of a lot for Dumovich to get embarrassed about.

"That and the grade transcripts. Each term we check to see if the client is maintaining a satisfactory academic standing in units taken and in grade-point average. If he or she is not, we bring him or her in for counseling—often he or she is carrying too many hours or working too much. And of course, if he or she fails, we terminate the funding. It's all strictly governed by federal rules and regulations and is part of the contract."

With him or her. Wager glanced at Axton, who nodded and bent to shake hands with Mr. Dumovich. Outside, leaning against the stinging grit of a sudden gust of raw wind, Max wagged his head. "It looks like everybody's telling the truth. Hard-working, honest, ambitious—not your usual target for a professional hit man."

That was true. And it meant they had exactly the same number of motives they began with—zero.

four

They spent the rest of Tuesday morning and all that afternoon tracking down the people on Max's "list of friends." Accentuated by a tone-alert call to a holdup in progress at a fast-food joint, and the discovery of one more nameless teenage victim of an overdose in a sagging crash pad off East Colfax, the day was a waste. Not one of the people they located told them anything new about Frank Covino; and not one had been with him on Sunday night. Covino had simply walked out of his house headed for a movie, and then turned up dead.

Axton rinsed the last of the day's coffee out of his cup and dried it with one of the paper towels used to wipe ink from suspects' freshly blackened fingers. "Any ideas?"

Wager looked down the list; all but a few of the names now had the little x in front which meant they had been seen and crossed off. "I'll try to get to the rest of these this evening. And maybe some of my old snitches have run across something new on the Scorvellis."

"Want me to help you with that?" asked Max.

"No. It's my turn for the overtime." Max had worked on the list the night before, and he was a family man who liked to look in at home once in a while. Wager knew exactly what his own empty apartment was like, and it wasn't going to change much in his absence. It did not change much in his presence, either.

Axton left five minutes before the four-to-midnight shift came on. Wager stayed to argue Fat Willy, an informant from Wager's stint in narcotics, into meeting him at the Frontier; he was hanging up the telephone when the two night-shift detectives—Ross and Devereaux—entered the office together.

"Don't you ever go home?" Ross tried to make the question sound like a joke, but it didn't quite come off. Since their first argument when Wager had come over to homicide, they got along like two dogs with one bone, and when either saw a chance to snap at the other, he took it.

"Some cops are more professional than others, Ross."

The man's hazel eyes bulged. "If you're so goddamned professional, Wager, why in hell don't you belong to the union!"

Devereaux grinned uneasily. "Either of you guys want some coffee?"

"The union doesn't make better cops, Ross. It just makes more lawyers." He closed his notebook and smiled as he stood, ready for whatever the taller detective felt like trying.

But the man with the angry face and carefully sculpted brown hair only glared at him while Devereaux busied himself pouring a single cup of coffee. Wager nodded pleasantly and stepped into the hallway, followed by Ross's half-strangled "Fucking spic runt!"

46

Wager had almost stopped smiling by the time he walked the two blocks to the Frontier Bar and Grill; at some time during the afternoon, the morning's cold, clear wind had blown itself out and in its place an April snow shower gusted off the icy mountains in wet, gummy flakes that fell like a heavy curtain across the prairie, soaking clothes and streets, driving people's faces toward the ground as they hurried. Already the dark sheen of wetness on the sidewalk was stippled with tiny grains of ice, and by early evening the dirty water running along the curbs would turn thick and scummy with yellow slush. Fat Willy had bitched about meeting him at the Frontier in this kind of weather, but Fat Willy always bitched about meeting Wager, anyway; the one thing worse than Willy's coming over here would be to have Wager drop by and give him a big friendly hello in front of his own people. "All right, Wager," Willy had grumbled into the telephone. "I be seeing you there at six o'clock. But it better be worth my valuable time."

That gave Wager a couple of hours to eat and to think. He wove between the crowded tables of the Frontier's barroom, where Red glided back and forth behind the long counter to serve happy-hour doubles at the gabbing men standing rib to rib against the dark rail. In the rear dining room, quieter with only a few groups scattered here and there this early, Wager slid into his favorite booth near the clatter of the serving window and raised a hand to Rosie, who said, "Be with you in a minute, Gabe."

When the woman came for his order, it wasn't with her usual smile.

He glanced over her worried face. "How are the kids?" There was a husband to ask about, but neither Rosie nor anyone else knew where he was.

"Fine, Gabe. They're all fine." The woman's dark, round

face relaxed into the familiar smile when she talked about them. "Inez is in college and doing just fine. I told you she's going to be a teacher? Her first year, and she's doing real good."

"The other two?" He never remembered their names, either.

"The kids are all O.K." She absently scratched her pencil across the order pad, and the sagging permanent that curled her graying hair quivered. Then she looked up. "They're closing us down, Gabe. They told us they're going to close the Frontier at the end of the week."

It took a minute to understand what she meant. "Why?"

"They condemned the building for a parking lot. For that . . . thing!" Her stubby, strong hand flapped at the wall, beyond which was the blank concrete face of the new concert hall. "They put up something like that, and the taxpayers get stuck for a couple million a year. While a place like this . . . This place has been paying taxes for eighty-two years!" She abruptly cut off the words and forced a tired smile. "And I feel like I been working here for most of them. You're hungry, Gabe—what's yours?"

He gave his order and, as he waited, gazed around the dimly lit walls at the rusty branding irons, rowels, yokes, varnished and crackling Wanted posters, samples of barbed wire, mining equipment, and various photographs of awkward posed figures with the occasional blurred face of someone who moved too soon. Eighty-two years of collecting junk from ranches and farmhouses that had once been a half hour's horseback ride across Cherry Creek or the South Platte; eighty-two years of customers bringing some piece of old mining gear from Leadville or Central City to see it mounted on the dark paneled walls with their name typed on a little piece of paper underneath. And almost thirty-five years that Wager had been coming here, too;

first as a wide-eyed kid with slicked-down wet hair when his father would take them for one of the rare treats of a meal out: Mother's Day or a birthday. Then, much later—and with that half-pleasant, half-itchy feeling of coming back to a place after a long time—when he was a uniformed cop. Lorraine, his ex-wife, used to say he spent more time here than at home. It wasn't true, at least not then. Now, of course, it was. There wasn't another place in town in which he felt more at home. And now it was going, too.

Rosie brought the dish of steaming chicken and rice with its poached egg and jalapeño sauce. "Watch the plate it's hot," she said automatically.

"What are you going to do when this place closes?"

"Mr. Harter wants me over at his Sixteenth Street restaurant. I'll have a job, sure; but it won't be the same." She, too, looked around the cluttered walls and listened to the hoot of male laughter from the bar. "I been here so long it's like home. There won't ever be another place like it. It almost makes me feel like I'll bust out crying." But she didn't; instead, she hustled back to the serving window, where the bell was ringing another order.

As usual, Fat Willy was late; it made him feel good to think that Wager was waiting for him. Just as it made Wager feel good to act as if he didn't notice the wide figure in the familiar white suit and broad-brimmed Panama hat as it floated across the room toward his booth.

"All right, Wager, you tell me what's so important I got to come out in this kind of weather, man."

"Vodka and Seven?"

The broad black face bobbed yes. "But I ain't got all day to socialize. I'm a working man—not a cop."

Wager ordered the drink, knowing that if Fat Willy ever did as much business as he talked about, he'd be living up in

Aspen screwing movie stars. "What do you hear about the Scorvelli people lately?"

The large man sipped and tilted his head back, letting a little of the room's dim light glisten on cheeks that swelled fully beneath his slitted eyes. "Not much. I thought you was out of that organized crime thing?"

"I am. But somebody with Dominick might have wasted a kid named Covino."

Fat Willy held the glass under his nose and thought before he drank long and deeply. "That's heavy. Very heavy. What's this Covino do to get that?"

"That's one of the things I'm asking you."

Fat Willy set his empty glass down; Gabe gestured for another. "You sure as hell don't ask for much, do you, Wager?"

"Just some information about that hit."

"Shit, Mexiboy, not from me. People who ask about hits *gets* hit."

"Just listen around and tell me what you hear. Nothing else."

"Look, my man, I don't mess with them Scorvellis. They been in town a long time and they got more connections than the whorehouse telephone. They work their side of the street, and I got my own little corner where nobody bothers old Willy. You want me goosing around for some Scorvelli hit man?" Willy's head jerked up with a short laugh. "Wager —you got what they call gall."

"You lay off your bets with the Scorvellis, don't you?" One of the actions in Willy's little corner was gambling, another was dope. He may have run a small stable of whores, too; more likely, he rented protection to their pimps. But he had been Wager's snitch for quite a while now; and as long as he dodged the other cops and didn't get too big, Wager let him run.

"Who says that!"

"Who else is there?"

"Man, I don't know nothing about laying off because I don't know nothing about betting. That is illegal!"

"You don't have to ask anybody anything, Willy. All you have to do is listen. If you hear something of a tie between this Covino killing and a guy who got bumped off the board a year or so ago, let me know."

"Which guy's that? There's been more than one."

"The Marco Scorvelli killing. The brother."

In the dark beneath the hat brim, two white circles appeared. "Jesus, Wager," he said, as if he couldn't quite believe Wager would ask him something like that. Then he sat silent, his breath coming with that steady lurch that some fat men have. Finally, he spoke in a very soft voice. "If there is a tie-in, there's a hell of a lot going down somewhere."

"That's why there must be talk somewhere." If Tony-O had picked up on it, Willy should, too.

"A hell of a lot." Willy finished his second drink and rattled the ice at Wager, who ordered another for him. "And that means I want less than nothing to do with this whole motherin deal, Wager."

"Just use your ears, Fat Willy. They're next to nothing."

"Ain't you funny! But supposing I do, my man? I would like to know what it's worth."

If he were still on the narc squad, Wager could flash the bills right now. But homicide's snitch budget rode on the Bulldog's hip, and he paid each dollar as if it was out of his own retirement fund. "I don't know."

For once, Willy's surprise wasn't faked. "Don't know! Mister Detective Sergeant Wager, this old boy don't chop cotton for nothing. Ain't you heard of Uncle Abe and that emancipation jazz?"

"I heard." Willy had been as far south as Pueblo, Colorado, where he was busted once for hustling a crap game in somebody else's protected territory. But he acted as if he'd been whipped, worn chains, and branded; to Wager it was as bad as the Return to Aztlán preached by some of the Chicano kids, and just as wearisome. It seemed to be a fear of standing naked without the masks of the past; it seemed that a whole generation of people was trying to cash in on what their forebears had survived. "Willy, if you get something for me, I'll get something for you. But I don't know how much. It's not like I'm begging you to dangle your fat ass in the wind; just keep your ears open."

"I ain't fat! I am *big,* my man, and don't you try leaning all over me, Wager. You are too *small* to lean on me."

"I can pop you like a cockroach, Willy. A fat one. You want to try me?"

The answer came in a sullen mumble. "One of these mornings, you gonna get out of bed dead."

Wager only smiled and waited.

Willy shoved his half-empty glass away with long, shiny fingernails that looked delicate and out of place on his thick hands. "I'll listen, Wager. And if I hear something, I might tell you. Only if the price is right—because it sure as hell ain't gonna be for love."

Among the four or five names left on the list of Frank Covino's friends, Wager finally found one who told him a little more.

"Yeah, I was supposed to go to the movie with him, but I got a call to work at the last minute." Peter A. Cruz, twenty, friend of the deceased, interviewed at his home at 3212 Wyandot, City-County Denver.

"Where do you work, Mr. Cruz?"

"At the Bahia restaurant. I'm a busboy. Last Sunday was

supposed to be my night off, but one of the other guys called in sick and I had to cover. Maybe if that hadn't happened, Frankie'd be alive now. Or I'd be dead, too."

"You were a good friend of Frank?"

"Yeah, sure. There's a bunch of us went through school together. We see each other a lot—well, maybe not as much as we used to, but still a lot."

"Is the Bahia a good place to work? You make good money there?"

The young man's alert eyes were set widely apart, and they said that was a strange question. "It's O.K. Next year, I ought to make waiter. Waiters got to serve liquor and I ain't twenty-one yet. I'll get some decent money then."

"But you don't make much now?"

"Maybe sixty-five a week. If I wasn't living at home, I couldn't get by. But it'll be O.K. when I make waiter. I'm learning the trade, like."

"Did Frank ever lend you any money?"

"Frankie? Naw. Where would he get it? He made more than me, sure, but not that much more. And he gave part of it to his mother, anyway."

"Tell me what happened on Sunday."

Cruz shrugged. "There's not much to tell. He gave me a call around five and asked if I wanted to see a flick. Said he'd be by about seven or eight. Then the restaurant called about six-thirty and told me to come down. So I tried to call Frankie and tell him, but he'd already left. I told Mom to tell him I had to work when he came by. Next I heard, he was dead. It's really too bad."

"What movie were you planning on seeing?"

"*Star Wars.* We seen it before, but it's worth seeing again. That space stuff is something. Really profound, you know? Frankie liked it a lot—all the computers and robots. He was always reading this science fiction, really heavy stuff. That's what he wanted to go into—space electronics or something like that."

"Where's it playing?"

"It was down at Cinema One, but I don't know if it's still there."

"Did Frank have any special girl friend?" There were a few females on the list, but so far none seemed to be deeply involved with the victim, and all had denied receiving any expensive gifts or money from him.

"A *novia?* Naw. That was something his mom was always getting on him about: 'When you getting married?' 'Don't you meet any nice girls at college?' " Cruz laughed. "My mom does the same thing, but I tell her I'm too young to die. I mean . . . Well . . . you know what I mean. Poor Frankie."

"But Frank dated girls?"

"Sure! Hey, he wasn't queer or anything like that. He just didn't find nobody to get serious about. He was like me, man, a Catholic. You stay married a long time when you're a Catholic, so why rush it? That's what I tell *mi angustiosa.*"

Angustiosa. Wager recognized the word as slang for "mother." "Are you going to college, too?"

"What for? There's already too many college people running around that can't get a job. Hell, a waiter at a good restaurant, he can make as much—more!—than a lot of people with college degrees."

"Do you have any idea why somebody might want Frank dead?"

"Not a one. He was a real good guy—the kind you have over for Sunday dinner with your family. Maybe one or two people didn't like him so much. Hell, you go through life, you can't help making some enemies if you got any *talangos* at all—I've learned that! But Frankie?" The youth shook his head. "He liked most people and they liked him. And nobody didn't like him so much they wanted to kill him."

Wager's next stop was the Cinema One, a neighborhood theater that made its living by showing the big hits a lot later and a little cheaper than the major theaters downtown. He stood out of the thick snow and under the radiant heat above the open glass doors to the lobby, waiting until the last couple in the short line bought tickets. Then he held his badge up to the glass window at the startled bleached blonde in the ticket booth. "Were you on duty Sunday night, miss?"

"Yes, sir."

He slid a photocopy of Covino's picture under the ticket window. "Do you remember seeing this man?"

She frowned at the picture. "I don't know. He looks kind of familiar. But lots of times I don't even look at people's faces any more."

"Was the same doorman on duty?"

"Yes, sir."

"Can I talk to him a minute?"

She looked worried and scratched at the dark roots of her hair. "I guess you can go in. I guess Mr. Paxton won't mind. I hope not."

"I'll only be a minute."

The doorman, a sallow kid in his late teens with a maroon uniform and freshly squeezed pimples to match, had been watching him suspiciously. "Yes, sir?"

Wager showed him his badge and the photograph. "Did you happen to see this man come in or leave last Sunday night?"

The kid held the picture and looked at it first from one angle, then from another, up close and then out at arm's length. Through the curtained entry to the auditorium came the quavering violin sounds of tension and pursuit. Another bleached blonde, perhaps the younger sister of the ticket girl, yawned behind the candy and popcorn counter. "I'm not sure, Officer," the kid said slowly. "He looks like a guy I saw. He was standing in line to buy a ticket and some guy came up and said something to him and they left."

"What'd this other man look like?"

"Well, he had his back to me; I couldn't point him out in a line-up. And I didn't really notice either one until they left. It was a long line—you know how Sunday nights are when we got a big bill. And if this is the suspect"—he tapped the picture—"then he was only two or three back from the ticket window when they left. That's how come I noticed him—he waited all that time in line and then went off when he got near the window." He added confidentially, "I'm supposed to kind of keep an eye on the ticket window in case of a stickup so I can identify the criminal. We haven't had one yet, but I'm ready."

"Was this person who spoke to him tall or short?"

"Kind of short. Maybe a little shorter than you."

"Did he have a beard? Was he wearing any jewelry or anything that would make you notice him?"

"Like I said, I only saw him from the back . . . excuse me." He reached past Wager to say "Thank you" and take the tickets of a middle-aged couple coming in. "I was busy collecting," he said to Wager, "and I just looked up to see this man say something and then the two of them left. I don't even know where the other guy came from."

"Any idea about his age?"

"No."

The kid would be a real asset in case of a stickup. "Was he noticeably fat or skinny?"

"I guess thin. It's hard to say because he had a coat on, but his shoulders didn't look too wide."

"What color was the coat?"

"Light. Maybe gray or tan, something like that. And long. I mean below the knees. That was something a little different —I noticed that," he said with a pleased smile.

"Color of hair?"

"Right—that was something else I noticed! He had a hat on, one of these black things—a beret. I couldn't see his hair, but you don't see too many hats like that around any more. There used to be a lot of Brown Berets, but this one was black."

"What color was his neck?"

He thought back. "Light—it was a white guy."

"How long did they talk?"

"I'm not sure. A minute, maybe. I tore a couple tickets and when I looked up again, they were walking off." He couldn't hold it back any longer. "What's this guy done? The suspect in the picture?"

"He's a homicide victim."

"Jeez!"

"Did the man in the coat walk in any special way? Have a limp or anything?"

"Not that I noticed. They went off pretty fast."

"Can I have your name?"

"Sure. What for?"

"In case I have to come back to verify some of these facts."

"Oh. Bill Paxton. I'm here all the time; my dad runs the place."

The boy didn't seem overjoyed about working for his father. "Can you tell me what time the show started last Sunday?"

"Like always—shorts at seven-twenty, feature at seven thirty-five."

Wager took a business card from his wallet. "Here's my name and number. If you think of anything else—no matter how small it might seem—call and ask for me or leave a message, O.K? Think it over real well—you just might have seen the man who killed this kid."

"Jeez!"

It was almost nine now, and Wager was starting to feel the heavy hours of the long day press on his shoulders and stiffen the small of his back. Still, there was one more thread to tug before calling it a day: Gerald Covino's arrest. He called in to the dispatcher for Detective Franconi's location; the reply came that he was on Code Seven at an all-night truckers' restaurant farther down on Wyandot, where the freeway ramps and railroad spurs looped in tangles around each other. Wager found him in the last booth, scraping egg yolk with a piece of toast and half listening to the crackle of his radio pack standing on the small table.

"Hi, Gabe. I heard you asking for me." Mario Franconi, about Wager's size, had on a navy-blue blazer with neat silver buttons that looked out of place against the simulated leather and greasy chrome of the restaurant. He wore a closely trimmed mustache in a thin line over his wide upper lip, and with the blazer, it made Wager think of a hotel manager or a jewelry salesman. But the man had a pretty good reputation as a burglary detective, and Wager tried not to hold against him the fact that Franconi was studying to be a lawyer.

He slid into the facing seat and shook hands. "I'm after some information on Gerald Edward Covino. You popped him about eight or ten months ago, remember?"

Franconi slid the egg yolk back and forth with a corner of toast for a second or two as he mentally thumbed through the arrest reports he carried in memory. "Covino. Yes, indeed. Burglary, but he bargained for breaking and entering. Yes, indeed. We had a four-square conviction on the lesser charge." He dabbed gingerly at his mouth with a folded napkin, ran a finger along each side of the thin mustache, and neatly tugged his jacket sleeves up to loosen them before propping his elbows on the table and leaning forward. "He was found with his burglary tools on him, so we might have gotten him on intent, but the D.A. didn't want to waste time pushing for it. Covino had taken nothing—opened no cash drawers or safes—so the strongest charge was breaking and entering. We suspected he had accomplices, but he was the only one we caught; and he wouldn't name anyone else." The thought suddenly landed in Franconi's eyes. "Wasn't that the name of the latest homicide victim? Any relation?"

"Younger brother. First name Frank or Frankie."

He stroked his mustache a moment or two more. "I don't recall that name. Only Gerald's."

"Do you remember anything about the bust?"

"Yes, indeed! It was almost comic. The uniformed officers received a ten-ninety, silent type, at approximately 3:45 A.M. It was at a drugstore on the north side of town off the I-25 and Thirty-eighth Avenue intersection. The exact location escapes me, but it'll be in Covino's trial record. I was on graveyard and of course responded, too. When I arrived, the patrolmen had been there perhaps two or three minutes ahead of me, having come up without lights or siren. They found the front door still locked and one of them was looking for a way to the back of the store. Let's see . . . one of the officers was McBride—Pat McBride. I can't remember the other's name. It was this other one who was looking for a way to the back entrance. But the building was one of these long series of stores side by side, so of course there was no immediate access to the rear of that particular store," Franconi explained carefully.

Wager took a deep breath and forced a patient smile and nodded. Franconi was going to make a fine lawyer.

"I picked him up and we swung around the corner and came down the alley. At that time of night, we naturally made some noise driving up, and fully expected to see the suspect or suspects running down the alley, so I had my high beams on. And remember, the patrolmen had already rattled the front door, so that anyone inside must have known an alarm had gone off and that officers were on the scene. But no one was visible. We stopped and tried the back door and found it open. Later investigation revealed that the dead bolt had been picked and the snap lock had been slipped by a piece of plastic. We thought we were too late, but in we went, anyway; I covered while the uniformed officer entered, and then he covered for me. We stood on each side of the doorway for a few seconds to let our eyes adjust, and then began moving through the stockroom toward the front of the store. We couldn't find the light switch, of course, so the officer whose name I can't recall was shining his flashlight around as we went forward. Still nothing—no sound of anyone running, no heavy breathing, no scurrying around. We reached the main part of the store and by the streetlights coming through the front window could see the pharmacy station on the left. The cash register was near the door, and so the two of us started down the left side toward the pharmacy and then we were going to sweep the cash register area and unlock the front door for McBride. All this time, we were keeping our eyes wide open in case someone was still in there and bolted for the back. We didn't really expect that —as I've said, we had made enough noise to scare off an army. Anyway, we made it past the pharmacy, and since none of the drawers behind the counter were pulled out, we again thought the thief had been scared off. When we drew near the register, we could see that the cash drawer was closed, but it was approximately then that we smelled him."

"Smelled him?"

"Drunk as a skunk and twice as fragrant. Apparently, he had passed out before he could rifle the cash register, and there he lay sound asleep and soaking wet, with an empty bourbon bottle in his hand and a puddle of booze deep enough to drown in. Kentucky Royal, it was—foul-smelling stuff.''

"He pulled the job while he was drunk?"

Franconi's eyebrows shrugged. "It's not so unusual. Granted, you're more likely to get stickups from drunken impulse than you are burglary. Still, it does happen, especially with your younger class of criminal."

"I thought Covino had a little more going for him than that. I thought he was a pro."

"Granted, that's generally for the amateurs. But Covino wasn't *that* much of a professional. We placed him in a holding cell until he sobered up and then tried to clear as many cases off him as we could. And there just weren't that many. He admitted to half a dozen break-ins and burglaries, and that was all."

If a suspect stood a good chance of conviction on one charge, it paid him to confess to all the others he had gotten away with. That way, he couldn't be prosecuted on those after he was given his time for the first one. But Wager still felt something slippery underneath the surface of facts. "Covino has been out of Buena Vista for five or six years. Are you telling me he only pulled half a dozen burglaries in that time?"

"That's all he admitted to. What would he gain by lying about that?" ·

A shorter sentence. But most wouldn't gamble that against further convictions. Unless there was something Wager could not yet see clearly. "Any idea what else he was up to before he tumbled?"

"Nothing concrete. We of course asked around when we checked up on his claims to the other burglaries. But you know how that is—if you have someone who wants to help you clear your books, you're not going to try very hard to paint him as a perjurer."

"Any talk about him at all?"

"Only that he was very hungry for the big time. But most of our respondents thought he talked a great deal more than he accomplished. It merely adds up to the familiar picture of a small-time hood with dreams of glory."

If that was the case, Covino would have been likely to exaggerate his other jobs. "Did you ever hear of a tie between his name and any of the Scorvellis?"

"No. I don't recall any. I don't think it's likely, though. Covino was a nonentity. Indirectly, of course, he may have known them through his fence—the Scorvellis have a finger in that pie, too. But Covino never named his fence. He was quite arrogant about not spilling a thing."

"You said he wasn't alone on this drugstore thing. Any leads?"

"None. And the only reason I think he had accomplices is because he had no transportation in the vicinity."

Wager thought that over. "West Thirty-eight's not too far from where he lived. He might have walked."

"That's possible, but not likely. My experience shows that most burglars will have a car within a block, either to pull up and load the goods or to put a lot of distance between them and the crime scene. There were no abandoned cars in the vicinity, and it's likely that the accomplices were parked at the back door, waiting for him to come out. Remember now, at this point in time, Covino had been in there long enough to pass out. A burglary like that should have taken, at the most, three or four minutes once the door was open. By the time I reached the alley, some eight or ten minutes had passed since the alarm went off. If Covino's accomplices were as amateurish as he was, they would be extremely nervous and might have left as soon as McBride and the other officer

62

tried the front door. Or they might have had a police frequency scanner and heard the dispatcher call McBride. That technique's becoming quite popular of late. Either way, if they drove out the other end of the alley, I'd never have seen them."

And, Wager thought wearily, that left things about where they had been. "Come on, I'll walk you to the cars."

"Be with you in a minute. I want to wash up and comb my hair."

five

Wednesday mornings were still conference mornings at the Organized Crime Unit's headquarters in the old office building that gazed through the trees of the state capitol grounds toward the gold dome. Wager and Axton, following the Bulldog's suggestion, stood outside a small pane of plexiglass at the second-floor landing. Security person Gutierrez remembered Wager by name and smiled widely as she pushed the loud buzzer that unlocked the door. "They're all in conference, Detective Wager, but they'll be out in ten minutes or so. If you gentlemen want to wait in the interview room, I can get you some coffee."

"Thanks. I'll say hello to Suzy first."

"Oh, do! She'll be so glad to see you."

Wager led Axton past the desks jammed into a warren of open cubicles to the corner that had been his. On the whole, the place was the same; but here and there, in small details such as a new wall chart or a different arrangement of office furniture, changes had been made. Wager felt that curious mixture of familiarity and distance, as if he remembered the location better than the location remembered him, and it brought home the fact that he was no longer an O.C.U. agent but just another visitor from an outside unit.

"Gabe! I mean, Detective Wager!" Suzy, whose plainness was one thing that would never change, looked up from her typewriter. "I heard you were coming by."

She shook hands and he introduced her to Axton. "Is Ed in conference, too?"

"Sure—same old Wednesday routine. It looks like your new job really agrees with you! You're looking just fine."

"You do, too. I heard the unit was re-funded—that's real good."

She held up a thumb and forefinger, a quarter of an inch apart. "Gee, it was that close, but Inspector Sonnenberg really put on a good budget presentation. He really deserves a lot of credit."

"That's real good," said Wager again, because there wasn't much else to say, and all the words he'd used so far seemed awkward and strained. Odd, how things that seemed vital when he worked here weren't worth talking about after he left. He glanced at the three desks, empty at the moment, lining the wall beside the old, square window. His had been the middle one and he had kept its surface clean. Now it was littered with a wad of papers and had somebody's family album propped at one corner; on the other corner, beside the window, grew a potted marijuana plant with a small sign: "Keep Off the Grass."

Suzy followed his glance. "That's Detective Beasley's desk. He's real funny—he uses the plant for lectures to junior high kids."

It made no difference to Wager whose desk it was any more or how messed up he let it get. "Do you know if anybody's working on the Scorvellis?"

"I'm sure someone must be, but no one ever tells me anything."

That wasn't entirely true, but Suzy knew how to keep her mouth shut. That was how she kept her job, and Wager didn't hold it against her. "Can we wait in Ed's office for him?"

"Sure. I'll get you another chair. Gee, it's good to see you again!"

When they had been settled in the unit sergeant's cubicle with a third chair and the usual cups of coffee, Axton murmured, "I think you've got a girl friend there, Gabe."

"Suzy?" It was hard to imagine her as anyone's girl friend, let alone his. "She's a real nice girl. Like a kid sister." More like somebody else's kid sister, because Wager's was a real bitch who still blamed him for his divorce.

"Ah," said Axton.

"She takes pictures in her spare time. Photography."

"Ah."

They sat in silence while Wager wondered what the hell Axton meant by "Ah." The cubicle's plywood partitions were covered with the familiar pale-green paint and various framed awards and certificates that marked the points of achievement in Ed's professional life. Through the rapid thump of Suzy's typewriter and the pop of transmissions from radios scattered around the old building's second floor, Wager picked out the raw squeak of the electric clock's hand as it lunged ahead each minute. It used to be a sound as persistent and steady as the pulse in his own ears, and he had grown just as unconscious of it in the hours and days and months spent at that desk beside the window. Now the noise was new again, and it irritated.

Ed finally came in, his sloping shoulders and neck as stooped as ever, his pale-red hair a strand or two thinner in its sweep back from his forehead to cover the balding spot on his crown. As tall as Axton, he weighed half as much, and Wager thought again that Ed looked less like a detective than a rawboned dirt farmer broken by the hard prairie and bent under the weight of mortgages. As usual, Ed went through five minutes of preliminaries to find out briefly how Wager was doing, and to tell them at length how he was doing, the O.C.U. was doing, the inspector was doing, and finally to ask for a pat on the back for getting the unit re-funded all by himself. "Well, me and Sonnenberg worked hard on that budget presentation, Gabe. I did the pencil work and the inspector presented it. He's the senior man, so I guess it's the thing to do. And I guess they liked it. We're still suited up, anyway, but I tell you it was a long fourth-and-ten."

At last the sergeant asked, "What can I do for you?" and Wager told him.

"The Scorvellis?"

The wrinkle between Ed's sandy eyebrows told him that the question had poked at a sensitive area. Wager said, "We're still looking into the murder of Marco. We think there may be some connection with a homicide that happened last weekend."

"Well, sure, we're scouting the Scorvellis—we always are. The whole game plan's to keep the pressure on, you know. But I don't see that I can give you much that you don't already have."

"I haven't heard a thing since I left a year ago, Ed. Max and I would like to be brought up to date."

"Right, sure! Has it really been that long? My, my."

"Let's start with what happened to the organization after Marco was killed."

"Wager, I'm not starting anywhere! This Scorvelli family's a very touchy issue around here, and I'm not about to be called offsides on it."

"Ed, we're on the same side. I used to work here, remember?"

"Then you ought to remember the inspector's security regulations. Sure, we're working on the Scorvellis—I'll tell you that much. But I'm not about to tell you what it is or what we know. Period."

"If I have to, I can take this right up to the D.A., Ed. You know that. And you know Doyle over in homicide, too. If I tell him that you've refused to cooperate in a legitimate investigation run by his department, he will raise such a stink you'll have to fumigate this place. Think about that when funding time comes around again."

The stoop-shouldered man ran a hand up his narrow forehead and across the wedge of thin red hair, then patted it back down. "Maybe you'd better talk to Sonnenberg."

"Maybe we had."

The unit chief, Inspector Sonnenberg, was lighting a fresh maduro from one of the long kitchen matches he kept in a glass at the very edge of his almost vacant desk. Wager and Axton each were issued one of his rare smiles with their handshake, then Sonnenberg sat back down in his dark-green swivel chair. "I take it you're after something that Ed won't give you. What is it?"

Wager was just as direct. "We want to know what the Scorvelli organization's done since Marco was killed. It may have some bearing on another homicide that happened last weekend."

Sonnenberg swiveled so that they could see only his angled profile. He rolled the cigar between pursed lips and held it just off his mouth; out of its wet end a tendril of brown smoke curled like a small question mark. *"I* haven't heard of their involvement in any recent homicide. What is it exactly that you're looking for?"

It would have been a lot easier if they had questions on

68

specific points, Wager knew. But just now they were groping, and that was on a rumor from an uncorroborated source.
"We're not sure," he admitted.

The inspector swiveled back quickly. "You mean you're
fishing?"

"We have a tip, but . . . yessir, a lot of it's fishing."

"I can't allow you to blindly poke around, Wager. The
subject is extremely sensitive, and I don't want anyone making waves right now."

"A good informant told me that Marco Scorvelli's hit and
this latest homicide were linked."

"What informant?"

"Tony-O. He told me Sunday afternoon that one Frank
Covino knew something about Marco's death, and on Sunday night Covino was killed."

"Lord, is that old man still around? He goes back as far as
the Scorvellis. Further, even."

"Yessir."

"But he's also been out of the action for a long time. His
tip could be wrong; we never had a whisper to indicate who
actually killed Marco."

"Yessir, he could be wrong. But Tony-O knows the street,
and you have to admit it's a weird coincidence. So there's a
chance that he could be right, too."

"Wager, if you had some specific questions, I could answer
them. But as it is . . ." Sonnenberg shook his head.

"It's the only lead we have on a class A felony, sir. Homicide." Wager did not spell out the threat the way he'd had
to for Ed.

The inspector played with the cigar again. Wager heard
Axton beside him shift his weight in the groaning captain's
chair. Ed, restless as ever, slowly rocked from one thin ham
to the other.

"All right. I'll let you have as much as I feel you need to

know, Wager. But for God's sake keep the lid on it."

That wasn't necessary; Wager kept his mouth clamped and gazed back into Sonnenberg's blue eyes.

"We have a contact inside the Scorvelli organization. You know what it would mean for him if anything I tell you gets out."

"I know."

"Well, you remember it. And remember this, too: the only reason I'm telling you is that you've worked with us before and I trust you." The chill blue eyes shifted to Axton. "And if Wager's told, his partner has to be let in. But nobody else. Absolutely."

"Yes, sir," said Axton.

"All right." Sonnenberg drew another mouthful of smoke and then lowered his voice and leaned across the desk toward them. "The contact is an agent—not local, but you don't have to know anything more than that. He tells us that Dominick had his brother Marco killed because he —Marco—objected to the direction in which Dominick wanted to take the organization. It involved a possible loss of local autonomy, but you don't need to know about that, either. Who the hit man was, we have no idea. A local soldier, somebody from out of town—we just don't know. Apparently Dominick made the arrangements very surreptitiously in order not to create any divisions in the organization after his brother's death. But the fact, if not the details, leaked out, and Dominick had to convince a lot of people that the move was the right one. In the last few months, it's become clear that he's consolidated his position and now feels that he can develop whatever it was that Marco objected to. Apparently, Dominick's organization is looking for new capital to finance a major expansion, but in what direction, our man hasn't found out yet. As usual, Dominick's very close-mouthed about his plans. But here's why

70

things are so very sensitive just at this time: our agent has a chance to be promoted when the expansion does occur. The organization trusts him that much. Dominick told him that the expansion's going to be in an entirely new direction, one that will require new personnel, and that he has our agent in mind for a very responsible position in the new division."

"That's really something!" said Axton.

Sonnenberg said with emphasis, "It is. And we don't want anything to shake him out of that position. Anything!"

"It's not a takeover of somebody's territory?" asked Wager.

"No. From Dominick's point of view, that's the beauty of it. The move won't cause any territorial disputes because so far nobody else has thought of it. And he's not about to let the idea out until the last minute, when the whole operation is set up and can be activated without opening doors for someone else to move in. He promised our man that he'll be —and these are Dominick's words—'in on the ground floor of a major new operation, a very big operation.' It's supposed to happen soon, but only Dominick knows when. Our man thinks Dominick's waiting to make sure of some out-of-town negotiations before he says go. At any rate, Dominick passed the word that nobody in his organization is supposed to stir up anything without his personal approval."

"When did this word go out?"

"Perhaps a month ago. So you see why I'm not inclined to lay your homicide at Dominick's door."

"Unless it was an emergency. Unless Covino somehow found out something about Marco's death." But, Wager wondered, how in the hell would a straight kid like Frank Covino learn anything about the Scorvellis?

Sonnenberg puffed out another stream of yellow-white smoke. "I suppose that is a possibility. I suppose you will have to consider that angle. But you can see what it will mean for us if we get our own man promoted to a lieutenant in Dominick's organization. If we can penetrate that far, we stand a good chance of getting Dominick himself, a good chance of flushing a big wad of filth down the toilet. And by God, I'd like that!"

Axton let out a long breath. "Jesus. It's like a pile of toothpicks. We can't wiggle one without shaking the whole mess."

"That's exactly why I don't want any wiggles at all. At the present time, anyway. And you realize that if you do find your killer, it won't be Dominick himself. He doesn't do his own work, even on his brother. Our only chance to nail someone as big as Dominick is through a conspiracy charge, and this is the best opportunity we have ever had."

"Jesus," said Axton again. "That really puts Gabe and me between a rock and a hard place, Inspector. The Bulldog's going to want to know why we're not chasing down that Scorvelli rumor, and you don't want us near the guy."

"I know Chief Doyle," said Sonnenberg. "And of course there's absolutely no question about his reliability. But, Wager, you know as well as I do that the greater the number of people who know something about an operation, the greater the chance is for a leak. It may be unintentional, but all it takes is a hint or a careless word; and the Scorvellis have ears everywhere—clerks, janitors, perhaps even some officers. The Scorvellis pay well for information, and this item would be worth a very great deal."

What Sonnenberg said was true, and Wager went along with it. From the last estimate he had seen, the Scorvelli organization had a payroll half the size of the police department's. Tax free. They could—and did—buy people wherever they needed them. "I suppose we could keep searching for other leads for a while, and the chief wouldn't get uptight about it. For a few days, anyway. But what you're asking for is anything from a couple of weeks to a couple of months. I don't see how we could stall for that long if Scorvelli's name keeps popping up."

"I've tried to explain the necessity of it."

Wager said, "Let me ask you, Inspector: What's the first thing that happens whenever there's a gang killing?"

Sonnenberg studied the ash of his cigar. "You mean it's routine to pull in a Scorvelli for questioning?"

"Yessir." It was just as routine to let him go again, too, but Wager didn't like to admit that. "And if Tony-O heard that rumor about the Covino kid and Marco, there's a good chance Scorvelli picked up on it. After all, Covino ended up dead, didn't he?"

Sonnenberg shifted his study from the cigar to Wager, and the sharp angles of his face drew closer in a frown. "So despite what I've told you, you want to pursue this rumor? Despite the strong probability that the rumor's false, you still want to step in and stomp around?"

"What I'm saying is, if we don't follow the routine of picking him up, he might want to know why. And if, on top of that, he's heard that rumor, it would tell him that we're holding off for some reason. He'd begin sniffing for something rotten somewhere, and that would really put your man's tail in a crack."

The inspector spoke with increasing anger. "I disagree, Wager. I think you'll arouse far greater suspicion by forcing it on his attention. But it's obvious that you intend to continue despite the danger you might cause a fellow officer. I hope that you still have enough sense of professional responsibility to keep what I've told you absolutely confidential. Because if you don't . . . if my man gets hurt . . ." He jabbed the threats back in his mouth with his cigar and glared at the two homicide detectives.

73

If Wager had not noticed the distance between him and his old unit before, it was stark now.

Axton broke the tense silence. "Our interest is in the murder, Inspector. Most of what you've told us doesn't bear on our case, so there's no need for us to say anything about it."

"See that you remember that."

Wager drove.

"Is Sonnenberg always that way?" Max asked.

"If you're working for him, he's behind you. The bastard got sore when he saw I wasn't still working for him."

"Well, I don't know as I ever want to work against him."

"He's wrong about Scorvelli." Wager was still angry at Sonnenberg's crack about professional responsibility; a lot of times that phrase meant "Do what I tell you," and that was one of them. It was as though he believed Wager had used his past ties with the O.C.U. and then betrayed Sonnenberg when he had the information he wanted. Well, Wager thought, maybe he *had* leaned on his old relationship for the information; but that stuff about betrayal was nothing more than crap. Because Wager knew that Sonnenberg was wrong in his reading of Scorvelli. If the police did not question him as always about any professional hit within a five-hundred-mile radius, Scorvelli would grow more suspicious than he already was by habit.

"Where are we headed?"

"Back to the office. We need a probable cause warrant," answered Wager.

"You still want to talk to Dominick?"

"Hell, yes."

"Jesus. Today was the day I should have called in sick and practiced my bagpipes."

The p.c. warrant was routine. The familiar Scorvelli name and the familiar phrase "known criminal activity" ensured a judge's signature without a lot of questions. However, it still took time for the departmental clerk to find one free to sign; and while he and Axton waited in the homicide office, Wager called down to Baird in the police lab. "Did the autopsy on Sunday night's shooting come in yet, Fred?"

"Wait one." Wager, holding the telephone to his ear, nodded when Axton gestured to ask if he wanted more of the office's hard, bitter coffee. "Right," said Baird. "It came in this morning. It doesn't change the cause of death; I'll get it right up to you."

A secretary brought it five minutes later. Wager untied the brown routing envelope and dumped out the Xeroxed sheets. His glass desktop was gritty from next door's construction dust and the dirt constantly churned by the traffic two floors below, and the heavy sheets crackled slightly as they slid over the surface.

"Anything new?" Axton's wide figure loomed at the corner of the desk.

"Not much." The description of the wound was more detailed, the path of carnage ticked off by a list of parts mutilated and missing from inside the victim's head. Lead pellets picked from the brain and various bones gave evidence supporting the shotgun theory. Not that it was needed; one look at the entry point and you knew what had done it. The analysis of body fluids revealed no drugs, no alcohol. The stomach contents showed he'd eaten about one to three hours before he was killed, and that was a little something. Wager thumbed back through his notebook to find his interview with Covino's mother: before he left for the movie, they had finished supper at about six o'clock. Wager tapped the entry in his green notebook and held it for Axton to read.

"That puts the time of death at between seven and nine, Sunday night," Axton said.

"Yes." Wager skipped down to the conclusions section of the report and scanned through it. "And the doc says absolutely that the body wasn't moved after it fell."

Axton rubbed a thick finger down the line of his jaw to scratch at the bump of an ingrown whisker. "Seven to nine . . . The time fits what the kid at the movie told you." Then a second thought came. "That's pretty early, even for a deserted place like the warehouse district."

A lot of winos prowled the loading docks, especially the fruit warehouses, looking for rotting oranges and grapefruits to mix with gasoline drained from pump hoses when they couldn't find anything better to drink. A chance existed that some had been prowling that early.

"Detective Wager?" The office clerk, in her mid twenties, short and chesty like a pigeon in the starched blue shirt, handed him the probable cause warrant. "Chief Doyle said he'd like to see you before you go."

"Oh, Lord," muttered Axton.

"Thanks, Kay." He waited until the squeak of her crepe-soled shoes was well down the hall before asking Max, "Any suggestions?"

"Yeah—you do the lying."

"Thanks."

The Bulldog looked up from one of the numberless forms that pattered onto his desk like bird droppings and were just about as useful. Wager had heard the chief complain about them, but the man also seemed to find a deep pleasure in the process of itemizing, totaling, charting, and cross-referencing data. It was one of several reasons why Wager never thought seriously about straining for a gold badge. "Good morning, gentlemen. What's your progress on that homicide?"

"Not a whole lot. The doc gave us the time and place of

76

death, and we have a poor description of a possible suspect. That's about it," said Wager.

"I see you asked for a p.c. on Dominick Scorvelli."

"Yessir. But it's just routine more than anything."

Doyle looked hard at Wager. "You did go over and talk to those people in O.C.U., didn't you?"

"Yessir."

"Well? Is this p.c. related to that?"

"Not really. They didn't know of any possible link between Scorvelli and Covino."

"Wager, are you giving me the straight skinny? I got the feeling you're holding something back from me, and I sincerely hope that's not the case." Those thrusting lower teeth showed briefly in the way that had earned Doyle his nickname, and his voice rose. "I sincerely hope you remember who in the hell you are working for now."

Axton's voice rumbled in a nervous gargle. "Gabe and I went over together, Chief. Both of us. Inspector Sonnenberg provided us some—ah—updating on the Scorvelli organization. But none of it was—ah—pertinent to our case. At least, not so far. It may prove later—ah . . ." His voice faded out.

"What kind of 'updating'?"

"Facts and figures, mostly. Operational information. That kind of thing," said Axton.

"Is this information confidential?"

"Yes, sir," said Axton and Wager together.

"Those people over there scream 'confidential' every time they break wind." Doyle studied each of them; in the corner of his office, the Bulldog's personal coffeemaker gave a muffled pop and hiss and a short, small dribble somewhere inside. "All right. Let's leave it at that for now. But I want no question in your minds about where your loyalties lie. Do you understand me, Wager?"

"Yessir."

"And I will not let the O.C.U. or anyone else put me in an embarrassing position by withholding information about my own goddamned cases. Is that clear?"

"Yessir."

"And you'd better remember that your files and fitness reports are in homicide. I don't give a tinker's damn if Sonnenberg claims confidentiality or not. If there's vital information concerning one of *my* cases, I want to know about it. If some other agency seeks priority over my department's activities, that is *my* decision to grant. Not yours or anybody else's but *mine*. You two got that?"

"Yessir."

The blue, slightly bloodshot eyes fixed on Axton. "Don't disappoint me, Max."

"No, sir."

Neither detective spoke as they entered the elevator, which moved jerkily downward. Wager was half angry about things he should have said when he had the chance and half puzzled over how someone like Doyle could make him act like a guilty schoolboy. Axton must have been feeling the same thing, because he finally whistled between his teeth and said, "It's not like we were selling secrets to the goddam Russians."

"Maybe Doyle and Sonnenberg are both rupturing themselves to be deputy chief." The anger at Doyle was spreading to anger at himself: He was the one who had let Sonnenberg put him in this position; it was his own damned fault for giving a promise to Sonnenberg, and for not coming right out and telling Doyle that to start with. That had been a mistake, and Wager was not the kind to shrug off mistakes, his own or anyone else's.

"If we screw up with Sonnenberg, we'll never get anything out of him again."

"That's right," said Wager.

"But if we screw up with Doyle, it's going to be our fannies."

"He needs us as much as we need him," said Wager. "If he wants to come down on us, there are ways we can get even."

"Sure—but that's a shitty thing to have happen in any department. I'd hate to cause something like that."

Axton was right; Wager had been in units that had gone sour with infighting and jealousies and favoritism, and the result was a total waste—waste of energy and effort, waste of purpose, waste of men and careers. "I guess we'll have to keep them both happy while we go out and catch the bastard, won't we?"

"Yeah. But, Gabe, let's use a lot of couth, O.K.?"

" 'Smooth' is the word." The elevator doors pumped open on the ground floor as Wager's radio popped his call numbers and the code that he had a message at the Motor Vehicle Division.

"Sounds like they located Covino's car," said Axton.

They would find out. At the main desk, Wager asked to use the telephone; a sergeant with cropped white hair handed it to him and turned placidly back to the woman standing on the civilian side of the desk and loudly wanting to know why she couldn't see her Jason right now. Wager poked the buttons for the M.V.D.

"We've located a vehicle registered in the name of Frank Covino," answered the police person. "His address is 2901 Quivas Street; the vehicle was ticketed this morning for a parking violation—it wasn't moved for the street cleaner last night."

"Have they towed it away?"

"We haven't put a tow order on it yet. The ticket just came through."

"Hold off on that; we'll get the lab people over there."

"Yessir," she said.

Wager hung up and then dialed the laboratory. The desk sergeant, voice as expressionless as a recording, was again telling the woman that her Jason would be kept in a holding cell until released or until transferred to County Jail, and that the only visitors allowed upstairs were the prisoners' lawyers.

"Lab. Baird speaking."

"This is Wager. That homicide victim's car turned up on Eliot Street. Max and I are going over there now."

"Wait a minute, let me get the address and description—"

"Forty-two hundred block," Wager read from his notes. "A 1972 Chevrolet Impala, license BF 7479."

"I'll try to get somebody over there after lunch. Don't screw up the evidence too much, O.K?"

"We won't touch it. Let us know when you're through so we can tell the family where to find it."

"Right."

The car was at the end of a block on a residential street that was quiet because it ran parallel to a main artery that took away most of the traffic.

"We're not too far from that theater Covino went to," said Axton. "It's one block over."

That was so. Wager walked once around the car with its slip of yellow paper tucked under the wiper blade. A film of dust had settled on it, and yesterday's wet snow, burned away by this morning's hot sun and clear sky, had left little circles and streaks in the dust. But there were no large dents in the fenders and the chrome had been polished free of rust. As his mother had said, Covino kept the car in good shape.

Max peered through the windows. "It's locked. Didn't the victim have his car keys on him?"

"Yes. GM keys." Wager, too, looked at the car's interior; then he turned to gaze around at the small homes, some with

80

brick porch pillars, others fronted by turned wooden posts painted white.

Axton read his glance. "What side of the street do you want?"

"This one, I guess."

As Wager worked his way from one door to the next, showing his badge and asking the same questions about that car parked by itself and anyone who might have been noticed with it, he could see his partner keeping pace across the street and occasionally hear the rap of Axton's knuckles on a doorframe. Wager did not expect much, and that's the way it turned out; but if they had not tried, he would have felt that his work was sloppy. In a lot of ways, it was like the carpentry his dad used to do before he had died: an extra brace inside where a lot of finishers might not put one because it couldn't be seen; a beveled edge or a countersunk screw that no one else would see. And the only explanation he had ever offered was to say, "It's *my* work." That was the way Wager felt, and that was why he wasted time knocking on doors when the chances were a thousand to one against learning anything. And, Wager was glad to see, that was the way his partner felt, too.

"I suppose it had to be done." The large man settled into their car's front seat and Wager felt the vehicle bounce a little under the weight. "Now what?"

"We've got a warrant to serve."

six

Dominick Scorvelli's office was a booth in the rear of the Lake Como restaurant. The sign over the entrance was outlined with pink and green neon scroll at night, but in the hot morning light, the painting of stiffly symmetrical mountains surrounding a splotch of blue water had peeled in large scales to show the dull red primer beneath. Even this early, two cars were nosed into the building's blank side; one wore a glow-pink bumper sticker stating "Thank GOD I'm Italian."

"There's some ethnic pride for you," said Wager.

Axton read it. "That's more than the Pope can say."

Wager drove once through the circular driveway that isolated the square building from its neighbors; Scorvelli's black Coupe de Ville with its leather bumper strips and half-open sun roof was parked in its own slot at the rear.

"That's exactly where we found Vern the Gimp six years ago," said Max. "They killed him in the back seat of his own car and parked it in that same spot."

And it was like Dominick to place his car right there; it was his challenge to the ones who had shot his uncle—and to anyone else who might have similar ideas about him. "Did you ever clear the books on that one?" Vern the Gimp had been a medium-sized name in off-track betting on the northwest side of town, and his death was one of a series in the Ortega family's attempt to take over that corner of Scorvelli territory.

"We had a little luck that time. Vern was killed by some people the Ortegas brought in from L.A. But when they got home, they shot off their mouths and the L.A.P.D. picked them up on a tip. I guess they're still in Cañon City, though a couple other states wanted a look at them, too. Wherever they are, they'll be locked up a long, long time."

"The Scorvellis didn't go after them in the pen?"

"Not that I heard. Maybe they figured it wasn't worth the trouble."

"That doesn't sound like the Scorvellis."

"You're right. But I learned that somebody got Bruce Ortega when he went out to L.A. about six months later. Shot him in the knees and then set him on fire while he was still alive. I guess that got the message across; the Ortegas cleared out of Denver after that."

"Now, that sounds like the Scorvellis." Wager parked and they sat a minute looking at the restaurant's quiet doorway. It stood open to show a dark drapery that had the powdery stains of dried mud splashed up from the sill.

"Gabe?"

"What?"

"Remember—we do this very smoothly. Just a routine pop."

"Por supuesto. Let's go."

Past the curtained doorway, the entry turned sharply right toward a bar where the counterman, when he was on duty, could see whoever came in. Now the long, straight bar stood empty of all but a white glare from the fluorescent light beneath the shelf. The small ceiling bulbs gave a shadowless yellow glow, and when Wager and Axton turned into the room, a quiet murmur of voices from a knot of men at the back booth suddenly stopped.

"The restaurant's closed, gents." A hefty young man, tieless and mod in a blue denim leisure suit and wavy black hair, hopped up from a chair near the booth and came toward them. "We don't open till one."

He was new, but Wager would recognize him the next time they met. Wager showed his badge and went past the kid without answering. Behind him, Max muttered, "Keep your cool, sonny," and strolled closer to the bar for a better angle of vision into the booth—and a different line of fire if anything came to that.

Four peering faces were pale ovals in the dim ceiling lights. Next to the wall on the near bench was the Scorvelli accountant, Sully O'Brien; across from him was another face new to Wager, fifty or so, trimmed mustache and white hair plastered down across a wide skull. As Wager pushed past the kid in the leisure suit, the man's eyes widened into a startled look at Scorvelli.

"Police," said Wager clearly, holding both hands open in sight. "You people just sit still."

Richard Scorvelli—"Wet Dick" because of the drop of spittle that always seeped out of the corner of his twisted mouth—sat with his back to Wager, scowling over his shoulder; across from him and beside the man with the mustache sat Dominick. His cheeks were fuller than Wager remembered, and their flesh hung heavier from the jaw, but the dark fringe of hair around his balding head was the same, as were the clear brown eyes that lifted up and down once behind glasses as if measuring Wager for a coffin. Behind

84

him, Wager heard blue-denim's voice: "I'm sorry, Mr. Scor-velli—they're cops."

Wager's smile was wide. "Mr. Scorvelli! You are Dominick Scorvelli?"

"You know who I am, Wager. What is it this time?"

"I just need positive identification to lay this on you." He leaned across the table and stuffed the oblong paper into the man's coat pocket, wadding it on top of the three ears of the white handkerchief that peeped out.

Scorvelli tugged it loose and opened it, knowing what paragraphs to scan and which to read carefully. Then he tossed it onto the dark table among the tiny coffee cups and ashtrays holding half-smoked thick cigars. "Just what in hell is this for?"

"An invitation, Mr. Scorvelli, to visit our downtown office as the guest of the proud City and County of Denver. Let's go."

"What is this shit?" Wet Dick tried to stand, but Wager clapped a hand to his shoulder and pressed him back to the seat.

"Mr. Scorvelli, you are not required to say anything to us or to answer any questions. Anything you do say can be used against you in court. You have the right to talk to an attorney before we question you and to have him accompany you during questioning. If you cannot afford—"

"Goddamn it!" Wet Dick lurched upward again. "What crap is coming down, cop?"

"Sit down and shut up, dribble-chin. I'm doing my constitutional duty. If you cannot afford an attorney and you want one, an attorney will be provided for you. If you want to answer questions without an attorney, you will have the right to stop answering at any time. And last but not least, Mr. Scorvelli, you have the right to remain silent until you talk to an attorney. Do you understand these rights, Mr. Scorvelli?"

"I understand you're on my private premises," said Scorvelli.

"Cut it, Dominick. You've got the warrant and it's all legal. You've been through this enough times. Let's go."

"The hell you do!" Dominick's cousin tried for a third time to bounce out of his seat. "You can't just come busting in here like this!"

Wager turned to the angry face whose left side was clutched into a permanent scowl. "I am talking to your keeper, Wet Dick. You are interfering with an officer making an arrest, Wet Dick. One more squeak and I will include you without a warrant, Wet Dick."

"Don't call me that!"

Wager's grin was wider. "It's your known alias. Wet. Dick."

"Richard!" Dominick's voice was low, but it cut like a knife through Wet Dick's anger. "Just what is this harassment, Wager?"

"We'll talk about it downtown." He looked at the other two. Sully O'Brien was pushing back against the dark paneling of the booth as if Wager had bad breath; the man with white hair sat motionless and—the initial start of fear gone—without expression. Wager leaned closer to study the man's features. His black eyes blinked once and a small muscle strained along his jaw, but he said nothing and didn't move. It was the same blank look that Wager had seen in a thousand mug shots, and he bet there was one somewhere for this face, too. An old one, on file in a city back east, to judge from the three-piece suit and the pearl-gray homburg placed on the table in front of him.

"Sully, call Freiberg and tell him to come down and get me out right away."

"Yes, Mr. Scorvelli." The accountant leaned toward Wet

86

Dick to slide out of the booth, but Wager kept both of them pinned in the seat with his hip.

"You got any identification?" he asked the white-haired man.

Under eyebrows whose color matched the homburg, black eyes moved slowly up Wager's shirt to his face. "I might have."

"Mr. Scorvelli, here, is a known felon. Wet Dick, here, would like to be known as a felon, too. So you're consorting with known felons. I'd like to see your I.D. Either here or down at headquarters."

Silently, the man slipped a narrow hand inside the smooth tailoring of his coat and lifted out a long snakeskin billfold; holding a white card with two slim fingers, he flicked it on the table for Wager to pick up. It was a business card that said only "Victor Galen Associates."

"You're this Victor Galen?"

"I am."

"You want to watch who you associate with, Vic. It could hurt your reputation." Wager took the card by a corner and slipped it into his shirt pocket, then he tapped Scorvelli's shoulder. "All right, Mr. Scorvelli. Let's get the cuffs on."

"I don't need those."

Wager tugged the handcuffs from the back of his belt. "It's department policy, Mr. Scorvelli. All prisoners get to wear them. Otherwise they get rusty—you know how it is."

Scorvelli's lips, usually full, pressed into a tight line and his brown eyes seemed as brittle as the lenses in front of them. He slowly picked up a cigar and drew deeply, held the smoke in his lungs for a long moment, and deliberately mashed the fire from the tip. Then the corners of his mouth lifted in a thin smile. "All right." He stood and offered Wager a cigar. "No hard feelings, right?"

Wager did not smoke, but he sniffed the cigar appreciatively and tucked it in his pocket. "No feelings at all." He snapped on the handcuffs and quickly frisked Scorvelli.

"Richard, make our friend comfortable," said Scorvelli. "I'll be back in an hour."

Max was standing behind the kid in the blue denim suit, who looked worried when Dominick passed him, as if he thought he should do something. Wager gave him his chance. "What's your name, punk?"

"Fuck you."

"The name fits your face. Let's see your I.D."

"What for?"

"Consorting with felons, witnessing an arrest, wearing an ugly suit, and because by God I told you to."

The kid's eyes again shifted to Dominick and a red flush rose up the side of his neck; behind him, Axton cleared his throat with a low sound like distant thunder.

"Show him your I.D., Henry. Detective Wager likes to act a lot bigger than he is. He gets his pleasure from harassing innocent taxpayers. But all he ever gets out of it is a joke. A very small joke."

Henry took his cue and relaxed; high-class hoods didn't lose their cool in front of cops. He snapped open his wallet and pulled his driver's license from a small inside pocket. "I don't trust you with the whole thing," he said. "There's money in it."

"You shouldn't trust your birth certificate, either, if it's got your father's name on it." Wager noted the address of Henry Clark and handed the license back to the kid. "It's a real pleasure to make your acquaintance, Henry. I'm sure we'll be seeing each other again."

"I can't wait. Believe me."

Wager steered Scorvelli toward the glare seeping in around the curtain across the entryway; Axton lingered a step or two behind until Wager had his prisoner at the car. They

88

set him alone in the back and Axton drove, slowly, as Wager leaned over the front seat to talk to Scorvelli. "We're interested in what you know about a murder."

"What murder? That's this what's-his-name on the warrant?"

"Frank Covino, yeah. Somebody did it to him, Dominick, in a very professional way. Naturally, your name came to mind."

"For Christ's sake! What's with you people? Somebody dies, you come see me like I was supposed to write his obituary. I don't even know who this guy is!"

"You never heard the name Frank Covino?"

He shrugged. "Maybe I have; maybe I haven't. Hell, I don't know all the names I've heard. What you think, I keep a list of every name I hear? Bah! I got nothing to do with this guy getting killed. Anything else you want, talk to my lawyer. Come on, let's get down there so he can spring me."

"How's your mother doing these days, Dominick?"

"What's that supposed to mean?"

"Is she still taking Marco's death hard? I remember she was pretty upset at the time."

That got home; Scorvelli's right eyelid, the one behind the thicker lens in his glasses, suddenly drooped. He shifted his arms behind him to a different position and glared at Wager.

Who could not help another slow, wide smile. "Anybody ever claim that reward?"

"There's nothing illegal about offering a reward—for the arrest and conviction of."

"Not a thing. And it was a nice touch, Dominick. Real class. Now, why did you want Frank Covino killed?"

"I got nothing to do with that and nothing to say without my lawyer."

"He's probably waiting at the station for you now."

"He'd better be."

89

Freiberg was there, a dapper figure in a double-breasted brown suit and glasses whose wide horn arms disappeared into the carefully dyed silver hair curling at his temples. He trotted down the half-dozen steps of headquarters' front entrance, squawking about his client's being in handcuffs and about how the chief would be held responsible for this travesty of justice. Axton and Wager led Scorvelli through the small foyer with its two long benches, one on each side, crowded with friends and relatives waiting in silence for the bailed-out prisoners to be processed somewhere along the waxed and echoing corridors behind the front desk. On the end of a bench, his restless eyes never looking at the person he murmured to, Watson James—sole owner and operator of the Angel Wings Bail Bond Service—stifled surprise at glimpsing the handcuffed Scorvelli, and quickly found something else to gaze at.

"How's business, Watson?" Wager asked loudly.

The man smiled uneasily at a corner of the room. "Could be better, Officer Wager. Business could always be better."

"We're trying to help." Wager patted Scorvelli's shoulder and steered him to the front desk, where the sergeant with the cropped white hair, impassive as ever, hauled out a blank admittance form and beckoned Scorvelli closer.

"Maybe Counselor Freiberg, here, can give you some work, Watson," said Wager.

"I don't think so, Officer Wager. I sure don't think he'll need me at all."

Behind Wager, Axton gave a little moan and whispered in his ear, "Gabe, no waves, and very quiet—remember?"

"Did I break his thumbs? Haven't I called him Mister Scorvelli?" Wager whispered back. "I'm being as smooth as I damn well can."

"Smooth as a sledge hammer. That bondsman will have the word all over town in an hour. Let's just get him upstairs before the goddam reporters get here."

The desk sergeant took his time with the form, finally looking up to ask in a bored voice, "What's the charge, Detective Wager?"

"No charge yet, Sergeant. He's only here for questioning. Better give Counselor Freiberg a pass—he might want to go with us."

"I certainly do! And what's more, on behalf of my client, I indignantly protest—"

"This way, Counselor." Axton clipped the plastic card to the lawyer's silk tie. "You know where the elevator is."

"I also know where the chief's office is, and I assure you that he will hear—"

"Shut up, Freiberg." Scorvelli had glimpsed the black turtleneck of police reporter Gargan coming up the outside steps, and he roughly shouldered the short attorney toward the elevator. "Just get the goddam habeas corpus and get me out. I don't like the stink around here."

As the doors opened, Axton shielded the prisoner from view. Wager started a friendly wave at Gargan, but Axton's wide hand pressed him firmly into the elevator.

Once in the crowded homicide office, Wager unlocked the cuffs and offered Scorvelli the only hard, straight-backed chair in the room. Wager sat in one of the swivel chairs with its well-worn cushion, and Freiberg wasn't offered a seat anywhere.

"I'll stand, Wager," said Scorvelli. "I'm not going to be here that long."

"You'll be here seventy-two hours if I want it."

"What the hell's he mean, Freiberg?"

"He—ah—can hold a person for seventy-two hours before advisement if the charge might be a felony."

"You can't get me out of here right now? What the hell kind of lawyer are you?"

"Good question, Mr. Scorvelli!" Wager was enjoying this.

"Mr. Scorvelli, the law's clear on this point. Until you are formally charged, the need for a habeas corpus is unrecognized. A judge wouldn't waste his time hearing an argument for—"

"Waste *his* time! What about *my* time? I'm the goddam taxpayer around here and I don't know a goddam thing about this goddam Covino wipe or anything else, you bastard!"

"Mr. Scorvelli, please!" Freiberg's face turned splotchy with red and gray patches and he aimed a quivering finger at Wager. "You're overhearing privileged conversation—you can't bring a word of this into court! My client's addressing his remarks directly to me!"

"And accurately, too," said Axton.

"Suppose your client starts by telling us where he was last Sunday night," said Wager.

Scorvelli had put himself under control again; he beckoned to Freiberg and whispered something in his ear. Freiberg murmured back briefly and Scorvelli shook his head. "Bullshit, Counselor. I'm not going to spend seventy-two hours in this crap hole." He turned to Wager. "Is that when this what's-his-name got hit?"

Wager said yes.

"Jesus." His look asked Wager how dumb cops had to be to think a Scorvelli would put himself in the neighborhood of a killing. "I was out of town the whole weekend."

"Where?"

"You don't have to answer a thing, Mr. Scorvelli."

"What's to hide? My wife and me went shopping in Chicago. We took a flight out Friday midday and got back maybe noon on Monday. It was United Airlines."

"You're sure?"

"Sure I'm sure. I always fly United. I like to support local businesses."

92

Axton looked up from his notebook. "Do you remember the flight number?"

"Naw. But how many morning flights do they have to Chicago? Just call up and ask. The first-class section—I always go first-class."

"You used your own name?" asked Wager.

"Certainly! Whose goddamned name you think I'd use?"

"You've got a few aliases."

"What other people call me, I can't help. But my name—the Scorvelli name—that's what I use. It goes all the way back to the fourteenth century. I paid a guy good money to look it up and he drew me one of these—what you call them—family trees. Count Scorvelli in the fourteenth century. He had his own castle and everything up near Monte Sirino. Now, that's *real* roots."

"You've made it a name to be proud of," said Wager.

"You're goddam right. Now, like I told you, Wager, I don't know this guy that was wasted; I wasn't in town when it happened; you got no right to keep me here. So let's go, Freiberg."

"Just stay right there. We've got a few more questions."

The eyelid drooped again. "You got shit for brains, too." Scorvelli pulled one of the massive cigars from a silver case in his coat pocket and nipped it with his teeth, spitting the end on the floor. "Gimme a match," he said to Freiberg, who quickly leaned to light it.

Axton spoke into the telephone. "That's right—to Chicago last Friday. A Mr. and Mrs. Dominick Scorvelli."

"Where'd you stay in Chicago, Mr. Scorvelli?"

"My client doesn't—"

"The Palmer House. I like to stay there because it's too expensive for cops to go to."

"Is there anybody who can say they saw you there?"

"The registration book, Wager. When I checked in, and

when I checked out. Even you can figure that one."

"Under the name of Count Scorvelli?"

"It's a democracy, right? I just use 'Mister' in a democracy."

"When's the last time you saw Frank Covino?"

"Hey, hey—you're sharp. By God, what dazzling technique! Penetrating questions! Counselor, you should take lessons from this man." Scorvelli wiggled his fingers as if tying a shoelace. "He can twist a witness in knots."

"Well?"

"I never saw Frank Covino because I don't know Frank Covino."

"Who do you know who might want him dead?"

"Don't answer that, Mr. Scorvelli!"

"But I never heard of the guy, Freiberg!"

The lawyer whispered into Scorvelli's ear and the man with the cigar too thick to fit comfortably between his fingers nodded. Freiberg turned to Wager. "My client refuses to answer."

"On what grounds, Counselor?"

"On the grounds that it might incriminate him."

"Right," smiled Wager.

"A Mr. and Mrs. Scorvelli took flight number 236 at 10:25 A.M. on last Friday, and returned Monday on flight 263 at 11:32," Axton read from a scrap of notepaper.

"Where was Wet Dick over the weekend, Mr. Scorvelli?"

"Hey, you shouldn't call him that. People with an affliction, you shouldn't make fun of, you know? Didn't you have a mother to tell you that?"

"Was he in town?"

Scorvelli shrugged and plugged his mouth with the cigar. "Talk to Freiberg."

On a vague hunch, Wager asked, "What about Gerald Covino? Ever heard of him?"

94

"Not that I remember. Who is he?"

"Frank's brother. He's inside the walls for breaking and entering."

"And you want to blame me for getting him busted? I should get a medal for that, right?"

"Did you ever know or have you ever had dealings with Gerald Edward Covino?"

Scorvelli waved his cigar and Freiberg answered for him. "My client refuses to answer on the grounds that it might incriminate him."

"Who's this Victor Galen you were sucking up to in the restaurant?"

Again the cigar. "The question is irrelevant. My client refuses to answer."

The telephone rang and Axton picked it up. "Homicide Division, Detective Axton."

"Maybe you're trying to get at Gerald by having his brother killed?"

"My client refuses to answer on the grounds that it might incriminate him."

Axton's voice rose and he caught Wager's eye. "That's right, Gargan, for routine questioning. I don't care what Watson James told you, but it's only for routine questioning. No, no leads. Whenever there's a gang-style killing, we routinely talk to certain people."

Wager smiled at Scorvelli. "How's it feel to be so famous?"

"My client refuses to answer on the grounds that it might incriminate him."

"Do you wipe yourself after going to the toilet, Scorvelli?"

"My client refuses to answer on the grounds that it might incriminate him."

Axton hung up and bobbed his shaggy eyebrows. "Gargan wants to come up."

"Gargan can go to hell. Well, Mr. Scorvelli, I certainly want to thank you for your cooperation in this matter. Can we give you a lift back to the restaurant?"

"I got a ride." Scorvelli thumped the ash from his cigar onto the desktop and straightened his black overcoat. "There's a lot of things wrong with cops, Wager, and you got them all. If you'd of used your head, I might have asked around some and maybe could help you out, you know?"

"Mr. Scorvelli!" Freiberg's fingers clutched at the air.

"Maybe somebody would of picked up on something." Scorvelli tossed the long cigar into a crowded ashtray and straightened his glasses before leading Freiberg from the small office. "Now you can burn in hell for all the help I'll give you. And I'll laugh, Wager. I'll split my sides watching it."

When Axton returned from escorting Freiberg and his client past the security gate, he slowly poured himself a cup of coffee and then gently asked Wager, "What in the name of God did you want to do that for?"

"What?"

"Make a big show of bringing him in, Gabe. Pretending you were on TV or something."

"I want him worried. If he's worried, he might let something slip."

"But we were supposed to handle him with discretion, remember?"

"We didn't do one thing to tip him to Sonnenberg's operation."

"I hope not. I truly do. But we didn't show much goddamned couth, did we? We made Sonnenberg a promise to go slow, and then for Christ's sake we're telling Watson James and Gargan and everybody else about Scorvelli's bust.

96

Sonnenberg's going to hear about that, Gabe. And he's not going to like it one bit."

"I handled Scorvelli just like I would every other wad of puke. Anything different, and he'd start to wonder why."

"I hope to hell you're right."

So did Wager, but he wasn't about to say so—especially not with Doyle leaning through the doorway to pick up every word.

"You just had Dominick Scorvelli up here?" asked the Bulldog.

"Yessir. But he told us about what we expected. Not a thing."

"If he's really mixed up in this, I'll be glad to give whatever help I can. I've been watching him for years. He goes around and around like a turd in a toilet, but he never gets sucked down." Doyle's palm slapped the doorframe as if he spotted a mosquito. "I'll be more than glad to help, Wager. As a matter of fact, eager!"

"Yessir," said Axton. "We'll yell if we need help."

"Be damned sure you do that. It would be very, very good to get Dominick Scorvelli."

Axton peeked down the hall after Doyle and then muttered to Wager, "You're going to make me paranoid, Gabe. A man my size shouldn't have to feel paranoid; when I look over my shoulder, I run into things. And I still don't understand why you want the entire city to know we picked up Scorvelli—or why you wanted to rub his nose in it."

"Aside from plain not liking the son of a bitch, I've got a feeling. . . . I can't give it any more weight than that—a feeling. I think Tony-O was right; I think there's some connection between Covino and Scorvelli."

"And you want him nervous about that connection?"

"That's it."

"Well, now I've got a feeling, too, Gabe. Call it 'sick.'"

seven

Wager had been reading a book on fur trapping, telling of attacks by grizzlies and Indians, winter storms and starvation, summer rendezvouses and prairie battles within sight of his apartment balcony. It was with some feeling of irony that he also listened to his new microwave oven thaw a couple of filets of trout. Behind him, the television chattered monotonously to make the living room seem less empty, but when the telephone rang, its sound still echoed slightly through the apartment. It was the duty clerk, trying to locate a stand-in for Munn, who, it turned out, was as ill as he had looked.

"He's on the midnight-to-eight, right?" asked Wager.

"Yessir. We tried to get either Detective Ross or Devereaux to extend their tours, but they're union members and have their quota of overtime this month."

That was all she needed to talk Wager into it. His watch told him he could still get three or four hours' sleep, though he had planned on using the time in a better way, to prowl the loading docks where Frank Covino had been found.

The duty clerk misunderstood his silence. "It's only this one time," she said anxiously. "Captain Doyle can get a replacement tomorrow, but the hospital called just ten minutes ago to say Detective Munn had been admitted with a perforated ulcer."

"I'll be there."

"Thanks a lot, Detective Wager!"

The lilting relief of the girl's voice made a distant refrain in his mind as he read and listened to the microwave's hum. He hoped the filets would come out all right; they would never taste as good as those rolled in meal and broiled over a campfire, but the simple instructions told him what to do and assured him that the fish would taste just fine. They had been in the freezer since he caught them on his one fishing trip last summer, bringing them home with some vague idea of someday having a trout fry for some friends. However, there was never anyone to invite over. Of course, there was Axton and his wife; he supposed he could invite them sometime. But that would mean asking another woman, to balance things out. Maybe Suzy or even Police Person Fabrizio, who wasn't going around any more with that tall blond cop from Personnel Division. Yet even as he thought the names, he knew he wouldn't invite them. He understood himself well enough to know he couldn't be serious about either one in the way she would expect if he ever did ask her to his apartment.

Still, there came the times like this, when the small landscape photograph and the Marine Corps N.C.O.'s sword hanging on the apartment walls seemed no more than feeble attempts at scrawling his own name against blankness—like the sprayed graffiti on rocks and buildings, which meant nothing to anyone except the "Rick" or "Sandy" who put it there. Times when it seemed as if he really could give someone the part of his life that Lorraine had asked for in vain. Except that he hadn't really changed. When he plumbed the deepest well of his mind, he found that what Lorraine had said of him was still true—he was totally complete without her. How had she put it? She always felt like an intruder in her own marriage. And Wager couldn't tell her otherwise, because it was true. So his marriage, like other things, had gone; but occasionally, in uncharted times like this, he felt that loss.

Wager wandered through the featureless living room and out onto the little concrete balcony to gaze at Downing Street below. There, beneath branches still leafless and winter-stiff, the mercury vapor lights drained the color from locked houses and cars and walks empty of pedestrians.

He wouldn't change. That being so, it was no good to drag someone else into his life. That mistake had been made once, and the anger and pain, the accusation, the guilt, were not worth the little happiness he and Lorraine had had at first. When they both realized that, it was over. And, oddly, the formal gentleness with which they treated each other when that point was reached had caused a deeper ache in him than any of the earlier loud arguments or tense silences. Nothing was worth reentering that magnitude of pain, or bringing anyone else into it.

Wandering back inside, he turned the television's volume up a bit, the dialogue as mindless and half familiar as the taped music or the mechanical laughter that accompanied it. Most of the programs weren't meant to do more than destroy silence and turn off thought—when they worked. Tonight they did not seem capable of even that.

Did he regret what had happened? Not any more. It was as matter-of-fact as his feelings about the old neighborhood whose disappearance he had perceived so sharply yesterday. Better if it had been he alone who had suffered and not

100

Lorraine, too. But *todo tiene su precio, y su valor.* If there had been a price, there was also value in learning the range of his isolation and his strength to match it. Not everyone could or wanted to be able to say that, but he found pride in it.

So there would be no one over to share those fish and that was fine. Because what Wager really wanted was not to fill his apartment with dinner guests, but to clap both hands on something concrete and to pull and tug until a shape emerged that would tell him who killed Frank Covino and why. He wanted something more solid than the feeling that what he was looking for was just beyond his fingertips. If a man's reach should exceed his grasp, it sure as hell wasn't in homicide.

The microwave had fallen silent; its dial rested at the off position. He lifted out the trout and sniffed at the aroma loosened when he unfolded the wrapping. The fish filets lay in their juices, pale brown skin and steaming white flesh traced here and there with butter and lemon and crumbled chives. Gingerly, he peeled them onto a plate and then tasted. One was mushy, the other raw at the center; the instructions, like so many other simple guides, turned out to be wrong.

Trimming off what small portions were edible, he opened a can of beans and turned back to his book. What the hell; the supper fit with the rest of the evening, and he would soon be on patrol again, anyway.

eight

Since little usually happened during the graveyard shift, only one homicide detective was assigned to that duty, and no partner was there to tell Wager if Munn had been working on anything. He found no notes about current cases, nor did the twenty-four-hour board hold any messages for the ill detective. It was as if for all the years he had served, Munn had not really existed; and, the routine of duty watches ruffled only slightly by the man's absence, a replacement would be in the schedule by tomorrow night. A lot of people might find that heartless or demeaning. Wager found more comfort than not in knowing that Munn, Wager, even the Bulldog himself, were all dispensable. It was the sense of totality that his ex-wife had complained of and his distant cousin—the one who joined the Jesuits—had praised. "Police force," "agent," "commission"—to Wager, these words had a range of meaning that many civilians and even some of his fellow officers didn't grasp; but it was enough for him that he knew what service meant. Just as there was faith in serving the church, so there was faith in serving the law—and, it was to be hoped, justice as well. Except that his dedication was not to the remission of sin, but to conviction and punishment.

Slowly, Wager guided his police cruiser down the tunnel of dim glow from widely spaced streetlights that converged on one of Denver's high-crime areas, the Five Points section. At this hour, the patrol was more from habit than need, since the life that used to fill the heart of the black neighborhood until long after midnight had ebbed as more and more inhabitants moved into east Denver or to the suburbs in the surrounding counties. Soon developers in search of cheap land for expensive offices would move in; soon this area, like Wager's own, would be ground to powder under the steel treads of bulldozers and blown away in puffs of dust from collapsing walls.

He headed southwest, toward the brighter lights of Larimer. Almost by itself, the cruiser wove through alleys and side streets, tracing a pattern as random as the thoughts that ran like stray mice through his mind. And kept returning to nibble one thing: Covino's corpse. Those thoughts gradually led him toward the empty streets of the Denargo area and the site of the shooting. But in the widely spaced circles of dim streetlight, no figures shuffled across the pavement or scurried away from the headlights that swept over wall and doorway. Wager would try again tomorrow. And the night after. And the night after that. Since bums, like stray cats, had their territories and trails, and maybe the one he was looking for would show up. The one who had seen something last Sunday night. It was another long shot, but that was the only kind of shot Wager had, and there was nothing lost but a little time and a little patience.

The routine cruising through Denver's empty streets helped prop the sagging hours of Munn's tour; so did surveillance of Scorvelli's restaurant, which, Wager knew, never had many customers until near midnight, and then, for three or four active hours, large and flashy cars swung in and out like teen-agers cruising a drive-in. Wager, parked in the shadows of a vacant lot across the street from the Lake Como, absently watched the male figures, always in twos and threes, cross the brightly lit parking area to the cloth-draped front door. Once, a face turned to squint over at his still car, then the figure went inside and a few minutes later the curtain was held back while another face—that of young Henry Clark—came to peer out at him. Wager yawned and poured one more cup of coffee from the large Thermos that always rode the night tours with him. So they knew someone was watching. Good. If it bothered them, that was even better. Because Wager was bothered, and it always made him feel better when he could spread his irritation around.

He was deeply bothered. His irritation had gradually tilted into a subterranean anger because there was nothing to show that Covino had deserved what he got. It had been no accident—the boy had been selected to die. He had been executed not in fear or jealousy or blind madness—none of the things that civilization accepted as excuses for slaughter. He had simply been discarded like a thing empty of value, and Dominick was capable of doing that. But always for a purpose, and that's what chafed Wager's thoughts. Nothing, not one thing, even hinted that Frank Covino ever crossed over into Scorvelli's world, where laws and codes and values were distorted reflections of the so-called normal world. "Satanic reversal," Wager's Jesuit cousin would call it. From Wager's angle, the old-fashioned name for it was "underworld." And just as his Jesuit cousin was at the border between two worlds, so Wager paced the line between this and that nether world, part of neither. But sometimes he felt pulled closer to Scorvelli's realm than he liked to admit.

He sipped at the plastic cup, the coffee's stinging heat gone but its metallic flavor just as hard. The radio that tied him into the sporadic traffic of District Two muttered with that monotonous, level tone that always came halfway through the graveyard shift, announcing the ripples and swirls that bubbled to the surface of that world surveyed by Wager and other cops. Flipping the cold dregs of coffee out his window, he watched another Cadillac roll heavily and incongruously past the grimy pink stucco of the small restaurant whose mountain and lake glowed brightly over the dark door. Then Wager's radio buzzed an all-channel alert and the dispatcher's voice woke with excitement.

"Any homicide detective!"

Wager was it. "X-85; go ahead."

"We got a reported shooting in the one hundred block of South Broadway, and the assault team's tied up over on Colfax. Can you cover it?"

"I'm available. Is this a verified report?" It was the dispatcher's job to make certain that night calls were legitimate before sending a cop in; like the routine of surveillance and patrol, there had developed the routine of the false emergency that lured an officer into a dark alley to be shot in the back. "Revolutionary action," it was called; "ridding society of oppressors." The national figure for officers killed in the line of duty last year was 123; Wager didn't know what the score was on assassins, but he bet it wasn't that high. Otherwise the Civil Liberties Union would be screaming about police brutality.

"It's verified. A uniformed team is on the scene; the victim was still alive when the ambulance picked him up."

"I'm on North Federal; I'll be there in about ten."

"Ten-four. Time out: 0308."

Switching the car's radio to Channel Three, which carried the traffic of that police district, Wager wrenched the sedan around in a hard, squealing turn and headed south beneath the strobe-light flashes of streetlamps and through silent intersections blinking yellow. As he bounced across the short Cherry Creek bridge, the radio buzzed an all-channel alert for the suspect: a white male, around twenty-five years old, blond hair, wearing a light-colored sweat shirt and Levi's, southbound on Broadway on foot.

Wager eyed the empty sidewalks lit by dull neon and glanced into streets that whipped past like fence posts. But the suspect had already slipped away into some dark crack. Two minutes later, Wager slid the car behind a blue-and-white unit parked in the middle of the block.

A small apartment building sat behind a shallow lawn sandwiched between the unpainted concrete block walls of two flat-roofed commercial buildings, one a paint store, the other a garage. The apartment was square and plain, with four units in front, two up, two down. In the yellow light from the marquee of a large porno theater across Broadway, its color seemed pale blue. In the identical dark windows of all four living rooms, faces gazed out against the marquee's glare. On the lawn stood two uniformed officers and three or four civilians. Wager recognized one of the patrolmen, Adamo, who had been a rookie on Wager's beat ten years ago.

"Hello, Walt."

"Gabe, *amigo!* I heard you moved over to homicide. Hey, a lot of people wanted that slot; I'm glad you got it."

Walt Adamo was one of those who had wanted it, but with him, at least, there was none of the suspicion that the job had been given to Wager because he was part Hispano and the department was hungry for the federal money that came with compliance.

"What's the story here?" Wager asked.

Adamo led him away from the witnesses and snoopers clustered near the small landing that served as a front porch. "We got a man shot twice by a male assailant; witnesses say he ran south on Broadway past the furniture store. We put out an alert on him."

"I heard it."

"The victim's Charles Porfirio. You know him?"

"He's been on the street five or six years? Pushes a little dope now and then?"

"That's the one. A little dope, a little fencing, maybe some burglary, though I haven't been able to land anything definite on him in that line—just rumors. Anyway, the witnesses say they were sitting on the porch, talking, when the assailant came out of this path here between the apartment and the paint store."

"Got their names yet?"

"Yep." Adamo tilted his notebook to catch the glare from Bunny's Adult Arcade across the street. "The first one's Jesus Quintana. He lives in apartment two."

"Which one's he?"

"The fat one over there by the steps, smoking."

"Anything on him?"

"No. He's been around the neighborhood for a while, but he hasn't attracted any attention. That's his wife in the front window of the right-hand apartment, first floor."

The woman caught Adamo's gesture and stared their way, a frown of worry pulling lines into her thin, dark face, and Wager half remembered the same expression, the same worries, on the faces of women in his childhood. It was more than the worry of a witness; it was the anxiety of someone involved. She said something to her husband, who looked at Wager and then went into the house. A moment later, he showed in the window, herding three small heads away to bed.

"According to him, the assailant walks up and says to the victim, 'I been looking for you,' and the victim says, 'Well, you see me. What about it?' Then the two of them walk over near the corner of the garage and onto the sidewalk, right there. They talk for a couple minutes and then the victim turns around and starts back to the steps to where Quintana's sitting and talking with another witness, who's staying with him. This second guy was leaning out the same window there where Mrs. Quintana is."

"Pretty busy around here for three o'clock in the morning."

"Yeah, well, some of these people don't like to be seen in the daytime. The second witness is one Ernie Taylor. He's the black kid talking to my partner. He's new to the neighborhood, but he's working some deal or other. You can smell it all over him."

"What happened next?"

"The assailant shoots Porfirio once in the back of the shoulder, and as far as we could tell, the bullet stayed in. Then Porfirio starts running for that path next to the paint store, but he trips on a kid's tricycle and while he's trying to get up, the assailant runs up and pops him right in the back of the head. Then he takes off that way down Broadway."

"He didn't threaten or shoot at the witnesses?"

"No. They say he never even looked at them. Only at Charley. They think he was drunk or high, and that fits the behavior."

"Where'd the victim fall?"

"Over here." Adamo led Wager to a patch of yard worn to gray sand by foot traffic and children's games. "That's the blood there." He pointed to a small, very soggy spot. "He was still pumping blood when the ambulance got here, and the attendant said he had a chance."

"None of the witnesses recognized the assailant?"

"Crap, no. They swear they never saw him before. Never ever."

"I hear you. Can you and your partner hang around long enough to keep an eye on this Taylor while I talk to Quintana? I'm working alone."

"Let me tell the dispatcher I'll be here a little longer."

Wager went into the dark, narrow hallway of the apartment building and knocked on the door of number two; the husband opened it. "Mr. Quintana? I'm Detective Wager. You think you could tell me what you saw?"

"I already told the policeman. That tall one there."

"I'd like to hear it from you. Maybe you could show me exactly where they were standing and where you were when everything happened." Over Quintana's thick, sloping shoulder, Wager could see his wife sitting stiffly in the dark; the lights from the porno marquee invaded the small room and fell across her tense face. From a half-open door came the excited whispers of children. Wager nodded hello; she didn't answer, but watched with wide eyes as her husband led Wager into the yard.

"Well, I was sitting here, and Ernie was at the window over there, and Charley was standing on the walk here, talking to me and Ernie."

"What about?"

"Aw, nothing. Just shooting the—ah—bull about this and that. You know how it is on a warm night."

"And then?"

Quintana scratched at the stomach bulging beneath his brightly patterned shirt. "Well, I didn't see the guy at first; he come from around there, and I'm sitting over here. But Charley says, 'My, my,' or something like that, and this guy says to him, 'I want to talk to you. Come over here.' And Charley, he don't really want to go. He says, 'We got nothing to talk about.' The guy says, 'I been looking for you. I want to talk to you.' He was acting high, you know. Drunk, maybe.''

"Did Charley say his name?''

"No. And I never seen him before.''

"Ernie's a friend of yours?''

"Yeah. I met him a couple weeks ago. He needed a place to crash tonight and I let him use my couch.''

"Did Ernie know this guy?''

"No. Neither of us ever seen him before.''

"What next?''

Quintana walked to the corner of the small, treeless yard near the corner of the garage and struck a pose. "They stood here and talked a little and then Charley turned around like this and starts back and the next thing I know, pow! This dude's shot Charley in the back. Charley starts running.'' Quintana jogged heavily a step or two and then tumbled gently across the apartment's short sidewalk, looking up from the ground to speak to Wager. "And then he trips over a goddam tricycle. It ain't my kids'; it belongs to them people up in four. They let their kids leave their crap all over the place.'' He stood to brush the dead grass from his shirt and then backed up two or three steps and hunched over, holding an arm out in front as if he had a pistol. "Then this guy just runs right up like this and lays that pistol up against Charley's head and lets fly, man! That son of a bitch must of been high —he aimed for the head and he still missed, this close. The bullet come out right here.'' He tapped the hollow of his throat. "Charley flopped over twice, kicking like shit, and got this far.'' He pointed to the bloodstain, black as a hole in the cold sand. "In the meantime, this dude's cut out, heading south.'' Quintana loudly smacked a fist into his palm. "Loaded or not, that son of a bitch knew what he wanted. He came here to waste Charley and he tried like hell to do it.''

"What were you doing while all this was happening?''

"Man, it went down so fast, I didn't do nothing! I mean, here I am shooting the shit with my cousin and a friend, and along comes this nut and out of nowhere starts wasting people! You'd think them kind of people would be locked up, man. But the—ah—patrolmen, they got here real quick. The police did real good, getting here so quick."

"The victim was your cousin?"

"Did I say that? Well, yeah."

"Who called the police?"

"Ernie did. I got a phone in my apartment, but I guess he didn't know it. He jumped out the window and ran to the booth on the corner. Sometimes it works; it's all the time getting vandalized. This is a very bad neighborhood, you know?"

"Did anyone besides Ernie see anything?"

"Well, I guess my wife saw a little bit. She come out of bed running when that first shot went off. At three o'clock in the morning, man, that son of a bitch was loud."

"Can you describe the assailant?"

"Yeah. He was maybe twenty-five. Anglo. Blond hair. I already told that to the other cop."

"Did he have a mustache or beard? Was he clean-shaven? Any scars? Jewelry? Was he wearing a hat?"

"No. He wasn't wearing no hat. But I didn't see him good. He was just a guy."

"Would you recognize him if you saw him again?"

"No."

"He stood this close and you wouldn't recognize him again?"

"It was dark, man, and everything happened fast. And I never seen him before."

Wager slipped a sheet of paper from his clipboard. "I'd like you to write down what you told me. Just put it in your own words, everything you told me."

111

"Yeah, sure. I hope that son of a bitch didn't kill Charley. If he did . . . !"

Wager left Quintana squatting in the pale light that splashed across the street and over the apartment's steps, and knocked once more on the door of number two. The wife opened it.

"I'm Detective Wager, Mrs. Quintana. Is Charley your cousin or your husband's?"

"His—my husband's." Both her hands clutched at her corded neck.

"I'm sorry all this had to happen. It'll help us get the man that did it if you can tell us what you saw. Are you up to it? Do you think you can just write down what you saw?"

"I . . . I think so."

"Did you ever see the assailant before?"

"I . . ."

She didn't want to say any more. Wager waited, smelling the familiar odor of chicken and rice floating through the small room toward the coolness outside the open window. Across the street, under glaring bulbs that spelled "Sugar Buns and Teeny Teasers X X X," a chesty girl in a pink miniskirt and shiny white boots stared toward the police cars, absently swinging her white plastic purse back and forth. Finally, Wager said, "Here's what I think, Mrs. Quintana. I think maybe your husband knows who it is and won't say because he wants to get even. *Soy hispano, señora; y comprendo la familia.* But suppose this guy has cousins who feel like your husband does?" Wager let her think about that. "You've got three children."

"Oh, God!"

"I'm not trying to scare you, Mrs. Quintana. I'm trying to tell you that it's best to let the police handle it. If we go after this guy, your husband's clear; if he goes after him, there's no telling where it might end."

112

She stared out the window above the marquee and into the lightless sky, looking at her choices and burdened by them all.

In the old days, it would have been the *jefe*—someone like Tony-O—standing here trying to prevent a blood feud from ripping through the neighborhood. Now it was just a cop, and there wasn't much neighborhood left to tear apart. Only a family. "The sooner we get the assailant, the less time he'll have to build an alibi. The law can handle him, Mrs. Quintana. If your husband tries to, there's going to be a hell of a lot more trouble. He might even end up in jail—no job, and you and the kids on welfare. You understand that, don't you?"

"Yes, yes, I know it. Jesus, he's . . ." She took a deep breath and turned to face Wager. "Yes, I seen this guy before. Today. We went to the park with the kids and Charley, for a picnic, and this guy showed up."

"What park?"

"I forget its name—the one off Speer Boulevard with all the bushes and a place to play baseball. The kids like it there."

"The Sunken Gardens?"

"Yeah. We was there and this Anglo kid comes up and hassles Charley. Aw, Charley's into something . . . We all know it—Charley's always got something going. But not Jesus! He's got a job, you know? And he's got the kids, too. But Jesus likes to think he's in on Charley's action. But he's not—not really; he just likes to talk. And he's Charley's cousin. Family's important to us."

"*Sí. La familia es todo.*" It was his mother's phrase whenever someone needed help. The family helped its members, regardless. If it didn't, no one would.

"Yeah. *La familia.* You really are Chicano, ain't you?"

"What happened in the park?"

"Well, Charley and this guy got into a fight, a little shoving and some loud words, and Jesus, he made me take the kids down to the creek to watch the water for a while. He loves the kids, you know—he really does—and he didn't want them seeing all that. After a while we come back and everything's cool; the guy's gone."

"What was the fight about?"

"I don't know." She meant that she had said enough about that to a cop and would not cross the line between a present worry and a new one.

"It was the same person who shot Charley tonight?"

"Yeah."

"Was Ernie at the park, too?"

"For a while, yeah."

"Did he know this guy?"

"He didn't say so."

"Would you mind coming down to headquarters to look at some pictures?"

"Jesus, too?"

"Yes. And Ernie."

"I'll have to get somebody to watch the kids. They're still excited. They shouldn't see things like this. This is a lousy place for kids to grow up. A lousy place!"

"It won't take long."

"O.K. I guess so."

Wager left her slowly pushing a ballpoint pen over a sheet of paper as she wrote down her version of what happened. Adamo and his partner, flanking Ernie, looked anxious to get back on the street; patrols and checkpoints waited, and they had an entire neighborhood to survey.

"You through with us, Gabe?"

"Yes—and thanks. Have the lab people come yet?"

"Jones was here while you were inside. He shot a couple pictures of the blood and poked around a little for the slug.

He said they got the other bullet out of the guy's shoulder, so they got good evidence."

"What's the victim's condition?"

"Too early to tell." Adamo said, "See you," and the patrolmen pulled away, glad to leave the routine of investigation to Wager.

He turned to the slender Negro youth. "You're Ernie Taylor?"

"Right, man."

"Where do you live, Ernie?"

"Well, I'm new in town. I don't really live nowhere, much."

"How long have you been here?"

"In Denver? About two weeks. It's a nice town you got here. I dig it, you know?"

"You looking for work?"

"Well, yeah. But I come here to go to college. I'm gonna start at Community College next semester, man."

"Where's your home?"

"Kansas City. But I done left home."

"You must stay somewhere, Ernie. Where's your mail sent?"

"I don't get no mail. I just leave my stuff at a friend's and crash around, like."

"Where's this friend?"

"Come on, man—he's just a friend. I just put my suitcase in his closet is all."

"What's the closet's address, Ernie? I have to put something on this piece of paper for an address."

"That's all? I mean, my friend's just doing me a favor. I don't want him to think I got him in wrong with the police, you know?"

"What kind of wrong?"

"Nothing, man! He's straight! It's just that a lot of people

115

don't like their names give to the fuzz, you know?"

"The address, Ernie."

"It's 525 Inca. Number eight."

"Now, how about telling me what you saw."

"I just went through it all with that cop!"

"I'd like to hear it." The small of Wager's back was beginning to ache, but he stood without moving; he stood as if he had all night and all the coming day. Which he did.

"Who else I got to tell this to? You think we could get them all together so's I could tell it just one more time?"

"This should do it."

"Yeah. Well, I was leaning out that there window . . ." He told his story while Wager noted what new items cropped up in Ernie's version.

"Did you ever see this man before?"

"Naw."

"Would you recognize him if you ever saw him again?"

"It was dark. I didn't see him that good."

"What kind of pistol was it?"

"It sounded like a twenty-two—you know that little pop they make. But it looked like it was on a thirty-eight frame. Chrome-plated."

"You could see all that, but you couldn't see his face?"

"Yeah—the light was on it. And he held it out like this. And I'll tell you something else—I wasn't studying his face, I was studying that gun!"

"What's his name?"

"I just told you I never seen him before!"

"Jesus Quintana knows his name. He thinks he's going to keep it from us long enough for him to go after that dude. I know you were in the park today when they had the fight. If Jesus wastes this dude, you're going to get fouled on, Ernie."

116

"Hey, I'm just visiting around here! I didn't even know this stuff was going down!"

Wager shrugged. "It's your butt. You'll be ahead if we get this guy before Jesus does."

"What you mean, it's my butt?"

"You saw these two fighting in the park. You're an eyewitness in the chain of circumstances. There's all sorts of crap an eyewitness in a chain of circumstances has to go through —maybe even protective custody." Wager didn't know if there was any legal handle called a chain of circumstance, but it sounded good.

"Protective custody? That means jail?"

"For a few days. Maybe a week. Until we get things cleared up."

Taylor made up his mind. "Shit—it ain't worth that! I mean, it ain't really my worry, you know?"

"That's right. Just tell me everything the way it really happened and you're clean."

"Well, all I heard was Charley calling him Francis."

"Where'd you hear that?"

"In the park after the beef."

"O.K. Let's go over here and get comfortable." Wager led Ernie to the police car and keyed the radio for Officer Adamo. A moment later, the dispatcher cleared the patrolman through. "The suspect's name may be Francis something. Do you know any Francis that matches his description?"

"Francis Innis," said Adamo. "I should have thought of him. You got a positive on that?"

"Not yet. I'll let you know as soon as I do." He handed Ernie a pen and paper and told him to sit in the front seat. "Can you write down everything you told me? Do you want me to write it for you?"

"I can write, man—as good as anybody. I'm going to college!"

"O.K. Do it on the way downtown."

Wager drove the three witnesses to D.P.D. headquarters. Quintana and his wife sat in the back saying little—she still with that worried look which, Wager knew, would become permanent in too few years; he silent and lip-heavy, glaring sullenly at the passing streetlights. Ernie, awkwardly printing his statement, said once, "It's a drag, man."

"What is?"

"This stuff. People. They ain't no need for people to act thataway." Then he was silent like the rest.

Wager guided them through the brightly lit but empty corridors, whose stale odor was being overlaid by the smell of fresh wax. Placing them separately in vacant offices, he gave the bored Records clerk Search Applications for Charley, Jesus, and Francis Innis. Charles Porfirio listed convictions for assault and burglary, and then went up a notch to fraud and receipt of stolen property. Francis Innis had a long list of petty charges and convictions going back to 1967 and beginning in San Diego. Jesus Quintana had no record.

From a drawer in the homicide cabinet marked "Cases Closed" he pulled a large envelope filled with identification photographs of past suspects. Spreading a handful on his desk, he carefully selected a half dozen who roughly fit the description but who didn't look too much like Innis, whose photograph he had taken from the suspect's folder. One thing Wager didn't want was a conflict between eyewitnesses on an identification. He went into the burglary office, where he'd placed Mrs. Quintana by herself.

"All right, Mrs. Quintana. Why don't you sign your statement right here at the bottom and put today's date on it. Then I'd like you to go through these and see if you can spot the man."

118

"You sure this is right? Jesus is awful mad that I said anything at all."

"We both know it's right. He will, too, when he cools off a little. I'll talk to him."

She chewed at dry lips; Wager went into the hall and came back with a paper cup of cool water.

"Gracias."

"De nada, señora. Now, just take your time and look through the photographs."

"I don't need no time. This is him." Her finger prodded Innis's face.

"You're positive?"

"Yeah. It's him."

"O.K. Just put your initials on the back of his picture." He waited until she had, then gathered up the collection. "I'll be back in a few minutes."

Ernie was on his feet, peering around at the Wanted posters and the patrol schedules of the homicide section's office. "How much longer, man?"

"Just a few minutes. You finished with your statement? Want to sign and date it there at the bottom?"

"Yeah, sure."

"Now, take a look at these and tell me which is the one."

Ernie squinted slowly through the pictures and pulled out a chubby, balding face. "This might be him."

Wager drew a long, slow breath. It was Ernie's moment of glory and he wanted to stretch it out. "Do you see anybody else that might be him?"

"You mean this ain't it?"

"Maybe; maybe not. Just look through the pictures again."

" 'Maybe; maybe not.' Ha." He squinted once more through the series and then started again, slowly flipping the photographs onto the table with a grunt of "Maybe . . . maybe not."

The bastard was having a lot of fun, but Wager was getting wearier. "Do you wear glasses, Ernie?"

"Naw! I ain't no four-eyes."

"Then what do you see?"

"This one. Here it is!" He slapped Innis's picture onto the table like a high card. "I got eyes, man, good ones!"

"You're sure this is the one?"

"Sure I'm sure!"

"Then put your initials on the back, right here."

"How much more of this draggy stuff I got to go through?"

"Just a few minutes. Make yourself comfortable."

"Comfortable—sure."

Quintana had been saved for last. He made a show of refusing to look at the pictures when Wager spread them on the glass surface of a desk in the bunco office where he sat alone.

Wager shook his head sadly. "You mean to tell me you don't know Francis Innis?"

"Who?"

"And that you weren't in the park this afternoon when Innis and Charley had their beef?"

"I don't know Innis."

"Quintana, it's almost five o'clock in the morning. I go off duty at eight," lied Wager. "The people coming on are going to ask the same questions, but they won't understand why you don't want us to get Innis. They're Anglos—they're going to think that maybe you set up Charley so Innis could waste him. They're going to think of you as a suspect—an accomplice—instead of just a witness." Wager rapped Quintana's signed statement. "Because this isn't true, Jesus. You signed a false statement, and if it gets into court, your ass is grass and mowed short."

"Hey, I didn't . . ."

120

"I understand, Jesus. Believe me. If somebody dusted my cousin, I'd want to get him myself. But we have a good case on Innis; he's not going to get away. If you go after him, it'll cost you a hell of a lot more than Innis is worth. If something happens to him, you know who we'll come looking for."

"I ain't afraid of that!"

Wager could see it in Quintana's eyes: he had cooled off enough to want to get clear, but he still had to puff a little. "Nobody said you were. I know you're *un caballero.* But you don't want anybody to call you dumb, either. And it's dumb not to let us handle Innis when we already know what happened. Think about how dumb that would sound on the street."

"Well . . ."

"It would be a dumb thing to do to your kids, too. For somebody like Innis."

"Well, I ain't doing it because I'm scared of that son of a bitch."

"Scared has nothing to do with it; just dumb. Nobody's going to call you scared for helping us nail the guy who shot your cousin; but they'll call you dumb for not letting us do the work. Now, which one's the man who did it?"

There was no hesitation. "Here's the fucker."

"You're positive?"

"Yeah."

"All right. Now, you write another statement and make sure everything in it's the truth, and I'll tear up this one."

"What about the park?" His hand hovered over the blank paper. "You gonna want to know what went on in the park?"

"If it's got nothing to do with the shooting, I don't need to know."

Wager returned to his desk to finish his report while Quintana wrote. He was stapling the sheets together when Walt

Adamo stuck his head in the doorway. "You got a positive I.D. on Innis yet?"

"Three. I'm just finishing up."

"Three! You sure got the son of a bitch. Is the victim dead?"

"I haven't heard."

"Can I use your phone?" The patrolman dialed Denver General Hospital. "Uh huh. I see. Thanks."

"Well?"

"He's in good condition. Want me to take your report over to the Assault Division? Those hard-working lads have just solved another case."

Adamo was right; the win wouldn't go on homicide's statistics. "Fine."

Laughing, Adamo paused in the doorway. "Ain't that the way it goes, Gabe? When you got a suspect identified, the goddamned victim never dies."

From his corner, where he had been sleepily propping himself in a tilted chair, Ernie asked, "You mean all this was for nothing?"

"It's still an assault charge. If you want to take off, you can; if you want a ride, it'll be a few more minutes." He went to tell Quintana that his cousin was alive.

"That's good," said Quintana. "What's it mean for that son of a bitch Innis?"

"Five to ten, with his record."

"That's good, too."

Wager eyed the paunchy man for a long moment.

"What's the matter? What you looking at?"

"Your cousin's got a good-sized jacket, Jesus."

His wide face closed like a fist. "So what?"

"So you're smart enough not to have a record. But from what I've noticed tonight, you see your share of the action."

Jesus's expression twisted between suspicion and a flat-

122

tered smile, then it settled back into the mask of a hard case talking to a cop. "Maybe I do; maybe I don't."

Wager read through Jesus's new statement and then slowly tore up the old one and dropped it into the wastebasket. "I'm doing you a favor, right?"

Quintana's upper lip peeled away from his teeth like flypaper. "So what's this got to do with the price of eggs in China?"

Wager pulled up a chair and sat so his head would be on the same level as Quintana's. Leaning forward, he dropped his voice to a murmur that died before it reached the open doorway and the hall beyond. "Here's what. You have a lot of contacts, you hear a lot of talk. I'd like you to listen around for me—I'd like you to do me a favor now."

"You want me to do what?"

"I helped you." Wager tapped the wastepaper can with his toe.

"But you're a cop!"

"And I'm trying to catch a hit man, Jesus. It's some heavy action, and there's some danger in it. But if I didn't think you could handle it, I wouldn't ask you."

"Well, yeah. I see what you mean." Quintana scratched once more at the soft mound of flesh lifting the red and orange designs on his shirt. "What can you give me to go on? I mean, I ain't saying I will or I won't—I'm saying I might."

"I understand, Jesus. You got a wife and kids, so if you think it's too dangerous, I understand."

"I didn't say that."

"I'm just telling you I'll understand if I don't hear from you. And I won't blame you, believe me, because the guy I'm after is a professional killer."

"Hey, I'm not afraid . . ."

"I am. It's one of the reasons I want the guy so badly. Anybody would be dumb not to be afraid."

"Well . . ."

"But a guy with your connections can hear things that a cop never gets close to. If you want to, you can really help me out. And I won't forget it."

"Well, if I feel like it, maybe I will. I'll think it over and see if I feel like it."

"You do that. And if you do feel like it, here's what I'm after: anything you hear on two brothers, Frank Covino and Gerald Covino. The first one got killed last Sunday, the second's in Cañon City for breaking and entering. Maybe your cousin Charley knows something about him."

"Covino. O.K. I maybe got some people I can ask. I got plenty of contacts on the street."

"One thing more. I heard they were mixed up with the Scorvelli family. I'd like to know more about that, too."

"The Scorvellis—holy shit!"

Wager pushed back his chair and stood, hoping he had not gone too far. But even somebody like Quintana had a right to know which shoulder to look over. "Come on—I'll give you and your wife a ride home. And if I don't hear from you, I won't lay a thing against you, believe me."

nine

His regular tour with Axton went by with that determined blur which comes from too many hours without sleep. While he was on his feet chewing gum or drinking coffee, he stayed awake; whenever he sat and tried to do the paper work that never ceased, his eyes burned and the words wouldn't make that long jump from the page to his mind. Most of the sheets he initialed and dumped in the out basket; the few pieces of any importance he read while striding back and forth between desks in the small office. Just before noon, the lab report on Frank Covino's car came in and, propped by another cup of coffee, Wager forced his mind to read each entry, but the effort wasn't justified by the result. The car had plenty of prints inside and out, on trunk, hood, and mirrors, but most of them were the victim's, and those that weren't matched no known prints in the files of police or F.B.I. The best guess was still the one that had the victim parking his car and walking alone to the theater, being approached by the man in the long topcoat and beret, who talked him into leaving with him, and then being driven to the warehouse area, where he was shot. It wasn't a bit more than they already knew, and that didn't make the weariness any lighter or the hard sun less harsh against the window. And the telephone call that came in to a frowning Axton did not lessen Wager's irritation, either.

Holding the receiver toward Wager, Max said, "For you. It's Sonnenberg."

He muttered "Damn" under his breath and then said politely, "Detective Wager, sir."

"I want to know what the devil you think you are doing, Wager. I confided in you with the express agreement that you would be circumspect in your investigation. Now everything I hear and every paper I read tells me that you frog-marched him in as if he were a two-bit dip or a pimp!"

Frog-march. Wager had not heard that phrase since he was a kid; Sonnenberg came up with an old-fashioned term like that every now and then. "I don't think he *is* any better than a dip or a pimp, Inspector. So he got equal treatment."

"Equal be damned! We had an agreement, Wager. You know what's at stake, and so help me, if I have to I'll go over Doyle's head. And I'll come back with yours!"

Wager tried to keep the exasperation from his voice. "He got the same handling he always does when there's a professional hit, Inspector. Anything different and he'd get suspicious. He may be pissed, but at least he believes things are normal."

"I won't have you disrupting my operations. This case is more important than that homicide. You will keep out of it from now on!"

Nothing was more important to Wager than that homicide, because that homicide was his case—his jurisdiction—

126

and by God, there was such a thing as interfering with an officer's duty, even for Sonnenberg. Some of this feeling slipped into his voice when he said, "Why not wait until you're hurt before you scream, Inspector?"

"By then it will be too late, Sergeant. You stay out of it or there will be plenty of hurt to go around!" The line went dead with a loud click.

Axton looked at him wordlessly.

"He wanted to express his appreciation for our smooth arrest of Scorvelli," said Wager.

"Sure he did. When's he coming over to slice off our ears?"

"It wasn't exactly our ears he had in mind."

"If what we did to Scorvelli puts his agent in danger, Sonnenberg can slice whatever he wants to, and I don't think the Bulldog or anybody else will do much to help us out." Axton heaved himself out of the swivel chair, which creaked with relief and sagged slightly to one side. "And to tell the truth, Gabe, I don't know if I'd want them to. I was awake half the goddam night worrying about that."

Wager had been awake the whole goddam night. "We had to act as if no agent was in place." Each word came out with the measured rate of worn repetition. "We did exactly what Scorvelli and everybody else expected. If we hadn't brought him in, the street would think we knew who did it. And then, when we didn't come up with a suspect—because we don't have a damned suspect—people would start to wonder why we let Scorvelli alone. That would be more dangerous than busting him."

Axton's mouth set in a tight line as he picked up the ringing telephone and smothered it in one fist for a last comment. "Gabe, it sounds great when you put it that way. The trouble is, Sonnenberg sounds good, too. Homicide, Detective Axton."

This time it was Gargan, and Max told him that Scorvelli's arrest had been strictly routine and that nothing helpful had come of it. "That's it, Gargan. The most we can say is that we're still chasing leads, but we don't have many. No, we haven't gotten very far at all." He hung up. "Let's get some lunch, Gabe. If I worry about this on an empty stomach, I'll end up worse than Munn."

They ate at the Frontier, arriving too late for Wager to get his favorite booth, near the clatter of the serving window; instead, they had to take a small table out in the middle of the big room, which was more crowded and noisy than usual. Rosie, wearing a quick smile and a shine of sweat on her face, brought them two beers without being asked.

"Why all the people? Another convention?"

"Tomorrow's our last day, Gabe. Everybody's heard about it, so they want to say they've been here before we close."

Wager had forgotten that, and the reminder made this long day chafe a little rawer. Nor did it help to have Axton take the closing so lightly.

"To the last of the old Frontier!" Max lifted his glass. "Rest in peace."

Wager glared around. "Bunch of damned buzzards."

Max drank and looked from the cluttered walls to the ceiling filled with ranch and mining gear, to the cigar store Indian tucked in a dim corner. "They really do have a collection of junk here, don't they? What in God's name are they going to do with all this?"

Wager shrugged and spooned hot sauce on his refritos.

"They should sell the good stuff to a museum. They should try to keep some of the history that's here," said Max.

"They shouldn't build another parking lot. Who in hell needs it? Who in hell needs the goddam bulldozers coming in and scraping away everything?"

128

Axton studied him through the thin light. "You come here a lot, do you?"

Wager shrugged again; he wasn't asking for one damned thing from Axton or anybody else.

"Well, I guess it's a shame. Whenever a place gets a little feel of history, down it comes. But they're starting to preserve some of the city's old houses—people are moving back in and rebuilding them. It's really important to keep something from the past."

"Like bagpipe lessons?"

"Sure—anything, as long as it means something for you. It's kind of like"—Max looked around for the word or simile that would fit—"an arrow. Your past is the tail of the arrow and if you know where it is, you have some idea what you're bringing along with you. Even some idea of where you're headed."

Max was getting weird again, but this time Wager's patience was too tired to stretch. "The past is dead, Max. It dies and gets buried and you forget about it. The only goddam thing that counts is right now and what's coming. I tell you what: why don't you shoot an arrow in the air and tell me where Covino's killer is? Or tweedle your goddam bagpipes —maybe he'll come out like a snake."

Even in the dim light from the wagon wheel chandelier overhead he could see Max's face turn red, and Wager felt —very faintly—a twinge of remorse. A man shouldn't stomp on his partner; a man should have greater tolerance for the things his partner says, more latitude for foolish ideas, because partners were supposed to relax with each other and be able to say things they felt but hadn't really thought through. You weren't supposed to have to keep your guard up with a partner, and Wager had that feeling of having hit Max when he wasn't looking and didn't deserve to be hit that way. But apologizing was something else; Wager hadn't much practice at apologizing. "You want another beer?"

"No." Then Max saw what Wager meant. "Well, why not? Sure."

Wager ordered and they kept the talk on Covino; Max said no more about history or bagpipes, and gradually their voices lost the strained note and warmed again like those of people who cared what each other thought. But beneath that, Wager had the feeling that maybe he had been a cop too long —that maybe he needed to step somewhere out of the scum he crawled through and be reminded that the world wasn't filled with only dope and arson, bunco and rape, contraband and killing. He had the suspicion that he should look for some kind of island outside himself that would let him view a world without the insanities that hid the horizon of each day. An island to tie to instead of being forced to rely solely on his own internal bearings, never sure that they coincided with the fixed bearings that must exist somewhere, since so many others seemed to know them.

"You have kids, Max?"

"Yeah, two—boy and girl. Thank God the girl looks like her mother."

"What do they think about you being a cop?"

"The younger one, Annie, she's still excited about it. She sees all that stuff on TV and thinks her old man's a fat Clint Eastwood. Tom couldn't care less any more."

"I mean, do they resent it? Sometimes people feel—ah— jealous of this kind of job."

"Sometimes, sure. They don't like it when I have weekend duty or the four-to-midnight shift. And I don't like to miss things that are important to them, either. Annie was in a school play when I had night duty last time and we both felt bad about that. But I'm home other times. It balances out."

"And your wife?"

"She's used to it. Most of the time, anyway. It's a lot better now that I'm in the detective division. I think the years in uniform were the roughest for her."

If regret came now to add depression to the restlessness he felt, then that was something Wager would have to hold off until it went away again, because you don't look back. The dark time after the divorce had convinced him of that. It wasn't much in the way of a philosophy, but it—and his work —had provided the only anchor he could trust. For the most part, anyway.

"Say, Gabe—why don't you come over for dinner some night? Polly would really like to meet you."

"I don't think so."

"You've got to sooner or later. Polly keeps telling me to ask you over; she really enjoys knowing the other people in the department, and she'll just keep after me until she gets to meet you. Hell, I won't get any rest until you've been over."

Wager looked suspiciously at the blue eyes, but there was nothing in them of laughter or pity. "We'll see."

"Good! I'll tell her to plan on it."

Axton talked him into going home just after lunch. "Your eyes look like two piss holes in the snow. If anything comes up this afternoon, I can handle it until Ross and Devereaux come in." But though Wager was half undressed and sound asleep by 2 P.M., he was awake and staring at the ceiling five hours later. Too much coffee, maybe, or too many questions about Covino that prevented the deeply relaxed feeling of work well done. He tried the pillow doubled under his neck, then over his face; he lay with his eyes closed and swept at the jumble of thoughts that kept tumbling back into his mind. Finally, he gave up and, with watery, puffy eyes, soaked in a long, hot shower that was as good as another four hours' sleep. In the emptying refrigerator he found the last frozen dinner—roast beef and mashed potatoes, the picture said; and by eight at night he was cruising in his own car under the heavy dark band of the viaducts bridging the area where Covino had been found.

The first slow, aimless pass showed a few early groups walking quickly and noisily down the center of empty and badly lit streets toward the old Oxford Hotel, which advertised the return of the Queen City Jazz Band. An almost vacant Union Station was partially lit, a white fluorescent contrast to the lightless windows of the buildings surrounding it. Past that, closed warehouses and bare loading docks slid by the car windows like fruit crates and timber bobbing in a black river. Wager pulled to a halt beneath the Twentieth Street viaduct and got out, locking the car. The people he wanted to find tended to lean out of sight into alleys and doorways whenever a car cruised by slowly, but they did not hide from a person on foot and alone. Neither the police nor the hoods patrolled this area on foot, and never singly.

Unconsciously, Wager lightly touched first the Star P.D. holstered over his kidney and then the oily chrome circles of the handcuffs looped over his belt at his spine. In the silence, a solitary car crossed the viaduct overhead, its tires a tiny sizzling zip in the black sky. Traffic from the city's center and from the Valley Highway across the South Platte River made a steady rushing sound like distant falling water; nearer, the only loud noise was the quick blat of a switch engine's air horn signaling backup. Clearing his ears with a forced yawn or two—a trick he learned on Marine patrols when danger was no less real or imminent but only more constant—Wager felt himself slip into that familiar air of threat that a cop, especially a uniformed cop, moves through on every street.

He walked down the viaduct's shadow to a corner whose old streetlight struggled sullenly against an older dimness, then he crossed quickly into the murky gloom of warehouses

132

and the unlit, barred windows of sagging brick offices. Trying to avoid the clink and scrape of broken bottles, Wager moved slowly toward the site of Covino's murder on Denargo Street, listening as much as looking. Once, a car wagged its stiff beams down the bumpy street toward him and, like those he sought, Wager melted into the strip of black lining a deeply recessed door, easing out again when the taillights blurred with distance. He had passed the narrow gap where the boy had been found and turned along one of the pale warehouse walls, when he heard, on the other side of the street, the clatter of a stone and a thick, muffled cough. Against the dark surface, a darker form moved slowly but steadily with the slightly awkward movements of a beetle on a fixed course. Wager let the figure get halfway down the block before crossing over behind it. Then he sprinted forward on tiptoes.

"You there—hold it right there."

The figure jerked and turned to stare bug-eyed at Wager, an arm's length away. "Don't hurt me! I ain't got nothing— I got some cigarettes is all. I'll give you my cigarettes if you don't hurt me!"

"Whistles? Is that you?" The whistling sibilants sounded familiar, but Wager couldn't see the thin face clearly.

"Who's that?"

"Sergeant Wager. Remember me?"

The figure thought hard. "Sergeant Wager? No. But I don't remember names real good. You won't hurt me, will you?"

"No, Whistles. I only want to ask you some questions. Come on over here in the light."

"All I got's some cigarettes. I got four, but you can have them all."

"Look at me—now do you remember?" Wager pulled the slight figure under the streetlight. His face was even thinner than Wager remembered, but the man's broken nose was the same, as was the left eye, which wandered frantically whenever he was afraid. "I'm not going to hurt you. And I don't want your cigarettes. Do you remember me? Sergeant Wager."

"I remember now. Now I seen you, I remember you. You're a policeman."

"That's right." It seemed that the man really remembered and wasn't just saying what he thought Wager wanted to hear. "I'm a policeman. I want to know if you walk down this street every night."

Whistles frowned, the left eye beginning to settle in slower arcs, like a marble rocking to a halt. Wager didn't recall how old the man was; he looked sixty, but he was somewhere in his forties. His record said he had been a battered child who, when he reached twenty-one, had been "graduated" from the state school as a legally defined adult capable of contributing to his own welfare and that of the great democracy to which he was born. And which found it cheaper to dump him into the street. He was one of those that Wager used to haul down to county jail once a month for washing and delousing, for a little hot food and a cursory medical check.

"Sure, Sergeant Wager. I go by here every night. I got a nice place I live in now." He poked a grimy hand toward the dark railway yard. "You ain't going to bust it up on me, are you? Nobody said they want me to move yet."

"Not if you tell me about coming by here every night, Whistles."

"I got to go by here every night. I got to go from my place to Manolo's restaurant. I got a job there!"

"What kind of job?"

"I take out the garbage in these buckets and dump it in these barrels out back. And sometimes Mr. Zapata even lets me sweep out the front room. It's a real job!"

"How much does it pay?"

"You mean money? Oh, he don't pay money—he don't make so much hisself. But I get a meal, all I want to eat."

"How many hours do you work?"

Whistles thought hard. "There's four buckets and I take them out, and then sometimes I sweep, and then I eat. Mr. Zapata's nice. He ain't never hit me. He gives me seconds if I ask. Maybe it takes two hours."

"Did you come by here last Sunday night?"

"I . . . I can't remember. You gonna tear up my place? Please don't do that! Sure, I came by here. I came by here last Sunday night."

"I'm not going to hurt you or your place, Whistles. Is the restaurant open on Sundays?"

"Sure. It's open every day."

"Have you missed any days?"

"You mean not go to work? No! It's my job. I go even when it's raining or even if my head hurts."

"All right now, Whistles, listen hard. When you were going to work a few nights ago, did you see anything happen over there where those fruit warehouses are? Think real hard, now. Did you see anything at all?"

The broken nose aimed in the general direction of the painted brick buildings. A long, tiny whistle came out of his half-open mouth as he thought and tried to remember. Finally, "I saw a car! It stopped over there."

Wager carefully kept the excitement from his voice; he didn't want to spook the man. "What did the car look like, Whistles?"

"It was dark."

"The car?"

"Yes. And it had long fenders. Like wings that lifted up in the back. And it had two mirrors, one on each side."

"Wings? What do you mean, wings?"

Whistles looked frightened and his eye began to roll slowly back and forth. "I don't know, Sergeant Wager. Maybe it wasn't wings. If you say it wasn't, then I guess you're right!"

"That's O.K., Whistles; never mind the wings. Who was driving?"

"I don't know. I hid over there." He pointed to the corner of a building where a wire-mesh fence collected blown trash. "Whenever I hear cars at night, I hide. Lots of times they want to hurt me."

"What did you see?"

"It came up and stopped and turned off the lights. But nobody got out right away. I thought they saw me and was waiting for me to come out. So I stayed quiet. Then they got out and went between the walls."

"How many people did that?"

"I saw two. They went between the walls."

"Did they get out on the same side of the car? Or did each one use his own door?"

He began to look worried again. "I don't know. They went between the walls."

"When they went there, did you hear anything?"

"I heard a big bang. Like a gun!"

"You heard it?"

"It was loud and scared me. I don't like guns."

"How many people came back?"

A faint whistle from his sagging mouth. "One. And he got in the car."

"What did he look like?"

Whistles squinted toward the building as if seeing it all again. "He had a coat on. A long one. And maybe a kind of hat or maybe it was his hair."

"You could see all that from over there?"

"The lights at the roundhouse were on. That makes things

136

kind of brighter. I like it when they're on and it's all light and clean-looking. It's real nice when they're on and it's snowing."

"Did you go over to the building?"

"No! The other one was still there and he might hurt me. I went to my job."

"Did you see a gun?"

"No."

"Can you tell me anything more about the car? The license, maybe?"

"No. It squeaked."

"How's that?"

"It turned and drove off. It went over the railroad tracks and squeaked real loud."

"Did the man see you?"

"No. I hid like always. I'm real good at hiding," he said.

In court, Whistles's testimony wouldn't go as far as a bailiff's fart, Wager knew; all a defense attorney had to do to discredit him was ask Whistles to count his own fingers and toes. But for Wager's use it was good enough; the long overcoat, the gun, the beret—those points were corroborated and linked the man who had picked up Covino at the movie with the man who had pulled the trigger in the alley. The car was something else; cars with wings, cars that squeaked. Without some kind of supporting evidence, it wasn't safe to believe Whistles on that. Wager fished in his wallet for a bill—ten dollars—and held it out to the thin figure. "Here. Buy yourself some fresh cigarettes."

"Money? For me?"

"Go on, take it."

"No. I better not."

"Why in hell not?"

"If I got money they'll hurt me for it. I never have no money, so they mostly don't hurt me."

Wager didn't bother to ask why this piece of flotsam was ever born and why it was left to creep its painful way through these shades of terror. Questions like that were for people like Frank Covino's mother, who would ask and ask and ask and get the same answer Wager had found long ago: there was no reason for it. There was every reason against it, and not one goddamned reason for it. And even the reasons against it only went as far as a man could take them and no further; they were the things he could pretend to find meaning in, things he could pretend were important to try to do or to try and save. Beyond what he pretended, those reasons didn't mean a goddamned thing.

A cunning look almost closed Whistles's bad eye. "Can you gimme some matches? I got four cigarettes, but I got no matches."

Wager took from his vest pocket the pack of stale cigarettes he carried to offer witnesses and informants, and pushed a book of matches under the cellophane wrapper. "Here. Now you've got some more cigarettes, too."

"Gee!"

By the time Wager was in his car and driving toward Manolo's Bar and Grill, Whistles's dim outline had glided into the protection of other shadows.

Wager found the restaurant by its half-broken neon sign, which said "—nolo's." It was on a corner, the door angled to catch both sidewalks, and the small kitchen was at the far end, past the bar on one side and the hard wooden booths on the other. Three or four men sat near the kitchen end of the bar, leaving the booths empty, their varnished seat backs darkened by wide bands of oily dirt, head high. The bartender, heavy-set, with a handlebar mustache, smelled cop when Wager walked in. "You got a Mr. Zapata here?" Wager asked.

138

"Why?"

Wager showed his badge. "Because I want to know."

"I'm him. What you want?"

Wager glanced down the bar at the men nursing their small glasses of pale beer; they quickly turned back to their own business—staring at the small television set quacking high in the corner above the entryway. "Do you have a busted-up guy named Whistles working for you?"

"Whistles? Yeah—he thinks he works here. I give him a meal of leftovers and he takes out the slops. What's happened to him?"

"Was he here last Sunday?"

"Sure. He's here every day. Like I said, the son of a bitch thinks he works for me."

"You don't pay him for his work?"

"What, you some kind of labor cop or union organizer or something? I give the son of a bitch a meal for doing nothing. I could empty the buckets myself, but he likes to think he's got a job."

"That's fine with me." Wager put the ten-dollar bill on the counter. "Give him some cigarette change every now and then out of this. Tell him he's earned it for working so hard."

The bartender's dark eyebrows climbed up toward the point of straight hair that made a V high on his forehead. "What's this for?"

"He did a job for me. But he doesn't want to carry this much money around—he's afraid somebody'll roll him for it."

"Oh. Yeah. He ain't that dumb." Zapata rang No Sale, then said to Wager, "Just a minute." He came back with a small slip of paper and a piece of Scotch tape. He stuck the paper on an upright beam by the cash register. "I'll keep it on a record. I don't want no cop saying I'm cheating him."

ten

Leaving Manolo's, Wager drove slowly along upper Larimer. At this time of night, and before the workers had been rounded up for the sugar beet fields, the three blocks of Little Juarez were filled with *braceros* spilling from the red and blue lights of bars and onto curbs to stand in arm-wagging knots talking loudly, to watch cars roll past with windows shut and pale faces staring wide-eyed or away. Only an occasional black or woman could be seen among the swarthy men, but here and there Indians in denim jackets and shining, plaited hair reeled in or out of a doorway, or stood swaying and silent, staring at the pavement in hazy thought. The night was another warm one, the kind that came in late April and early May, hinting of summer and fooling the men and trees into thinking winter was gone. But of course it wasn't; there would be at least one more heavy, wet snow to snag in the new leaves and snap the tender branches or split the tree

140

trunks, because this high and this close to the mountains, winter was never far away.

He turned left on Seventeenth, the windows of the financial district almost as dark and blank as those of the deserted warehouse area. In this city of half a million or so, no one but cops, firemen, hippies, and drunks seemed to care much for it after dark; and more of the streets lay empty like this one than were filled with the gab and action of Larimer or East Colfax. When the offices and stores closed—when the papers were shuffled and the day's money made—Denver became a city of a few veins and no heart.

At a closed gas station, Wager joined the short line waiting to use a telephone booth; inside the transparent plastic box a fat young girl, braless in a T-shirt and bib overalls, laughed into the receiver. Anxiously waiting behind her stood a barefoot and stringy-haired kid, who, when his turn came, relayed directions to a shadowy figure in a New Jersey van parked beside the booth and sprayed with tie-dye blobs of random color. Bumper stickers scattered on its sides said "Make Love Not Atomic Bombs," "Go Solar Not Nuclear," "Think Trees," and "Save Our Whales." Finally, when Wager could drop his dimes into the slot, he leaned far into the booth to close out the traffic sounds while he dialed the bar that served as Fat Willy's office.

"Who wants him?" asked the voice on the other end.

"Gabe."

"I see if he's around."

He was, grudgingly. "I don't appreciate you calling me here, man. I told you that before."

"Don't hurt my feelings, Willy. I'll begin to think you don't like me."

"You'll begin to think right, then. What-all you want this time?"

"It's been days since I heard your dulcet tones, Willy. I want those tones to tell me what you've picked up on the people I asked you about."

"I ain't talking about it here, man."

"Fine. I'll see you on the corner of Colfax and Race in ten minutes."

"Wait a fucking minute! I got—"

Wager hung up. Behind him, the stringy-haired youth said, "It's about time, man," and roughly elbowed past him into the booth. Wager stepped aside, careful to scrape his shoe down the skinny Achilles tendon poking beneath the fringe of frayed Levi's. He left the kid dangling halfway between cursing at Wager and trying to save his coin in the telephone.

The swollen figure of Fat Willy in its linen suit and Panama hat was not on the corner when Wager drove past, and Wager wasn't surprised. He went a block down Race Street and pulled around in a U-turn, moving back slowly to wait just beyond the glare of the East Colfax strip. Sooner or later the big man would come sauntering past the brightly lit liquor stores, porno shows, pawnshops, and fast-food joints that lined Colfax from the city limits to the shadow of the state capitol. And in another five minutes, Wager's Trans Am rocked heavily as Fat Willy slid into the front seat beside him.

"How come you didn't meet me right out on the street, Wager? Out there in the light where the whole motherin world can see me talking with you?"

"Because I've got to watch my reputation."

"It ain't *your* reputation'll be hurt. Look, I don't know nothing about what went down this afternoon, so this is just a waste of my time."

"What do you mean? What went down?"

"You telling me you don't know?"

"What went down?"

142

Fat Willy's head tossed back with a loud "Haw! I swear to God, Wager, you couldn't find your own ass with both hands and a rear-view mirror. You call yourself a cop and you didn't hear about this Covino dude in Cañon City?"

"Tell me, Fat Willy."

"He was stabbed today, man. Somebody nailed him real good."

"Who told you this?"

"I heard it in casual conversation with a recent traveler from those distant shores. Haw!"

"Is he dead?"

"I do not know. And I did not ask. I don't want to look too interested in that dude or in his friends—because I ain't."

"Have you heard anything about him and the Scorvellis?"

The bulk settled comfortably against the seat. "Wager, I recollect there was some little mention that this information you are after might be valuable. You read me?"

"I can't tell you how valuable it is until I hear it."

"Well, start counting coin, my man—here's what I got." He canted his head so the shadow of the large-brimmed hat shielded his face from a figure walking past on the sidewalk. "The word I hear around is that this Covino maybe did a job for Dominick Scorvelli."

"The one in Cañon City? Gerald?"

"Naw, man. The other one that got hisself shot last week."

"What kind of job?"

"The word I hear is 'hit.' "

"Come on, Willy! We don't have a thing to show that kid ever crossed the street."

"They's a lot of things cops ain't got, Wager. One of them's good sense. Now, you want to hear what I picked up? Or you want to waste time disputing my solemn word?"

"Which hit?"

"Dominick's brother. Marco."

The hell he did. Wager sat and turned that information inside out, upside down, and backward, and it still didn't fit what he'd discovered about Frank's life. Unless there was a pot load more to learn about him somewhere. As Willy said, cops never knew everything. "How'd you hear this?"

"Around."

"It's important to know, Willy. I'm not coming down on anybody; I just want to corroborate."

"What's this here 'important' worth?" Willy rubbed together a thick thumb and forefinger, the flesh making a dry whisper.

Wager pulled out his wallet and counted out a hundred dollars of his own money. Maybe the Bulldog would pay him back. Then again, maybe he wouldn't.

Fat Willy counted the twenties against the light cloth stretched tight across his thigh. "Is that all? Hell, just sitting here is costing me more than this in business."

"It's all I have right now, Willy. If your information checks out, I'll double it. If you don't want it, you can always give it back."

"Just like you gonna give me back my information, right?" He folded the bills into a tight wad and slipped them somewhere beneath the expanse of linen coat.

"How did you hear this about Covino and Scorvelli?"

"I heard it in a couple places. Couple days ago some people was talking about it at a game of chance I know about. And I heard it today, too, down at the Ebony Billiard Saloon. It come up when we got the word on the other one getting stabbed. It's all over the place, man."

"Who was talking it up?"

"Nobody special. It was just talk, you know?"

"You think somebody could have planted it?"

"Sure! But how in hell's anybody going to know if it's the real skinny or it ain't? I mean, you got to get a lot closer to

144

them Scorvellis to know that, and I am as close as I aim to get." He opened the door and grunted his way out, then bent to the half-lowered window. "And another thing: why would somebody want to blow smoke like that? And another thing, too: somebody sure didn't like them Covinos for some real heavy reason. You dig? Don't forget, you owe me. I be waiting."

He was gone, a wide blur of white against the darkness of worn and cautious houses whose shades were pulled to pinch out the glare and noise and eyes of the Colfax corner.

Why *would* somebody plant that story? It would be easy enough to do—a murmur here, a whispered "did you know" there. Anything about the Scorvellis was news everywhere, and the person who could tell his buddies something first would stand a notch taller in their eyes. A day, two days, and the story would be all over town and impossible to trace back to the one who started it. But for what reason? The police weren't even close to a suspect in Marco's death, so there was no one trying to shake off attention. And there was no reason Wager could see in naming Frank the hit man after he was dead—no reward to collect from Dominick, no revenge against a corpse. And not one goddamned bit of the kid's life even pointed that way. But as Willy said, Frank was dead, and now his brother had been stabbed.

An uneasy chill ran up Wager's back. Frank had been shot just after Wager had heard the name, and Gerald was stabbed within three days after Wager had gone to see him. It was almost as if there was a connection—as if Wager, himself, was the connection.

But that made as little sense as the rumor that Frank killed Marco. As little sense as any other link between that and Gerald's stabbing. Wager swore again and started his car and turned it west on Colfax, toward headquarters.

"Well, jumping Jesus—it's Wonder Wager." Ross looked up from a mound of papers, his red ballpoint pen aimed at the line of type he had been studying. "Did you come down on your free time just to help us lesser minions serve and protect?"

"No. I came to find out something about that stabbing in Cañon City today. Did you or Dev get anything on it?"

When it came to business, Ross could forget his animosity toward Wager. "Only that it happened. Is it part of that shooting last weekend?"

"I don't know. It's the victim's brother, but there are too many loose ends to say they're tied together."

"Anything we can do?"

Wager ran a finger down the list of frequently called numbers, looking for the duty officer at the state penitentiary. "I guess just listen around. So far, there's not much to do anything with."

"What do you want us to listen for?"

Wager told him what Fat Willy had said. If Sonnenberg didn't like the Scorvelli name talked about, he could take it up with Fat Willy.

"My, my. The plot does thicken. Is there a jacket on this Frank Covino?"

"He seems as clean as a hangman's conscience. But unless there's some kind of truth in that rumor, nothing makes any sense." Wager dialed the number and waited four or five rings before the male voice of the duty officer, cadenced with routine, answered.

"This is Detective Wager, D.P.D. Can you give me a status report on the prisoner who was stabbed today—Gerald Covino?"

"Just a minute." The voice came back. "He died at approximately 10:30 A.M. without regaining consciousness."

Damn. "Any idea who did it?"

146

"Yes, sir. But we're not allowed to give that information out over the telephone. We can send a report if you'll give me your official address and a statement of need to know. Or you can come down here. It might be quicker if you came down here, anytime between 9 A.M. and 3 P.M."

"Has the next of kin been notified?"

"Yes, sir. They have."

Wager hung up and looked at Ross without really seeing him. Dead. Another thread cut—a thread of life, a thread in the case. Somewhere, Wager realized, half buried in the back of his mind, he had been putting some hopes on Gerald. Give him a little time to think about his brother, let his mother's suffering work on him a little; make another trip down to Cañon City in a week or two and then again until something broke in the case. Hell, Gerald wouldn't be going anywhere—and Wager had plenty of time on his side to chip away at the man's silence. But now Gerald was gone for good, and Wager couldn't help the recurring question about his own part in it; he couldn't help wondering if somehow he had set Gerald up like a mouse trapped in a box. Like poking a stick at a goddam mouse cornered in a box.

Ross was saying something to him.

"What?"

"Did Covino buy it?" Ross asked again.

"Yes. This morning."

Ross wagged the ballpoint pen in a series of short taps. "Convenient, ain't it?"

It was that. And again came that feeling, like a moth butting its head and shredding its wings against the screen to get at a light inside, that something was there just beyond him. Something that he should be able to get hold of. "The dumb bastard should have told me what he knew." Wager said it more to himself than to Ross. "The dumb bastard could have saved his life if he'd told me."

147

"Or had his throat cut for being a snitch."

"I suppose." Wager hadn't built that box; the mouse had found it all by himself and crawled in and was trapped by its own stubbornness. It was that simple. It should be that simple.

"Do you want Dev and me to start shaking the trees? We've got a few contacts that even you don't have, Wager; and if there's any word about the Scorvellis, they're bound to hear it."

Sonnenberg wouldn't go for that; he was already getting diarrhea over his project, and to have the whole Homicide Division snuffling at Dominick's heels would either give the inspector a heart attack or send him right up to the department chief himself. And that would bring in another variable, a political one, which Wager didn't want to risk right now. "No. Just listen around."

He could see it in Ross's eyes—the other detective figured that Wager was trying to keep the case entirely in his own hands, that Wager was afraid there wouldn't be enough glory to share. "Sure. If that's the way you want it." What the hell, it wasn't skin off Ross's fanny; he'd offered and he sure as hell wasn't going to beg to be let in on it. Ross turned back to the forms, the red ballpoint pen stabbing sharply at the lines of print.

Wager got out of the office; it wasn't his shift, so it wasn't his territory. Let Ross sulk if he wanted to; there were things that Wager could not explain to him. And there were things he couldn't explain to himself, either. Call it instinct or ESP. Or even Celestial Seasoning tea leaves. But damn Gerald and damn the feeling that padded after Wager like a hungry dog down the corridors empty of everyone but the night janitor swinging his heavy, noisy waxer from wall to wall like the weighty pendulum of a clock.

Sitting in his car, Wager fiddled with the GE radio pack that rode either on his hip or in the rack he had mounted just under the dash. The terse queries and replies filling the police band told him nothing. He knew they wouldn't, but neither did they bring that calmness which often came from half listening to the routine governance of the city's daily violence.

Maybe he should go back and start at the beginning. At this time of night, midnight, it was as good a place as any; and Wager knew he would not be able to sleep, anyway.

Turning up Lawrence, he parked just north of the cold symmetry of the main post office, with its government lions in frozen crouch and the scattered bums sprawling on the benches at their stone feet like sacrificial offerings. Two blocks over was the Little Juarez section, and this time Wager cruised it on foot, silent among the loud intermingling of broken Spanish and fractured English, and the louder, brassy music spilling from the bars. Panhandlers came a step or two toward him, recognized a cop, and suddenly found something across the street to interest them; men lining the small bars that he entered one after another watched him from the corners of their eyes or in the mirrors. An occasional bartender nodded hello, and Wager asked quietly if he'd seen Tony-O.

"He came in maybe an hour ago. I ain't seen him since."

"Any idea which way he went?"

A shrug. "Out."

"If he comes back, let him know I'm looking for him."

"I'll tell him, sure. But you know how he is—*mucho orgulloso,* that one."

"I know. Just tell him."

"Cómo no. Sure."

It wasn't in a bar that he found Tony-O; it was crossing the street in front of the wide concrete walls and blank, tinted plate glass of an office building that formed a barrier between this raw corner of the city and Old Larimer Square, where

149

tourists paraded in shiny shoes or imitation grubbiness through expensive bars and restaurants, looking for authentic echoes of the boom town that Denver used to be. The old man walked with his usual careful but erect stride through the bustling street life, his wrinkled face restless in its habitual scan of the people strolling the sidewalks or weaving through cars stopped for the traffic lights.

Wager cut across the street and caught up with him. "Tony-O! Wait a minute."

"*Quién es?* Wager?"

"Let's get a beer. I need to talk to you, Tony."

"What about?"

He gestured at a corner tavern whose plaster wall was still painted with a faded 7-Up sign, the last remnant of the neighborhood grocery store that had preceded the bar. An equally faded sign in the window facing Larimer said "Aquí hablamos Español." "I want to ask you a few questions. Something's come up, and maybe you can help me out."

The shoulders of the old man's coat, square and fragile as if draped on a wire hanger, rose and fell. "Maybe; we'll see." He followed Wager into the bar and they found a pair of empty stools at the far end of the counter, away from the wailing jukebox. Wager ordered two draws. A newer sign in the middle of the oily mirror behind the bar said "We Support the Boycott. No Coors." People had signs for everything; not arguments or discussions, just signs.

"What's this help you want?"

"Remember that name you gave me? Frank Covino?" asked Wager.

"I read in the paper what happened to him."

"Now his brother's been killed down in Cañon City."

"Killed? When?"

"He was stabbed sometime this morning. He died around ten o'clock."

150

The gnarled knuckles on Tony-O's hands made the bones of his fingers look thin and brittle as they slid up and down the lines of the small beer glass. "I didn't hear about that. That's too bad."

"Maybe there was a tie-in."

"Like what?"

"I really don't know. I don't have the whole story on the stabbing, but the coincidence is enough to make me wonder."

Tony-O's white head bobbed silent agreement. "So what do you want from me?"

"I need to know where you got your information on Frank Covino. It's all over town now, but you were the first one I heard it from. I need to trace it down, Tony-O."

The knotty fingers rasped over the gray bristles speckling the sagging flesh under his chin. "You need." It did not come out like a question.

"That's right. I need." And there was no apology in Wager's voice.

Tony-O's eyes beneath the lids with their net of deep wrinkles glided his way, and Wager felt the old man probe this harder tone as he rolled a cigarette on his tongue and poked it into the corner of his mouth with his fist. "I guess I can tell you. But I don't know what good it'll do you."

"Why?"

"The guy that told me ain't in town no more."

"Where'd he go?"

"He said he was going back to L.A."

"What's his name?"

"Chavez. Bernie Chavez. Know him?"

Wager knew half a hundred Chavezes, a few who had numbers following their names and a lot without; but "Bernie" didn't fit any of them. "Does he have a record?"

Tony-O shrugged and sipped his beer. "Maybe. He's been

around. He's an old guy like me—all washed up."

Wager jotted the name in the little green notebook. Bernie Chavez in L.A. There shouldn't be more than five thousand of them, but he didn't have anything better to put in his notebook.

"How did he know about this? Why'd he tell you?"

"He told me because he wanted to. Not because I asked him. You know what I mean?"

"I wouldn't be bothering you if it wasn't really important, Tony-O."

"Yeah. Well, I was over at Centennial watching the quarter horses, and Bernie sees me in the two-dollar line. He's one of them from the old days, before he moved out to L.A. He comes back every now and then." Another slow sip. "He come up and wanted to borrow some bucks, so sure, I let him."

Wager could see it in his imagination: this Bernie Chavez spotting the old man and giving him the "Hey—Tony-O!" routine, asking, "Do you remember . . . ?" and saying, "Jefe, I remember when you . . ." And Tony-O eating it like candy, even up to the part where Bernie drops his voice to a whisper and says, "Jefe, I got a good tip on this one, but nothing to lay down. I mean, it's just two bucks and it's against a sure thing . . ." And, as in the old days, the *jefe* tosses him the bills like they were nothing.

"Did his horse come in?" asked Wager.

He took a long drink, then said disgustedly, "Yeah, it did. At about thirty to one. He wanted me to bet it, but I was too smart to listen to him. I think mine's still looking for the finish line." He rinsed his tongue with another swallow and dragged thumb and forefinger along the deep lines at the sides of his mouth. "So then this big winner wants to buy me a drink. To make me feel better for not listening to him, you know? And that's when he told me."

152

"Do you remember what he said exactly?"

Frowning, the old man stared across the bar top somewhere toward the tequilas and cheap bourbons lined up in front of the mirror. "Not exactly, no. We started talking about the old days again and Bernie said something about how the wops took over Denver and how the Scorvellis had a habit of killing people in their own family. Which was something none of us ever did."

That wasn't entirely true, Wager remembered from neighborhood stories; but he didn't interrupt.

" 'Like Marco's getting killed,' he said. And I said, 'Everybody thought that was from the outside,' and he said, "No, *hombre.* It was one of our people did it, but he was hired by Dominick to make it look like an outside job; Dominick wanted somebody who wouldn't have no loyalties.' " Another thoughtful sip of beer. " 'Where'd you get this?' I said. 'From a guy out in L.A. He had some trouble when Scorvelli was pushing the Ortegas out and he still keeps tabs on them wops.' "

"Did Chavez say who that was?"

"I figured if he wanted to tell me, he would have. So I didn't ask. But he saw that I didn't really buy his word, you know? So he says, 'It was a kid done it—named Covino.' 'There's a lot of Covinos,' I said. 'Try Frank,' he said."

Wager gave the old man another half minute, but he added nothing. Tony-O drank his beer and stretched his thin upper lip with a silent belch, watched the bubbles rise through the yellow liquid and stroked the damp glass with thumb and forefinger.

"That's all?" asked Wager.

"That's all."

One step back. All Wager had done was push the point of beginning one step back, and it was still out of sight. How many more steps would he have to push? "I still don't see why this Chavez would be the one to hear it when nobody else did."

Tony-O's white head wagged. "He says he picked it up in L.A. That's where the Ortegas went when they left here. That's all I know."

"What was he doing in Denver?"

"Playing the ponies when I saw him."

"Did he have any other reason for being here? Family? Business? Anything that could give me a lead on him?"

The old man drained his beer and set the glass carefully on its ring of moisture. "He's street people. I didn't know him too good in the old days and I know him a hell of a lot less now. I don't know what he was doing here. But I do know this: I'm beginning to wish I hadn't said one damned thing to you. You really are starting to bug me with these questions."

Wager ordered another round from the bartender, who checked glasses whenever the TV set glowed a commercial that did not have bouncy, smiling girls in short shorts. *"Estoy apurado, Jefe, y no tengo compadre ni padre."* The saying—"I need help, Chief, and I don't have a friend or a father"— came from so far out of Wager's past that it brought with it the clean smell of fresh tortillas, the sunny rustle of cotton-wood leaves beyond the cool of the back porch. It was a phrase supported by the truth of murmured childhood lore, that if you were ever really in trouble from something you couldn't take to your parents or uncle or anybody, you could always go to Tony-O and whisper those words and he'd say, "I'm here."

But that was when Tony-O's shadow lay long through the barrio, and the barrio itself still had life. Now the old man's already straight back stiffened slightly as if he heard a long-forgotten voice. Then it relaxed with a slight shrug and he

154

said to the glass in front of him, *"No soy jefe.* Not any more. I can't help you, Wager."

"But I've got to ask the questions, Tony-O. It'll be a big help if you try to answer them."

"O.K., Gabe."

They both sipped at their beers.

"Did this guy know anything about Gerald? Is there a possibility that he meant Frank's brother did the hit?"

"The only Covino he named was Frank." The knotted fingers tapped against the glass, their dry, hard flesh making a muffled *tink.* "He could of been wrong, yeah. Or whoever gave him the word could of had it screwed up." He looked at Wager in the mirror. "Or maybe Scorvelli knew it wasn't Frank but Gerald that did it, and had somebody down there slip him some iron."

"That's what I was thinking," said Wager. But even if that made sense for part of it, Frank's death was still a puzzle. Unless . . . "Have you heard any rumors about anyone making a move against the Scorvellis?"

"Like how?"

"Taking over their action. Bringing the Ortegas back, maybe."

Tony-O's face dipped toward the floor and he bit off a small white blob of disgusted spit, which dropped between his feet. "No. The Ortegas, they're finished. There's not enough of them left to do anything. The kids these days . . . bombings, marchings, singing goddam songs! No, I ain't heard nothing like that."

"Something's got to explain Frank's death. Maybe somebody with big ideas heard the same thing you did and tried to tell Scorvelli something by killing a Covino. But they got the wrong man."

"I ain't heard nothing like that, either." The thin shoulders wagged once. "Hell, it's possible, though. There's a lot that's possible."

"Have you told anyone else what you heard?"

"No. Just you. But if it's all over town like you say, then Bernie must of told somebody else."

Like every other theory, that might be the reason—or it might not. So far, every thread Wager pulled either snapped off or frayed short. And one was cut.

"Could be it was Scorvelli himself," said Tony-O. "Could be that Bernie told the truth and Scorvelli heard it and measured Frank for a wooden overcoat. Then did the same for Gerald so there wouldn't be no revenge. Or because he was afraid Frank told Gerald about the hit. Could be Scorvelli's got some answers to that—maybe you should go sit on him awhile."

That, too, made as much sense as everything else. But there was a good reason why Wager wouldn't go running down that trail yet: Sonnenberg. "I've got too many ifs, Tony-O; what I need is hard information. Do you know anybody else around who might have a lead on this Bernie Chavez?"

"No." This time the old man spoke quickly, and like the shadow of a fast, thin cloud across his mind, Wager faintly wondered if it was too quickly.

eleven

When Axton entered the office the next morning, Wager first told him the latest on the case, then drew the day's initial cup of coffee.

"Let me call down to Cañon City," said Axton. "I know some people there, and maybe they'll give us the scoop and save a long drive."

He dialed and waited and then, as Wager handled the morning paper work, began asking questions of someone named Allen. "Right, Al, the one yesterday. It has a bearing on something we're working with up here. Right. Sure, I'll hang on." He covered the mouthpiece with two broad fingers. "Al's calling the officer in charge of the investigation," he explained.

Wager nodded and focused on the stack of requests and queries, the bulletins, alerts, advisements, and warnings, the reports, statistical summaries, graphs, and diagrams that flowed in rivers and rivulets through the police routing system. Many were to be noted and shoved elsewhere, others to rest in homicide in various files and with varying degrees of permanence. Most would never be looked at again, but only a few could be thrown out immediately. When Max hung up at last, Wager was ready for him. "Well?"

"They're calling it a local fight. Gerald and a black guy got into a squabble during a softball game the afternoon before, and the guard thinks they carried it over. They met the next morning and the other prisoners say Covino started it, and of course he's not around to say he didn't. Anyway, they tangled, and by the time the guard got there, Covino had a sharpened spoon handle in the heart."

"What's the black's name?"

"Ronald Greenlee, a.k.a. Ali Uhuru."

"Anybody mention Scorvelli's name?"

"Christ, Gabe, I wouldn't ask that!"

Wager would. But he let it pass—Axton was probably right not to talk the name around any more than they had already. "Any hints at all that it was a setup?"

"I asked him twice; he said no. Greenlee has been in for about four years on a murder conviction. About three months ago he was transferred out of maximum security into Covino's cell block; and as far as past records show, there was never any connection between him and Covino. The fight seems to be the first time the two ever talked."

"Do we have a jacket on Greenlee?"

"Yeah—they gave me his file number. Want to look at it?"

"Might as well." Besides, it would delay a little longer the thing they had to do today, which had awakened Wager this morning with that weary feeling of wanting to drop this day out of the calendar.

Axton brought the jacket back from the Records Section and they started going down the column of entries that was the man's life according to the law.

158

"Busy dude," said Axton.

He had been. The juvenile record started at thirteen; they skipped over that. The adult record, which began at eighteen with an arrest for attempted rape, listed a conviction for robbery, another for assault—this one with intent—and finally first-degree murder with life imprisonment. That usually meant parole in six to ten years. Greenlee's second known murder, that of Covino, would put off his parole a little longer. Nowhere in the official or unofficial entries was there any hint of a connection with either Scorvelli or Covino. But, Wager figured, if Scorvelli or anyone else wanted to arrange for Covino's death, then Greenlee was a good choice for the job: violence-prone, little to lose, and—since the payoff would come through a third or even fourth party—no direct link at all to Scorvelli.

Axton was thinking along the same lines. "It doesn't really help us one way or the other, does it?"

It was good when you and your partner could think together like that. It was like family. Better than family, from Wager's point of view, because the jealousies and secrets, the old regrets and newly twisted affections, the family memories and family jokes, did not tangle things up. It was a much cleaner and more precise bond of shared labor, a bond one wasn't just born to but which one chose. "It doesn't shut off any possibilities, anyway. Can you call your friend Al back and get a full report on Greenlee's prison record? Whose cell he shares. What gang he runs with or any recent changes of behavior."

Max picked up the telephone and dialed again.

Wager sorted through another half inch of paper work, pausing to read carefully an F.B.I. report forwarded to him through Baird in the laboratory. The fingerprints on the calling card of Victor Galen belonged to one Vittorio Galente, who was described as a figure active in organized crime, generally associated with operations in and around the Chicago area. Apparently, whatever expansion plans Dominick Scorvelli had, they involved closer links to Chicago through the white-haired man with the neat homburg and the flat black eyes. That tidbit meant nothing now, but later it might; Wager filed it in memory.

"Allen will send Greenlee's record this morning, and the courier should have it here late today or tomorrow," Max said when he hung up the receiver. "Al's really not sold on the idea of a planned hit. He says fights happen all the time down there, and this just looks like another black and Chicano run-in."

"If I wanted to cover a hit, that's exactly what I'd make it seem like." And besides, there was a lot less paper work if the killing was explained as being racially motivated instead of a conspiracy.

"Yeah," said Max. "You're right. I think we should have looked a little harder at Gerald when we had him. I think we screwed up."

"It's not 'we,' Max. It's 'me.' I screwed up."

"Hold it, partner—I've got a brain, too. And I didn't use it."

However Max wanted it. Though in his heart, Wager knew that if fault lay anywhere, it was with him alone. Wager should have thought out all the angles—should have looked ahead and asked for protective custody for Gerald. With the mere possibility of someone like Scorvelli mixed up in the case, Wager should have done a hell of a lot more than he did. It wasn't the first time he had screwed up, and probably wouldn't be the last; but it always felt newly bad when it happened. "You know who we have to go see?"

Max knew and winced at the thought. "Lord, I hate facing that Covino girl again."

160

The small house with its half pillars of brick had not changed a bit. There was still an odor of sadness about it, even from the street, which made the silence and dark of its windows seem more intense than the other houses on the block. Wager had noticed that before: somehow, when you were sent to a house of bad luck, you knew which one it was even before you read the address. There was something in the waiting stillness, something in the light—as if the house and small yard around it were listening. Not that they would offer any reply—but they were suddenly, and quietly, listening.

The daughter answered their knock, standing wordless behind the screen door with its scattered small patches of newer screen and a small puff of cotton pinned in the center to scare away flies.

"We're sorry to have to come back, Miss Covino," said Max.

Wager saw that she was picking through a dozen replies like a kid fingering stones, trying to find the one that would hurt most.

"You attack the dead. Now you kill the living. You don't want to leave us anything, do you?"

Axton's throat rumbled nervously. "We're still trying to learn who killed Frank. We're trying everything we can, even things that aren't likely, because we have nothing else to try."

"So that's why you got Gerry killed? You were 'trying' things?"

"He was killed in a fight with another inmate, Miss Covino," said Wager. "As far as we know, there's no connection between that and Frank's death."

"Oh? Then what the hell are you doing here? You just come by to say you're sorry about Gerry? You're not going to ask any questions about Gerry and Frankie, that so?"

161

No, that wasn't so. And grope as he might, Wager could not find a phrase that would make things sound nice. Things weren't nice—they hurt, and there was no path long enough to work around the edges of all that hurt. He would have to go through it. "As far as we *know,* there's no connection. But there may be, and that's why we're here. You're right about that." But Wager could not yet admit to her that he had anything to do with Gerald's death. "We have to find out if there's a connection," he finished lamely.

Grace Covino's wet eyes narrowed and she gave a tight little smile that was no smile at all. "You tell Mama that. You come right on in and you tell that to Mama!"

This time, Mrs. Covino was not in the tiny parlor waiting for them. Wager stood with Axton beside him, looming even bigger against the formal, close walls and ceiling and the crowd of overstuffed chairs and knickknacks, the small bookcase with its thinly gilded collection of Reader's Digest Condensed Books, the shelf with the madonna and the pictures and now three prayer candles glowing redly in their glasses. When Mrs. Covino entered, it was with the unseeing numbness of shock, the unnatural coldness of wearied but not exhausted anguish.

Max apologized again, but Mrs. Covino, gray hair combed and black dress neat with the touch of someone else's care, did not seem to hear him. She stood a long minute staring at the row of pictures and the candles, and, with a quivering breath, sat slowly on the heavy sofa. Grace Covino stood beside her, hand on her mother's rounded shoulder, and glared at them.

"Ma'am," said Axton, "is there anything more at all that you can tell us about Frank's death? Anything that might help explain Gerald's?"

Her voice, level and almost girlishly thin, prickled the skin at the back of Wager's neck. "You killed him."

162

"What?"

"You killed him."

"Why do you say that, Mrs. Covino?" Max asked gently.

"Gerry told me. He knew it was going to happen. He knew what you did to him."

"When?"

"He wrote a letter. When it came, I didn't even know the handwriting. We never wrote much, and I didn't even know my own son's handwriting."

"Can we see his letter, ma'am?"

"Gracie . . ."

The girl came back a moment later and handed Axton the envelope. The paper inside held a few penciled lines, and Wager could see a couple of wrinkled spots on the well-folded sheet, spots that had dried. Axton held it so Wager could also read.

Dear Mom

I heard about Frankys death and I am sorry for you and him. He was a good boy and did not deserve what he got. The cop who told me said some other things to which has me worried. If some thing happens to me in this place go see Pete Zamora. You remember him. Tell him what has happened and show him this letter.

Con amor y siempre su hijo,
Gerry

There was no date on the letter. "When did this come, Mrs. Covino?" asked Wager.

Grace answered, "Three days ago. Two days before it happened."

A stray hair on Mrs. Covino's head quivered. "Now my family has no man. First Frankie. Then Gerry. And Gracie's not married."

"Did you go see this Pete Zamora?"

"I went," said Grace. "Yesterday afternoon."

163

"What did Zamora say?"

"I don't have to tell you. Whatever Gerry did, he paid for it."

"Why not tell us, Miss Covino?" Max urged. "We really are trying to find out who killed your brother."

The girl studied his face and then said angrily, "He gave me forty-five hundred dollars. Zamora and me went to a bank and he handed me forty-five hundred dollars. He said Gerry left it with him in case something like this happened." Her jaw pushed out, and in that gesture Wager saw a dim reflection of her brother's last interview in prison.

There was a long silence as Wager and Axton weighed the implication of the money. "Where is it now?"

"I've got it safe. Mama don't want it, but we can use it to pay for all the funerals. I guess you'd like to take the money, too, wouldn't you?"

The state's tax collector might be interested, but not Wager. "Your money's none of my business, Miss Covino. Unless it gets in the way of our investigation. Can you give me this Pete Zamora's address?"

"All he did was hold my brother's money for him."

"That's not against the law. But we've got to talk to him. You understand that, Miss Covino?"

She seemed to, but it still took time to get her words out. "He's got a wrecking yard on the south side. Near Mississippi and Mariposa. It's called Pete's."

Wager caught Axton's eye for any other questions and the big man's head shook slightly before he said, "Thank you very much for your help, ma'am. And we're sorry all this has happened."

Mrs. Covino said, "Gracie . . ." and murmured something that only the girl could hear.

"What's that, ma'am?" asked Wager.

"She wants to know," said Gracie, "why you had to get

164

Gerry killed. She wants to know why you had to do that."

It was Axton's turn to drive; he headed the sedan south on Federal Avenue and, for the first dozen blocks, neither man said anything. Finally, "Gerald's death wasn't our fault."

"That's right," said Wager.

"We were following a lead on a homicide, like anybody else would do."

"That's right," Wager said again. It was useless to talk about it; anything Max would say Wager had already thought of, and none of it fully answered the self-accusation he felt. It had not been wrong to dig for a link between Covino and the Scorvellis. A lead was a lead, and by God, cops chased after them. But Wager still felt the sourness of not having done enough when he felt that small tingle of suspicion at the end of his interview with Gerald. It would have taken only one telephone call to have Gerald reassigned to a more secure area. One call, and Wager had not done it. He had let the chance go by and it had cost Gerald his life. And— something Wager didn't bother to explain to Max—it was less Grace Covino's sorrow at losing another brother than Wager's regret at losing a main figure in the case that affected him.

"What do you think about that forty-five hundred bucks?" asked Max.

"It could have been his Christmas account."

"Right—and the little elves helped him save it. Do you remember what burglaries he confessed to when he was busted?"

Wager didn't. He and Max would have to comb through the records and transcripts again to see if any or all of the stolen property added up to that much money. If it could not, then there remained that worrisome rumor about the Covinos and the Scorvellis; to kill Marco Scorvelli would be worth that much money. More, even. And if the case took a turn in that direction, then the self-accusation Wager felt would be truly justified, because his questioning of Dominick would have stirred fears about Gerald's reliability. "The arresting officer, Franconi, said he was small-time as a burglar. But that doesn't have to mean the forty-five hundred's Scorvelli money," Wager told himself as much as Axton.

It was Max's turn to say, "That's right."

He turned off Federal onto Mississippi and drove down as far as the Colorado and Southern Railway tracks before slowing to look for the salvage yard. They found it, a steel-mesh fence laced with metal slats to block the public view of twisted and stripped car bodies; but the patches of rust and the scrawls of spray paint along the fence didn't do much to help the beautification effort. Max pulled up beside a two-room box with the sign "Office" and a neighboring pen crowded with two wolflike German shepherds whose rough coats looked wild and angry.

Inside the small building, a kid was trying to fit a slightly worn generator into a cardboard box; behind him on a board shelf flanked by out-of-date Pirelli calendars whose girls looked too good to be real, two radios squawked—one with country wails and electronic twangs, the other, a shortwave band, carrying queries and replies for parts from salvage yards all over the Southwest. As they entered, it asked for a 1968 Olds 98 left front fender, location and price to A & S Salvage, Alamogordo.

"Can I help you?" The kid, in oil-stained overalls, glanced up.

"We're looking for Pete Zamora."

It wasn't the usual request for a Corvette transmission or a Kaiser grille; a little wrinkle came and went between his

166

brows. "He's in the yard, cutting. But customers aren't allowed out there."

Wager showed his badge. "Where in the yard?"

"Is this some kind of bust or something?"

"No. You expecting a bust?"

"No, man! It's just that I only started working here yesterday. If something's wrong, I don't know anything about it."

It wasn't hard to figure why the kid was nervous; last month the Colorado Bureau of Investigation had broken a five-state ring whose members were using a Denver junkyard to take stolen automobiles apart. Sold piecemeal, a five-thousand-dollar car could be worth ten or fifteen thousand. Plus very low overhead for the chop shop. "You think something's going on here?"

"No, man! Like, I've only been here two days."

"Is business good?"

"Oh, yeah! We got twenty, twenty-five pieces to ship this morning, and that doesn't count the walk-in trade."

Wager peered around the room, cluttered with ripped-out dash instruments and an assortment of dusty hoses and belts dangling from wire hooks. "Where does Zamora keep his records?"

"In the back there, I guess." He pointed through a doorless frame to the corner of a desk. "Maybe you should ask him."

"That's what we're trying to do," reminded Wager.

"Oh, yeah. This way."

He led them past the police dogs, who neither barked nor growled, but became ominously still. "Man, talk about your junkyard dogs. They scare the hell out of me, and I work here. I think Pete feeds them a little gunpowder to make them crazy mean, you know?"

Wager had heard of people doing that. "Is that Zamora over there?"

"Yeah—just follow the hoses."

The thin high-pressure lines, one black the other dull red, ran from scarred tanks of oxygen and acetylene to a gaping Dodge pickup. From inside the cab came the hiss and splatter of a cutting torch and a fiercely whispered "Come loose from there, you son of a whore!"

"Mr. Zamora?"

The stained green coveralls plunging over the seat and under the dash wiggled slightly and the hissing lessened. "What? What the crap you doing in the yard?"

"Police, Mr. Zamora. We want to ask you a few questions."

The gas shut off with a pop and Zamora, dust and sweat mixed on his wide face, wriggled out of the truck. He lifted the goggles and dragged his thumbs over the circles of cleaner flesh beneath them. "What about?"

"Some money you were holding for Gerald Covino."

"What money? Never heard of him."

He was about Wager's height, though half again as wide, and seemed to be in his early thirties; when Axton leaned toward him, Wager saw Zamora's eyes travel up the thick body like a woodsman measuring a tree.

"We've already talked to Covino's sister, Mr. Zamora," Max said quietly. "We're trying to find some reason for his death."

Zamora wiped again at his sweaty face, the soot spreading like war paint. "All I did was put a little money in the bank for him."

"No law against that," agreed Axton. "Do you remember when this was?"

"Nope."

"What bank was it?" asked Wager.

"I forget."

Wager deliberately gazed around at the lines of cars whose

168

metal ticked and creaked beneath the hot weight of the sun. "You have papers for all these vehicles?"

Zamora, face flushed and streaked, looked back without answering.

"Did you notify the Motor Vehicle Division to cancel the license plates on every one of these cars, and do you have evidence that those plates were in fact destroyed?"

"Come on!"

"The law's there, Zamora. And the M.V.D.'s very interested in the salvage business right now. When's the last time you had your records audited?" Wager continued.

"Last year. The inspector was out just last year!"

"I'm not talking about an inspection, Zamora. I mean a detailed audit of each number on every registered frame and motor. A careful audit that might take as long as two weeks to check out every number in this yard."

"Hold on now, Gabe. Mr. Zamora doesn't want that—he'd have to close down for the whole audit. He'd lose a lot of business." Axton turned his earnest eyes to the stocky, sweating man, who stood as silent and tense as his dogs. "It would be better all around if you helped us out, Mr. Zamora. Gerald's dead; he can't tell us where the money came from, so there's no possible accessory charge we can bring against you. And if you've got nothing to hide, what good does it do to withhold evidence in a homicide investigation?"

"You dudes are a real Laurel and Hardy team," said Zamora.

Wager smiled. "Guess who'll have all the laughs, Zamora?"

"All I did was put some fucking money in the bank for him and then take it out like I was asked to."

"Then you must have an entry in a bankbook," said Wager.

"Aw, shit! Come on." Muttering, he led them to the office

169

past the soft whine of the dogs and the glance of the busy kid. Rummaging through the drawer of the beat-up desk, he yanked out a small blue passbook embossed with the gold words "World Savings and Loan." "Here." He shoved it at Wager.

Wager had noticed before that people kept bankbooks even after the account was closed, as if the tiny numbers still had some value. Inside the book's cover, the blanks were filled in with two names: "This certifies that *Peter J. Zamora or Gerald E. Covino* has a savings account . . . issued at *Denver,* Colorado, on the *12* day of *June, 1978.*" The entries were only three: the date of deposit, which was the same as the opening of the account, and for an amount of $4900.00; an earnings notation of $261.66, for a total of $5161.66; the account-closed note was the same day that the interest was figured.

"You gave Grace Covino only forty-five hundred dollars," said Wager.

"That was the deal—if anything happened to Gerry, I was supposed to give his mother forty-five and keep four for my trouble."

"What about the interest?"

Zamora's face grew darker beneath the streaks of drying soot. "Gerry didn't say nothing about that."

"Neither did you. Any idea where he got this money?"

"No. And I didn't ask. It was none of my business. He was a buddy and he wanted me to help him out is all."

"How long did you know Gerry, Mr. Zamora?" asked Axton.

"Since we were kids. He was a year or two behind me in school, but he ran around with us. He liked to hustle for the older kids—what you call 'advanced for his age.'"

That was the second time Gerald had been called ambi-tious. And now there was a bank account to show that he had somehow furthered his ambition. How did a small-time burglar who was dumb enough to pass out in the middle of a job suddenly get his hands on five big ones just before he was locked up?

"Did you know Frank, his brother?" asked Max.

"No. I mean, I saw him around when I'd go by for Gerry. But he was just a little kid, you know. Maybe eight or nine."

"Have you ever been arrested, Zamora?"

"Yeah. And I did my time. So don't try hassling me for that."

"When was that?"

"Eleven years ago. I did six months in Buena Vista for car theft. I been clean since."

"Was that the same fall Gerry took?"

"Naw, he was smart on that one. Said he was just hitchhiking and that I picked him up and he didn't know the car was hot. I backed him up—hell, what are friends for? He was sent down there after I got out."

"Did you stay friends with him all this time?"

"Sure. We didn't run around like we did before, because I got busy with my business here. But we'd have a couple beers now and then."

"Did you know he was a burglar?"

"No. He had a job at a car wash, and I figured that's what his act was. But listen—I'm clean, man. This place gets me plenty and I don't have to run no risks for it."

"You never wondered where Gerald got that forty-nine hundred?" prodded Wager.

"He told me he won it, and that was cool with me. There's a few games around." He glanced at Wager and then out the window as he lit a cigarette. "The cops know about them, you know what I mean?"

"You want to file a report on that?" asked Wager.

"Hell, no."

Max interrupted. "Who are some of the people Gerald ran around with?"

"I don't know. I'm here from seven in the morning until seven at night, man, and that don't leave much time to be nosy about other people. Besides, we didn't see each other that much."

"You didn't see each other that often, but he trusted you with all that money?" asked Wager.

"What the hell you mean by that?"

"I mean, why didn't he give it to somebody he saw more of?"

"Hell, I don't know. Maybe he didn't trust them; too bad you can't ask him. But he was that way—when he needed help he'd go to somebody he ran around with in school. Me, too: I need a special favor, I call one of the old buddies. Hell, everybody keeps in touch with buddies from school. Don't you?"

Axton nodded; Wager did not bother to shake his head. "Can you give me some names of the people he ran around with before he went to Cañon City?"

"No. He didn't say much about them and it was none of my business."

True or not, Zamora wasn't going to name anyone to a cop. Wager looked closely at the man's eyes. "Did he ever mention the Scorvellis?"

They blinked surprise. "Not that I remember. No, I never heard him say anything about them people." Zamora was tempted to ask something, but he stifled it; Covino's activities were still none of his business.

"Did you hear from him while he was in prison?" Max asked quickly.

Zamora shook his head. "First I heard was when I read he was killed."

"Any idea why he might have been killed?"

"Down there? Yeah—because he was La Raza. Some nigger did it, right?"

Max tried one more time. "Do you know anybody who might have been with him on that burglary when he got caught?"

"Like I said, I didn't even know he was into that."

In the car, Wager once more read the entries in the passbook, then he turned back a few pages in the little green notebook that always rode in his shirt pocket. "Covino and Zamora deposited the money a week after he was arrested."

"After?"

"Yep. Now, think about this guy making minimum wage at a car wash, and suddenly one week after he's busted and has to make bail, he has almost five thousand dollars." Something else suddenly struck Wager and he leafed through his notebook, but did not find what he looked for. "Do you remember the date Marco was killed?"

Max scratched at his ear lobe as he thought back, and then finally shook his head. "We can find out." He keyed the radio and asked for the Records Section; the reply came back within minutes. "The body was discovered on the morning of June 4, at 0520."

Wager tapped his finger on the entry in his notebook. "That's the same night Gerald was arrested."

twelve

Max sipped a mouthful of coffee, winced at its heat, and set the cup on the gritty desktop; he shook his large head slowly. "It's hard to believe."

"What better cover could the bastard have?" asked Wager. "He kills his man, then trots across town to get himself arrested for breaking and entering. We run around looking every place in the country except our own hip pocket." Wager smiled to himself. "I kind of like it."

"But doing that much time—six months to a year—for only five thousand dollars . . ." Axton's head wagged again. "Even tax-free, that's not much of an income."

Wager's coffee was just as hot as Max's, but he made it a point not to wince as he drank it. "It's about a year's pay at minimum wage—which is all Gerald was making legitimately. A year of sitting on his tail at state expense instead of washing cars."

"I don't think so, Gabe. It's not enough money to go into the joint for."

People had gone for a hell of a lot less, but seldom voluntarily, it was true. "I think," said Wager, "he saw it as an investment."

"How's that?"

"With Scorvelli." Wager groped to put into words the picture he had been building almost unconsciously. "Say you're a guy who's been gnawing his knuckles off trying to move into the big time, and say a chance comes along to do a job for somebody as important as Scorvelli. You'd jump at it, wouldn't you?"

"It's conceivable, I guess."

"And say you figure that if you do the first job right—and it's a big one—Scorvelli will keep you in mind. Hell, maybe you've been told that. So this is your one chance to impress somebody who can open the door to all the things you've dreamed of since you were a kid swiping cars and pretending they were yours: plenty of money, clothes, cars, all the women that money can buy, and being on the inside of the real action. Being able to walk down the street and have the eyes of dudes on the corner follow you the way you've stood there and watched others walk past. Others who weren't a damn bit better than you, but who somehow got the lucky break."

"You make it sound mighty nice."

"It *is* nice. It's the chance you've been dreaming of all your life, and you grab it. The money's O.K.—it's great, in fact. But you've been so hungry for this break that you'd have done it for nothing."

"But to kill somebody . . . That's not just another burglary, Gabe. A man just doesn't jump from burglary to contract murder."

"Every hit man jumps from somewhere, Max. And the target's not just anybody. It's a Scorvelli."

"What do you mean?"

"It's somebody who's dipped his hands in shit all the way up to the elbows to get where he is. It's somebody who knew the chances and took them, just like Gerald knew them and figured it was worth trying anyway. He was asked to get rid of a puke that nobody—not even his own brother—wanted around. And the one who asked him was this 'Count' Scorvelli." Wager took the next step, too. "It could be that Gerald didn't see himself as a murderer, but as a soldier in a separate world, a mirror world, where it's not called murder but—I don't know—'liquidation' or 'political necessity.'"

Axton looked at Wager for a long moment as if seeing him from a new angle. "God help us when our language is a license for murder."

"I don't think Scorvelli called it anything but what it was. I think Gerald did that—he was the one willing to be used that way, and so he told himself something to make it sound better."

"Ambition?"

Wager would say it was something more; his name for it was hunger, or, stronger, starvation.

Axton sipped again at the coffee and gazed through the dusty window at the slabs of dark concrete rising from the new building next door, which would soon block the view of distant Longs Peak with its flattened tip and ribs of pale-blue snow—a tiny scene that, from here, was as unreal as the postcard picture it resembled. "Then if you're right, there was every reason for Gerald to do good time. He had a hell of a lot to look forward to when he got out."

Wager had not thought that far yet; he was still listening to Gerald talk himself into a murder. But what Max said was true, and again Wager appreciated having a good man for a

176

partner. "Yes. He had absolutely no reason to start that fight." And every reason to avoid being linked to Wager and all other cops, even when his own brother was killed. A man who could so neatly execute Marco Scorvelli, one who could write off his own brother, was a man who could avoid any fight if he had to. And Wager did not try to deny a spreading sense of relief—because such a man was also one whose death would be deserved.

" 'And grievously hath Caesar paid for it,' " said Axton.

"What?"

"Ambition. My kid's studying Shakespeare in school. Caesar paid for his ambition, too."

Wager vaguely remembered the white-haired old lady who stood erect and brittle in front of his class and made him and the other kids stumble through the thees and thous of a language awkward on his tongue. He had been too busy struggling with the foreign meaning of individual words to see the story that lay behind them. "I don't know about Caesar, but I guess you could say Marco had it coming. And Gerald, too. Hell, they both had it coming." And let that be Gerald's epitaph. "Except Frank. I still can't figure how Frank's death fits in."

"Even that makes sense if Tony-O had the right information but the wrong names. If he told someone else what he told you, and that someone went looking for revenge against the wrong person."

"I asked Tony-O that already, and he says he didn't. But he thinks the word might have gotten out through the guy who told him."

"Who was that?"

"Some old man named Bernie Chavez, from L.A." Wager sighed.

"Any leads on him?"

"Nothing."

Axton whistled a short tune between his teeth. "I suppose we could ask the L.A.P.D. But it's a hell of a long shot. There must be a thousand Chavezes out there."

"And half of them named Bernie." Wager finished his coffee and stood. "But we have to ask anyway. And we'd better let the Bulldog know we're moving back into Sonnenberg's territory. We'd better let the Bulldog handle him this time."

"That's fine with me!" Axton followed Wager down the short hallway to the corner office with its frosted-glass door bearing the flaking letters "Division Chief." Doyle looked up from the wash of papers over his desk and motioned toward the hard upright chairs along the wall; the Bulldog said his door was always open to his men, but those chairs ensured that none of them stayed too long.

"A lot of what you've told me is circumstantial—less than that, even; hypothetical," said Doyle when Wager and Axton had finished. "What I don't understand is why you're not out there crawling all over Scorvelli like flies on crap—why you're not out there squeezing everyone around him until you find someone willing to talk. If he had Gerald Covino scrubbed, somebody's going to know about it. And any links between Gerald and Scorvelli makes the possibility of links between Frank and Scorvelli all the better."

"Yessir. But we promised Inspector Sonnenberg we wouldn't put his operation in jeopardy. He's very nervous about what we've done so far, and we don't want to stir things up any more without him knowing about it first."

"And you still won't tell me the nature of that operation?"

Wager wanted very much to. "Well, we promised Sonnenberg to keep it confidential," he said. "But maybe if you talked to him and told him what we've found out, then he'd tell you what he's doing. Maybe he'd give us the go-ahead to move on Scorvelli."

178

"I'll be the one to give you any go-aheads—homicide's my territory." He chewed at his upper lip with those protruding lower teeth. "But I'd better call him and stroke his feathers. I suppose that's what chiefs are for."

It was, thought Wager, exactly what chiefs were for.

"All right, boys," Doyle went on. "You two work around the periphery of this thing until I can talk to him." He pressed the button on his digital watch. "It's eleven twenty-three now; check with me around two. I should have something by then."

"Yessir."

In the hallway once more, Axton said, "What about lunch? It's our last chance to visit the Frontier before it closes."

It had slipped Wager's mind that today was the end of the Frontier, and on remembering it, he really didn't want to go there for a last meal. It would be like helping time wash away another of those things he had called his. Those things would go—they always did—but it didn't seem right to celebrate them. Better to let them fade in peace and silence, better to let memory hold them as they were until their going was eased. But he could not think of any substantial excuse to give to Max. Like a lot of other things that were really important, the feeling seemed silly and even sentimental when he tried to frame it in words; he simply did not want to eat a last meal at the Frontier because he did not like to think of it as ending. But that wasn't something you could explain, even to your partner.

Wager was relieved that the snap of his radio broke the silence with his call number and saved him from answering Max. "This is X-85," he replied.

"You have a telephone call. What's your ten-twenty?"

"I'm in the building. Tell them to hang on." He walked quickly back to his office and lifted the receiver. "Detective Wager."

An unfamiliar voice asked cautiously, "You the detective that investigated that shooting the other night? The one over on South Broadway?"

"I am."

"This is Jesus Quintana. You said I should call you if I heard something about, you know, the Covino brothers or this certain other party."

Usually when Wager cast his bread on the waters, it sank. Maybe this time he'd get a crumb in return. "What have you got, Jesus?" He lifted a finger to Axton, who nodded and lowered himself to the corner of the desk.

"This is just between you and me, right, Wager? I mean, it ain't snitching or nothing, but I wouldn't want my name to, like, get around down there. You know what I'm talking about?"

"Just you and me, Jesus. I wouldn't work any other way —you're too important."

The man tried feebly to mask his pleasure. "Right!"

Axton made a sick face.

"O.K.," said Quintana. "I got this relation . . . well, he's a real distant cousin on my mother's side. Anyway, this relation was a buddy of the Covino down in Cañon City. You know, the one that got killed yesterday? The one that's in the paper this morning?"

"I know."

"Well, this relation is very important people in certain circles. You know what I'm talking about?"

"Yes."

"Well, the story came out in the paper this morning about this Covino getting it in Cañon City and this relation says to me, 'I knew it.' He says, 'I knew it would happen, him getting mixed up with them wops.'"

Wager leaned forward. "What's this person's name, Jesus?"

180

There was a long silence; in the background, a car horn beeped and the rapping sound of a motorcycle or truck passed, and Wager guessed the man was calling from a telephone booth. "I'd just as soon not say."

"He won't know it came from you. We'll tell him we're investigating all of Covino's friends and associates, and that he's just one more name on a list."

A second pause. Then, "O.K. His name's Huey Santos. Maybe you guys got a jacket on him down there. Maybe you could say you got his name and where he lives and all from his jacket or something."

So Quintana had thought it all out before he called, and Wager knew there was no "maybe" about a file on Santos. "That's what we'll do, Jesus. Good idea."

"Sure. I've cut all my teeth. This is pretty important info, right?"

"It could really be big, Jesus. It could be that you've just come through with something really big."

"All right!" The line clicked dead.

"We're looking for one Huey Santos, a friend of Gerald's," Wager told Axton. "He might know about something between Gerald and the Scorvellis. Let's take a look in Records."

The Santos file wasn't overly thick, but it was far from empty. The juvenile section finally noted a tour in the reformatory, and Wager checked the dates against those he had written in his little green notebook. "The same as Gerald. They probably met there." The subsequent entries were investigative and only one conviction was listed, a two-year-old sentence for burglary. Intermediate to nine, suspended. Wager guessed that the suspension was part of a deal between Santos and some prosecutor who didn't think the defendant was important enough to waste the court's time on. He flipped to the page of general information, and this time found that some nameless cop had made the effort to do things right. Sketched in on this page were some of the blank spaces of Santos's life, which fit nowhere else in an official sheet but were invaluable when—as now—Santos was wanted again.

"He likes that gin mill over on Kalamath, the Juanita," said Axton, reading over Wager's shoulder.

"And there's Gerald's name." Wager copied that and another half-dozen names from the list of known associates. "Let's go visiting."

Axton groaned and said with fading hope, "I thought we were going to the Frontier to eat."

Wager, already striding out the door, did not answer; given the present choice, he'd rather work.

Santos's room was in one of the shoebox-shaped apartment buildings whose narrow fronts lined lower Lincoln Street. From the back of the long, dim hallway came the odor of wood rot and rusty iron pipes; from somewhere indefinable —perhaps the brown wallpaper itself—was the added smell of old food scorched on illicit hot plates. Wager showed his badge and Santos squinted at it through the smoke of his cigarette as if he had seen badges before. Then, saying nothing, he let them in.

"We found your name among a list of Gerald Covino's acquaintances. Have you seen much of him?"

"Not since he was sent to Cañon City."

"You heard that he was killed down there?"

Why else would two cops be spending their afternoon with him? The cigarette in the corner of his mouth jerked when he spoke. "I read it in the paper. Too bad."

"We're trying to find out what he was doing just before he was arrested. We'd appreciate your help."

The wrinkles in Santos's forehead deepened momentarily.

182

"That was a while back. I don't know what I can tell you."

"How about starting with the burglary? Did Gerald do that one alone or with someone?"

Santos walked restlessly across the threadbare carpet of the narrow room to a small, dark bookcase under the single window. Its two shelves were scarred by puckered cigarette burns and held stacks of newspapers and an occasional centerfold magazine. Burglars tended to be avid readers of newspapers, especially the society sections. "You guys checked me out, right?"

Axton replied, "Yes, we have, Mr. Santos."

"*Mister* Santos!" He started a new cigarette. "What division you guys in?"

"Homicide."

"So you don't have the hots for crimes-against-property cases?"

"No, Mr. Santos. We're after information on homicides," Max said easily, and lowered himself to the arm of a stuffed chair whose nap had been rubbed away to pale bare threads and which creaked dangerously beneath him.

Santos's slow nod said that he had seen a lot of cops and some of them a man could get along with. A little bit, anyway; and there was no percentage in antagonizing any of them without good reason.

Wager spoke up. "Do you know who was with him on that last job?"

"That was a drugstore?"

"Yes."

"He would have been alone. Unless it was a heavy lift—you know, television sets or stereos, stuff that's hard to carry—he liked to work alone. A drugstore job where you pick up cash, pills, a couple packs of razor blades—that's a singles gig."

"You know for certain he was alone on that job?"

"No, not for certain. But it ain't likely he'd have somebody with him. I mean, why should he? The more people you got, the smaller the divvy and the easier it is to be spotted. And Gerry liked to work alone. The real artists are that way."

"Gerald was a real artist?"

"Not as good as some I could mention. But he liked to think so. He was all right—he was learning."

"Did Gerald usually get high before a job?"

Santos was shocked. "Hell, no! That's for junkies—that's kid crap!"

"Did you know that Gerald was caught because he passed out in the store?"

"Come on! You're blowing smoke. Maybe Gerald wasn't the best, but he was a professional. He took some pride in his work."

"It's true; you can read it in the arrest report. The officer smelled him before he saw him—passed out cold with a bottle of bourbon spilled all over him."

"Well, then somebody dumped him there! Because Gerry, he didn't even like bourbon. Vodka and gin, yeah, but bourbon always made him sick."

Wager and Axton glanced at each other with the feeling of still another rabbit popping out of this hat. "Why would somebody want to do that?" asked Wager.

The forehead's wrinkles deepened again. "You got me, because something like that really don't make sense. He never drank on a job and he never drank bourbon, anyway. But why anybody would set him up for a fall that way just don't make sense."

Damned little made sense. Just when they thought there was a pattern, just when one event seemed to explain another, something like this came and put question marks behind everything they believed. It was as if someone were

184

moving the things Wager reached for—as if some magician knew exactly which hand Wager was watching and then with the other hand shifted the facts before he could grasp them. He began a slow pace of three steps back and forth across the creaking floor as his anger at the slippery yet intractable facts began to build. "Did you ever hear Gerald mention the Scorvellis?"

Santos, standing beside the window, which—like the room and the scarred bookcase and the man himself—was long and narrow, did not hear Axton's tiny moan. The man's stillness told Wager that he was carefully judging what and how much to say.

"We've heard from other sources that there was some connection," Wager added.

"That's right," said Axton quickly. "It's all over the street."

"So you heard that." Santos started another cigarette and slowly pressed the long butt of the old one into an overflowing ashtray. "I heard it, too, but I never *saw* anything. Gerald talked to me, you understand, but his own jobs were his own thing."

"You met him in Buena Vista?" asked Wager.

Again the momentary deepening of wrinkles. "Yeah. You've checked all that out, too?" Santos sounded half pleased to be the center of so much attention. "Well, we got to know each other there. I met him around a few times before we got busted, but we didn't have much to say to each other. In Buena Vista, there wasn't much else to do but talk. He talked, anyway. He was always full of these big plans for himself."

Santos looked out the grime-coated window toward the brown stone wall of the apartment building next door, and Wager could see how it went: two second-story men, passing each other briefly in the stores or garages used by fences, finally ending up in a cell with nothing to spend except a lot of time. Wager studied the gray light from the window falling across Santos's sharp profile and wondered how really different from his life in a cell was the man's life in this narrow room. "What kind of plans?"

"Oh, the usual stuff—big connections, big scores, big man. Someday." The scorn in his voice seemed as much for himself as for Covino. "Everybody's got crap like that to dream about, right? Hell, I let the kid talk."

The kid. Santos's record said he was only four years older than Gerald, but there was some justification in his attitude; he was one of those people who had jumped from childhood to middle age without having touched youth. Maybe because he'd gone after those big dreams, too, and found out too soon that for him they were lies. "Did the Scorvellis fit into those plans?"

"Naw. Hell, those people never even knew Gerry was alive. It was just cell talk. But a funny thing—a month or two before Gerry took his last rap, he comes up and tells me he's got it made. 'Me and Dominick,' he says, and he holds up two fingers side by side like this."

"You knew he meant Scorvelli? You knew that for a fact?"

"What other Dominick is there in this town?" A tiny snort of laughter shot a plume of smoke from his nose and mouth. "But I asked him that. 'Dominick who?' I said, and he gets a little pissed like I'm making fun of him. Which maybe I was. Like I say, he was always trying to put on the dog, and I'd let his air out every now and then. 'The only Dominick,' he says. 'Mr. Dominick Scorvelli!' "

"Why'd he tell you this?"

"We had a—ah—business deal going at the time, and saw each other every couple days until we—ah—completed the transaction. He was real excited about meeting with Dominick. He told me somebody from the Scorvelli organization

186

scouted him and said Dominick wanted to meet him. So he went over to that restaurant—I forget the name—over on Federal."

"The Lake Como?"

"Yeah."

"Did he say why Scorvelli wanted to see him?"

"You got me. Gerry said that they shot the bull about business and all, and Dominick treated him like he was a junior member of the board or some such, giving him a big cigar, asking him how things were, what his plans were, crap like that." Santos paused to pull another cigarette from the crush-proof pack in his shirt pocket. "If Gerry wasn't blowing smoke, then I figure Dominick was feeling him out—sizing him up for a job, maybe. I don't think no deal went down at that meet, though."

"Why?"

"Gerry was hopped. It was like he'd been invited to the goddam White House or something. That's all he talked about for a week: what the Scorvelli connection was going to do for him, what a big man it was going to make of him. He didn't even smoke that cigar—just carried it around. Then all of a sudden he shut up about it. Not a peep. I'd ask, 'How are you and the wops getting along?' and he'd say, 'Fine' or something like that and get this worried look on his face. Finally, he got pissed and told me to shut up about them —that he wasn't seeing Dominick any more. So I shut up. I figured he learned what Dominick wanted from him and didn't like it."

"Did he go see Dominick again?"

"I don't know. Him and me finished up our business and he went his way. But he still had things on his mind. You could tell he was figuring something out."

"How?"

"Well, when we divvied the—ah—the profits, it wasn't as

187

much as he was counting on. But that's business, I told him; hell, he got just as much as I did, a fifty-fifty split. You couldn't ask anything fairer than that, could you?"

"I guess not," said Wager.

"Right. Anyway, he said that pretty soon he would be taking his off the top. 'Sure,' I says. 'See you next time.' 'Don't count on it,' he says. 'You don't have to work for a living no more?' I says. And he says, 'Not with you. Not for this piddly crap,' meaning the money, you see. It wasn't such a little bit, either!" Santos's voice said Gerald's words still stung. "It was like he was getting even because I'd tell him he was full of crap when he'd start blowing about all his big plans."

"How long was this before he was arrested?"

"Two weeks, maybe three. I don't remember exactly." Santos started another cigarette, talking while he puffed it alight. "But it's sure something, ain't it? He's got all these big connections and big plans and won't be working with me no more, and then he goes and gets popped on a two-bit job like that. Still"—this time the wrinkles deepened even further—"he didn't drink bourbon ever. That just don't make sense. It's like somebody planted him there."

Wager agreed with most of that. "Did you ever know Gerald's brother, Frank?"

"Nope. I knew he had family. His mother came down to Buena Vista to see him once, but we never talked about families. He kind of felt like I do—mine don't give a shit for me, so I don't give a shit for them."

"Do you have any idea who might have wanted Frank dead?"

"Dead? His brother's dead, too?"

"You didn't read it in the papers?"

"I might of. But I didn't connect the names." Santos scratched behind his ear. "Maybe Scorvelli, for something

188

Gerry did? It's like them wops. I told Gerry working with wops was bad news."

"Why would Scorvelli want to kill Gerald's brother?"

"You got me. Maybe Gerry talked too much, told him something, and Scorvelli found out about it. Like that bourbon—it don't make sense."

"About that," said Wager. "How many people knew bourbon made him sick?"

Santos shrugged. "A few friends, I guess. He never made a big thing of it; he just never drank the stuff."

"He knew that you knew?"

"Sure. He'd come over to talk business and I'd offer him a drink. I drink bourbon myself, so I'd have to get a bottle of something else for him."

"What kind do you drink?"

"Kentucky Royal. It's real good stuff for the money."

"That's the kind Gerald was wearing. Do you think he could have been telling you something about the drugstore job?"

For the first time, Santos's mouth hung open without a cigarette; he held it just off his lips and stared at Wager through the smoke. "He was telling me something?"

"That the job was a setup. That he set himself up to be arrested. He was telling you it was no accident."

"Son of a gun! That would be just like Gerry! Yeah—it would be just like that bastard!"

189

thirteen

They ate at a Cowboy Bob's Chuckwagon near Santos's apartment. The orange walls were hung with bent-wire outlines of bowlegged cowboys roping frisky little calves, and the waitresses wore fringed skirts and white patent boots. Except for the designs pressed into the Naugahyde booths—mesas, cattle brands, and six-guns—the restaurant was like all the other chain stores that based their sales pitch on some kind of image and not much else. Max had forgotten about going to the Frontier for lunch and simply aimed himself toward the nearest restaurant; Wager did not remind him. When they reached the homicide office, the twenty-four-hour board held an old message from Gargan and a new one from the Bulldog. Gargan's note asked somewhat plaintively for anything fresh on the Frank Covino murder; Doyle's said simply, "See me." Which meant immediately.

"Come in." Doyle gestured toward his private coffee-maker. "Pour yourselves a cup."

Max did; Wager didn't. He sensed in the offer a signal of some kind and did not want his guard down.

"I had lunch with Inspector Sonnenberg."

"Yessir."

"He went into great detail about his operation, something I wish he had done with me at the very beginning."

"Yessir."

"The upshot is, I want you two to cool your activity on the Scorvelli aspects of the case. Sonnenberg's made a good argument for his priority, and it looks like a great opportunity to not only get Scorvelli but also penetrate organized crime activities in other states as well."

So Sonnenberg had talked Doyle into easing off, and all the Bulldog's tough words about *his* territory and *his* decisions were just that: words. Wager leaned back against the hard angles of the straight chair and kept his voice carefully neutral. "You don't want us investigating the Covino homicide any more?"

Doyle studied him. "I said I don't want you approaching it from the Scorvelli angle. I'm sure there's a lot more you can do on the case that doesn't involve the Scorvellis."

"Everything that leads anywhere points at them," persisted Wager.

"Then dig up some other leads. What about that suspect with the long coat and the beret?"

"That's a real lead—yes, sir, it sure is. Just how long are we supposed to sit on this?"

"Until I damned well tell you otherwise, Wager!"

At his desk, Wager topped his cup with metallic coffee from the old urn and meticulously filled out a request for a reimbursement totaling one hundred dollars paid to a Confidential Informant for services on the Covino case. Then he just as meticulously filled out a second form, requesting another hundred for Jesus Quintana, C.I. The Bulldog would probably deny the money for Fat Willy and Jesus, but Wager went ahead because he knew the requests would irritate Doyle; when the chief turned them down, it would be one more instance of a lack of support, and both he and Wager would know it.

Max shifted restlessly from his desk to the dust-filmed window, where he stood watching the construction outside as if he, too, wasn't quite sure where to point his nose now. He belched and muttered something about eating too fast. Finally, he wandered heavily back to his desk to pick up the telephone and dial the mail room. When he hung up, he told Wager, "The courier's in from Cañon City. I'm going down and see if they have anything for us."

Wager nodded; he was finishing the justification section of the special funds request when the telephone rang.

It was Gargan. "Nice hearing you, Wager, but I'd rather talk to Max the Ax."

"He's out right now. Try again in ten minutes."

"If I had ten minutes, I would; but it's deadline time. What more can you give me on the Covino thing? I understand his brother's dead, too."

"That's right. Whether there's any connection, we don't know. We're still working on it." More or less, and more less than more.

"While you're sitting over there drinking coffee? It must be great to be on the city payroll."

Wager hung up without replying. Most cops got along with most reporters—but Wager wasn't most cops, and most reporters weren't Gargan. Signing and dating the forms, he slipped them into a routing envelope, which would make its way down three stories to the mail room, and then, sometime next week, wander back up those same floors to the office just along the hall. Doyle's procedure manual allowed only emergency correspondence to be hand carried to his desk; routine communications were to follow routine methods of delivery.

"Here it is, Gabe." Max returned, trying to kindle his own flagging enthusiasm, and opened the string on the envelope to slide the prison reports onto the desk. "Maybe we'll find something that doesn't have the Scorvelli name all over it."

"Something wearing a beret and long overcoat?"

"Yeah. Say, maybe the guy's a French flasher—maybe we should check the M.O. files." Axton's wide fingers sorted the papers held in small stacks by paper clips. "Here's Gerald's initial evaluation."

The prison admittance chart was full of jargon that, Wager decided, was designed to free the prison psychologist of responsibility no matter how the inmate turned out. It said that Gerald showed antisocial tendencies—which made sense because he was in prison for breaking and entering; and it said that Gerald could be rehabilitated provided he changed his attitude. Wager had that bit of wisdom figured out, too; but because he didn't have any letters after his name, he couldn't say it without being laughed at. He pushed that report aside and joined Max in reading the next, a brief survey of the inmates drawn from the turnkeys' logs. There was no indication of violence or insubordinate behavior. Gerald had been placed in a light-security cell block and seemed to be doing easy time; apparently he was working for an early release. His job assignment was the automobile compound, where he was busily being reeducated as a car washer by practicing on state vehicles, and the work reports were all "satisfactory." His log of visitors showed three. Just after he was admitted, he was visited by his sister, Grace Covino; the second was Wager. The third came two days before Covino's death and the name listed was Charles Smith. Covino also made a few telephone calls, but because of the new emphasis on prisoners' right to privacy, neither the number nor the conversations were monitored. But Wager noted that Covino had placed his final call on the evening of Wager's visit to Cañon City and before "Charles Smith" came down. He would give a lot to know who Gerald had telephoned—and strongly suspected that both Sonnenberg and Doyle would not want him to try to find out. The warden's summary said that Gerald was generally a loner and had no close friends, which included his cellmate; that he spent a little time in the library and a lot of time watching television; and that he had been involved in only one altercation, his first and last.

"Covino didn't start that fight," said Max.

Wager had already decided that. "But there's no sense wasting time with the kid who did."

"No. Scorvelli wouldn't leave any direct lines, and Uhuru's not going to say anything different, anyway. I think we're stuck with the official report—that it was a racial fight and Uhuru thought Covino was trying to kill him. He knifed him in self-defense."

Wager grunted agreement and picked up the telephone as if it were one last straw. Dialing the Records Section, he said, "This is Detective Wager. Did the L.A.P.D. come back to us on that query about a Bernie Chavez?"

"Just a moment, sir," said the police person. Then her voice returned. "The reply came in at 1217; they requested more on the description, sir. 'Insufficient detail for compliance' is what they say."

"Thanks." So much for that straw. He answered Max's glance. " 'Insufficient detail.' "

"Crap."

Which was the way Wager felt for the rest of the long afternoon as he and Axton made the rounds, backing up the uniformed officers on the street, supporting the other sections of the Crimes Against Persons Division at the inevitable

194

assault or robbery. After finally turning over the shift to Ross and Devereaux, Wager and Max stood a few moments in the afternoon shade of the old headquarters building before crossing the sun-scorched parking compound to their cars.

"Do you have any goddamned ideas at all, Gabe?"

"Sure. Go after Scorvelli."

"Other than that."

"Wait. That and keep our ears open. What the hell else can we do?"

"Yeah." The big man's disgust matched Wager's and he gave a slight whistle between his teeth like a steaming kettle. "By the way, Polly asked me to invite you to dinner Sunday night. If you don't already have plans," he added quickly.

Wager rapidly tried to think of something he could call plans, but he wasn't fast enough; Max took the brief silence for consent.

"Fine. Come on over about seven—that'll give us time for a drink."

"I—"

But Max strode out of earshot with a wave of his wide hand, and Wager had the feeling of being told rather than asked to come to dinner. He watched Axton's square Bronco pass between the steel posts of the parking compound's gate and swirl among the heat-shimmered car roofs surging down Thirteenth Street in rush-hour traffic. Feeling the twist of irritation that always came when someone pushed him into something he didn't want to do, he had an impulse to call and tell Axton that he had a date. One he'd forgotten about. Except that Axton wouldn't believe him, and the thought of being weak enough to have to lie his way out of something was more painful than the thought of going to dinner. Besides, Wager was getting tired of that book on fur trappers; the only reason he wanted to finish it was that he had started it. And what the hell, maybe Axton's wife was a good cook.

fourteen

At ten that evening, Wager quit forcing himself to relax. The lingering spring warmth had long faded from the stone of his balcony wall, and the restless glare of Friday-night traffic rose from Downing Street below to wipe away any stars that may have shown above the ragged black shadows of the mountains. He had again resisted as maudlin the impulse to have a last meal at the Frontier and instead ate a frozen dinner whose picture this time said it was turkey and green peas, though it tasted suspiciously like roast beef and broccoli baked in cardboard. Rinsing the silverware, he left it to dry, poured himself a beer, and sat down once more to the book on fur trappers.

But he was too restless to read.

Even the news on TV didn't soothe him. The small screen flipped pictures of rescue groups at plane crashes, police squads at crime scenes, political teams accusing other political teams, and platoons of demonstrators accusing everybody. Then the twenty-two-second editorial questioned earnestly if "our city" was going to become a hunting ground for organized crime since the police still had no suspects in the gangland slaying last week, and it ended by saying that the television station and this reporter certainly hoped not, and qualified persons having contrasting views were encouraged to respond.

Wager turned it off and stood, forehead against the cool glass of the balcony doors, to look out across the winking, gliding lights of the city below. Colorado had had its share of organized crime since the days of Soapy Smith a hundred years ago, and with varying intensity it was still here—all the way from Trinidad in the south to Fort Collins in the north. The Scorvelli family was only the best-known in Denver, having made contributions to the city's criminal code for the past thirty years. The family had large territories in Denver and Pueblo, and many members lived just north of Denver in a small ex-coal-mining town which called itself "the most law-abiding little city on the Eastern Plains." But there were plenty of other groups, some bound by loose ties, who had carved up the rest of the state. Sonnenberg's classified files were packed with reports and studies of them, and they came and went and changed alliances with the shifting flow of money and the rare convictions of an occasional leader. What filled Wager with mild wonder was the TV editorial's assumption that the Scorvellis and all the others had disappeared; that somehow Denver was clean and now ran a risk of being sullied by "new" criminal activity. It was a public blindness, a laziness, perhaps even a cowardice in the face of facts—one that Wager could not understand.

The afternoon paper, too, had carried a story about Covino's death: an article headlined "Police Still Baffled by Gangland Slaying," by police reporter Gargan. Since the reporter had got nothing from Wager, he apparently called

197

the Bulldog, because most of the short column on page 28 quoted what Chief Doyle had said—that yes, the police were still looking for the culprits; no, they had nothing concrete yet; no, all leads to well-known criminal figures had been exhausted; and no, the police had no further plans to investigate in that area.

And Wager, too, had better not have any plans to go near Dominick. Not the man himself, nor the Lake Como restaurant, nor any of the people close to the man—the only people most likely to know of any connections with Gerald, and who might be squeezed into talking if Wager had enough freedom to get his hands around their necks.

But he was free to get out on the street and find the man in the beret. He would never locate him. Wager was absolutely certain he would never locate him, since the coat and beret had been used for a disguise. But prowling through those streets down there was better than prowling through this apartment up here, kicking the two sling chairs from one spot to another and back again, straightening the Marine Corps sword and the framed photograph on the wall. He would not ask anyone about Scorvelli; but if someone wanted to walk right up and say, "Wager, I've got proof that Dominick wasted Frank and Gerald," he wouldn't say, "Don't tell me." Sure, someone was going to walk up and say that and everything would work out just fine! Just like the proud City and County of Denver was still a virgin.

He slipped his Star P.D. into its holster and shrugged into his light sports coat. At times like these, the street was better than his apartment. In fact, most of the time the street was better than his apartment.

Driving slowly on Downing to the Colfax light, he turned west, keeping in the right lane to glance along sidewalks already filling with summer crowds of shaggy transients and with night people lured from their close rooms and converted garages on the side streets to this glow of lights and restless motion. Especially the motion. It was the same thing that had drawn Wager out of the silence of his apartment, and as he eased his Trans Am along the trash-littered curbing he felt a kind of kinship with the quick-eyed movement of the street people who wandered looking for the action, watching for the fuzz, seeking what was going down, man. It beat hell out of staring at the four walls of a rented room and listening to the echo of your own breathing.

On Broadway, the character of the sidewalks changed abruptly from the topless bars and porno shops and nude photography studios to the ground floors of office towers that seemed to be faced with the same polished stone and vertical strips of aluminum. Inside, the foyers were dimly lit and empty, and even the banks of elevator lights were off. Here the few pedestrians were tourists and conventioneers who, crossing from one downtown hotel to another, had made a wrong turn and were groping their way back to the sheltering arcades of the Brown Palace or the Continental. Wager saw an occasional face that he recognized working the tourists, one of them being "Hey You" Jones, the demented and half-crippled Negro whose outstretched palm and "Hey you got a quarter?" drifted from street to street like a piece of blowing newspaper. Two or three blocks up Broadway, the sidewalks changed again, darker and lined with store windows papered over and painted with signs saying "Lease" or "For Rent—Easy Terms." Here the curbs formed triangular corners, and wedge-shaped taverns drew customers from the aging apartments and converted sanitariums just behind Broadway. The few trees in tiny, three-sided parks cast uneasy shadows over the figures on the grass, smoking, talking, passing wine bottles back and forth. Wager reached upper Larimer and parked on Twenty-fifth, locking his car and pausing to smell the odor of frying grease and spiced meat that drifted from one of the drooping houses between stubby office buildings and wholesale businesses. If a person looked hard enough, he could see the remnants of a neighborhood still here, stretched thin by the increasing distances between homes. Just how long it could last, and who—besides the old people clinging to the small houses with their cheap rent and low taxes—would care when it was gone, Wager didn't know. But right now, even with the torn and sagging screen doors, the pale glimmer of unpainted and warping boards at the porch edges, there was more life, more humanity to watch and to talk about, than in all twenty stories and two hundred units of his own apartment tower. Despite the violence and noise, despite the drunks pissing in the front yards or retching against doors or window screens, this was a place where life was not a television set, and because of that the residents struggled to remain.

As he strolled toward Little Juarez, his mind was divided between the present—this stretch of Larimer with its dim glow of lights behind pulled roller blinds—and the past: memories of his old neighborhood before the "developers" turned under the homes to turn up a profit. For the first time in a week, he was not really looking for anyone, did not give a damn about Scorvelli or the Covinos or Sonnenberg or Doyle. He merely walked and felt the loosening muscles in his neck and shoulders tell him that at last he was slowly relaxing.

But someone saw him.

"Wager!"

The call came from one of three small houses wedged between brick buildings across the street, and he saw Tony-O's figure stiffly erect even as he sat on a tiny front porch that only had room for two rusty patio chairs. Another figure sat beside him, and Wager crossed between the automobile traffic to the sidewalk that ran a scant four feet from the edge of the low wooden porch. "Is this where you live, Tony-O?"

"Yeah. I rent a room in back from George, here."

George, a thick-bodied man in railroad overalls, nodded without speaking or changing the gentle bounce of his metal chair.

"What's this crap I read in the paper about you cops giving up on Scorvelli?"

Wager started to say he hadn't given up on anybody. But it wasn't true. "No evidence."

"What about that tip I handed you? Hell, I told you about that Frank Covino!"

He wondered at the note of anger in the old man's voice. Tony-O's information had been offhand; at the time, he hadn't seemed to care if Wager used it or not. Yet now he was angry. Perhaps it was an old man's pique at having his word rejected; perhaps it was something else—Wager vaguely remembered something else . . . His thoughts, like the muscles of his neck, began again to clench. He remembered something that he should have paid more attention to: an attitude . . . a note in the voice . . . a tiny question in his mind. He tried to recall and at the same time mask his thoughts with a casual voice. "We checked it out. We couldn't corroborate anything you told us, Tony."

The erect shape remained wordless and accusing. From somewhere farther down Larimer, a hoarse voice whooped and a bottle shattered, followed by the frantic bark of a large dog. "But I told you what that Chavez guy said. You can work on Scorvelli with that."

"We haven't been able to find Chavez. And from you, it's just hearsay evidence—not enough to support holding Scorvelli. If you know where to find Chavez, then tell me and I'll go after him."

Tony-O's wrinkled face dipped in the flash of passing headlights. "All I know is L.A. He didn't give me his goddamned address and telephone number, Wager."

That was it—Wager remembered it now: he had asked Tony-O before about someone else who might know Chavez, and Tony-O had answered "no" a shade too quickly. In itself, nothing notable—just a feeling that the old man wasn't giving Wager all that he knew. And now the realization that Tony-O was eager to see Wager land on Scorvelii and disappointed that he had not. With chagrin, Wager realized the obvious—that Chavez, with good reason, might be afraid. Especially if he was still in Denver. "Have you heard anything else that might help? Anything on the brother down in Cañon City?"

"Naw. I ain't been listening." The anger was gone and now Tony-O's voice held threads of boredom and sullenness. "Why in hell should I, when you people don't use nothing I give you?"

"If you get us something we can take into court, Tony-O, we'll use it."

"I bet you will."

Wager, still feeling the air between him and the rigid old man, said it again: "You get us something we can use, Tony, and we will."

Tony-O no longer answered. George, his chair squeaking rustily, bounced in gentle rhythm and watched the street life flow back and forth just beyond the edge of the porch.

No longer walking without purpose, Wager quickly crossed Larimer Street toward the half-lit sign in the next block: "—NOLO'S." The round-faced bartender with the drooping mustache recognized him with a cautious nod and wandered down from the small group of men clustered at the far end of the bar. They looked like the same ones who'd been there the night before, still in the same positions, still falling into the same silence when a stranger walked in.

202

"Look." Zapata tapped a stubby finger on the scrap of paper taped to the post beside the cash register. "I gave Whistles a dollar last night. The damned loco didn't know what to do with it, but he was happy enough to wet his pants. He thinks I've hired him now like for a real job, you know? I'll never get rid of the son of a bitch now."

Wager took one of his business cards from his wallet and slipped it across the bar. "When that runs out, give me a call." He put a five-dollar bill beside it. "How about some phone change and a beer?"

"Mexican or Yankee?"

"You really sell much Mexican beer?"

Zapata shook his head. "Once in a while to some *borracho*. Hell, who can afford it? You want a draw? All I got's Schlitz —no Coors."

"Draw." He paid his quarter and took the small, cold glass and the handful of coins over to the wall telephone in the room's dim corner. The first number he dialed was Fat Willy's.

"Hey, I been waiting to hear from you, my man." Wager could almost see the fat man squeeze himself into the corner telephone booth of the bar that was his office. "You owe me a little something and I ain't seen you. Why is it I never see the people that owes me, but I always see the ones that wants?"

"I've put in a request for the funds, Fat Willy."

"A re-quest! How the hell long is a request supposed to take? I got expenses, man!"

"I'll know next week. Right now, I want you to listen up on somebody else."

"I will put in a fucking re-quest and let you know next week!"

"I want what you can pick up on Tony Ojala—Tony-O."

Curiosity drove the sarcasm from Fat Willy's voice.

"That's the old man who's all over Larimer? The dude who looks like a broke-off match stick?"

"That's him. I want to know where he goes and who he talks to."

"Hooeee. That old man's everywhere and nowhere; he talks to everybody and nobody."

"I want to know if he's been talking to somebody named Bernie Chavez, a man about the same age."

"Come on, Wager—get yourself a spic for that. I couldn't tell this Bernie Chavez from Pancho Villa. All you brownies look alike to me."

"There might be something in it for you."

"Yeah—another goddam re-quest. Count me out, Wager. Until I get the bread from that last little favor I done you, I ain't doing no more."

"You're going to want something from me sometime, Willy. Maybe soon."

"Yeah, maybe so. But right now *you* owe *me*. When the account is balanced, then I will worry about owing you. And hey, I see where you backed off the Scorvellis. What's the matter, them wop boys too tough for you?"

"No evidence," said Wager, and hung up. The next number was one he had not yet memorized, and he dialed it carefully. A woman's voice answered hurriedly on the third ring.

"Can I talk to Jesus, please?" asked Wager.

She held the telephone a few seconds without replying. "Who's this? Who wants him?"

"Gabe Wager."

"Oh! Sure—just a minute."

The relief in the woman's voice made it almost happy. This time it wasn't another of Jesus's suspect friends dragging him into one more scheme that would someday land her husband

204

in the clink; instead, it was a cop, somebody on the right side of the law, who would help keep her husband on the straight and narrow. Wager rinsed his mouth with beer.

"Gabe?" The voice sounded sleepy and slightly drunk. "You called late. Scared hell out of my woman."

"Sorry, Jesus. I didn't think what time it was. I need a little help with—"

"Say, *hombre,* it's good you called!" Jesus was waking up. "I been trying to get you, but them people at headquarters, they wouldn't give me your home phone, you know? They kept telling me to call back Monday. I told them it was real important, but it's like they don't know who I am. Maybe you better straighten them out or give me your number for emergencies, man."

Wager did the latter, repeating the number when the man on the other end of the line finally located a pencil. "Why'd you want me?" he asked Jesus.

"Because I got some information! You asked me to listen around for certain names, right?"

"What kind of information?"

"Good stuff, *hombre.* I got it from a guy I know who's just out of Cañon City. Got out yesterday. He was in the same cell block as that Covino dude."

"What did he tell you?"

"He says that somebody from the Scorvelli organization came down to visit Covino just before he was shivved."

"Did he know who Covino's visitor was?"

"Nope. But he was working as a trusty and he saw Covino's visitor. He knew the guy from before, and later Covino as much as told him it was a Scorvelli messenger."

"What's your friend's name?"

"You'll cover for me, right? Like before?"

"Trust me, Jesus; I'll say I got his name from Cañon City."

"O.K., that sounds decent. It's Ken Espinosa; I forget what he was up for. I think he's got a room down at the Binghamton."

"Did Espinosa mention anything about the knifing? About why Covino was killed?"

"He said what everybody else says—Covino got it in a fight with Uhuru."

"Nothing about a hit on Covino?"

"No. Hey, you think Covino was set up that way? You think somebody knew he was with Scorvelli and wanted to get rid of him?"

"Anything's possible, Jesus." At least, it seemed that way so far. "There's another thing I need some help with."

"You've come to the man who can do things, Wager."

"I know that, Jesus—*por supuesto.* What I want you to do is keep an eye on Tony-O. You know him?"

"That old guy? Sure, I see him around all the time. But what the hell's he got to do with anything?"

"He may be a lead to somebody I'm looking for—a Bernie Chavez, about the same age as Tony-O."

The line was briefly silent. "The only Bernie Chavez I know's about my age."

"It's this old Bernie Chavez I'm after. He might tie a tail to some of those very important people." Wager gave Jesus Tony-O's address.

"Hijole! This thing really is big time, ain't it? But the papers said you weren't laying anything on Scorvelli."

Gargan would wriggle and pee like a scratched puppy if he knew how many people had read that story. "Don't believe everything in the papers, and don't let Tony-O know you're behind him."

"Hey, don't worry about that—I'm no *bembo!*"

The third call was to Records. Police Person Fabrizio—she of the slender legs and large breasts—took Wager's request for information on Espinosa, Kenneth, and came back on the line in less than two minutes. "The subject was released on parole yesterday, Detective Wager," said her very nice voice. "He lists an address at the Binghamton Hotel, 2105 Larimer. His employer will be Greenland Sod Farms in Aurora. Do you want his parole officer's name and number?"

"This is enough. Thanks."

The Binghamton was nearby, a decaying red-brick warren of foul-smelling rooms inhabited by drifters and old people who couldn't afford more than eight dollars a week. Once a month, when the oldsters received their social security checks, the building rustled busily with muggers and thieves and muffled and hopeless cries for help. The assault and homicide sections knew it well.

In the cramped lobby, a black-and-white television set high in the corner flipped its grainy picture endlessly, but no one sat on the single broken sofa to watch it, nor was a clerk on duty behind the short and dusty counter. Wager reached under the wooden shelf with its circular blisters from old glasses and pulled out the register to read down the spotted paper for Espinosa's name. He found it listed with room 32. There was no elevator to the third floor; he groped his way up the creaking stairs, stepping into some mushy stench near the landing. A single bulb locked in its safety grate lit the hall. The metal numbers had long ago been pried off the doors, but he found Espinosa's room, the "32" scratched into the wood by a knife or screwdriver. He knocked.

A low voice came from just beyond the dark panel. "Who's there?"

"Detective Wager, D.P.D. I want to talk to you."

After several seconds of cautious silence, first one lock, then another rattled open and the door swung back an inch or so. "You got your I.D.?"

Wager showed his badge. "You're Ken Espinosa?"

The door opened wider to reveal a middle-aged man with close-cropped graying hair, and a pale and weary face that was almost twice as long as it was wide. He had high cheekbones and a hooked nose, and his dark eyes never seemed to rest long on one spot. "Yes," he said softly. "What you want with me?"

"I understand you were in the same cell block as Gerald Covino. I'd like to ask you some questions about him."

"Who told you that?"

"I checked with Cañon City. I've been waiting for someone to get out who could tell me something about Covino. Can I come in?"

Espinosa stepped aside to let Wager enter; he leaned against the warped door to work the locks back into place, then finished buttoning his shirt. "This dump didn't used to be so bad," he said in a quiet drawl. "I've never seen so many guns around since the goddam army. Of course, I can't have one—I'm a parolee."

Wager glanced around the tiny cubicle with its sagging bed and peeling chest of drawers. A paintless rod under a shelf served as a closet, and even if the single dusty window could be opened, the smell of stale urine would never be gone from the room; it came from a corner where the wallpaper had been washed away, leaving a patch of dark and rotting wood.

Espinosa followed his glance. "It's still better than Cañon City," he said. Then, "Wager. I've heard of you. You're a narc, right?"

"I'm in homicide now. Cigarette?" He held out the pack and Espinosa took one, lighting it slowly and then cupping it, prison style, between fingers that were as fleshless as his nose. "They already got the dude that did it to Covino. A black guy."

"How well did you know Covino?"

Something like a smile twisted Espinosa's lips. "You could call us next-door neighbors."

"Did you talk with him much?"

"Some. Nothing heavy. He was doing his time and I was doing mine."

Espinosa's sparring was automatic; without some kind of trade, he wasn't going to reveal much—not because he was worried or afraid, but simply because that was the way things were done in places where information was currency.

"We think Covino was killed on orders from the outside," said Wager. "His brother was killed, too. Did he get many visitors?"

"Killed on orders?" Espinosa mulled that over for a while. Then he said, "I don't know how many visitors he had. I just heard about one."

If there was a single word that Wager could use to describe the man, it would be "tired." Espinosa was like a tired runner or laborer; he moved with the economy of exhaustion, as if he had just finished a task that drew off the last quiver of energy and left him in that numb state where even saving his own life would bring a groan of effort.

"How about telling me?" Wager asked.

"Why not? This buddy I know—a trusty—told me that just before Covino bought the farm, somebody from the Scorvelli organization came down to see him."

"Did your buddy know who that somebody was?"

"Nobody important. This friend of mine knew him from somewhere, and he's what you might call a step-n-fetchit, a burro for the Scorvellis."

"Did your friend have any idea why somebody like that would be seeing Covino?"

"No. Every once in a while Covino hinted about some kind of connections. He wouldn't talk too much about them,

209

but you got the idea he had something going for him when he got out. But you hear that all the time; hell, sometimes it turns out to be true."

"Did Covino say anything after the Scorvelli man came to see him?"

"Nothing you could take to court. He hinted about getting out soon and seemed a little cocky and anxious at the same time—like a short-timer. We figured he was going to be sprung soon, but he got dusted first."

"Sprung over the wall?"

"Naw, legitimate. Get him a good lawyer, somebody to talk for him at the parole board and tell them he had a job and all. Covino had his good time coming, and they're hard up for space down there."

"Did Covino ever say anything about his brother?"

"No. He never talked about his family. Hell, who does? We all heard his brother got blown away, but Covino didn't say nothing about it. The padre tried to talk to him about it, but he told him to go to hell."

"That was before or after the visitor from the Scorvellis?"

"Before. I guess his brother's death made him a little uptight. Like I say, he was more like a short-timer after the visit."

"Loose enough to start a fight?"

Espinosa thought about that, drawing on the cigarette stub pinched and cupped beneath his palm. Finally, he said with conviction, "No. I didn't even think about that at the time —people are always getting cut down there. But no, Covino wasn't one of the crazies. If he thought he was getting out soon, he wouldn't of screwed that up with a fight. It looks like he really was set up, don't it? But you're never going to prove it."

"Did he ever say anything about his bust? Anything that sounded strange or different?"

Some of the weariness in Espinosa's eyes faded momentarily as surprise came into them. "You really do know something about Covino, don't you?"

"Why's that?"

"Most guys when they get there claim they got finked on or had bad luck—that it wasn't their fault they got busted. But Covino almost joked about it. I mean, he was pretty pissed at the judge for hitting him an indeterminate on a breaking and entering—that's pretty heavy, even for a second offense, and Covino really didn't expect that. But as for the bust itself, he acted like it was a big joke, like it was something he'd put over on somebody else."

Which he had.

fifteen

The horns and rapping exhaust of midmorning traffic woke Wager around ten. Saturday—especially a warm spring Saturday—made the streets on the east edge of Capitol Hill throb with young singles gathering other young singles into young groups for the day's run to the mountains or the tennis courts or the city parks and reservoirs for Frisbee and beer. Wager leaned on the balcony railing with his first cup of coffee and watched slender, long-legged girls in their jogging shorts and braless tank tops hop into cars or onto bicycles or motorcycles, freed for the weekend from stacks of typing or nurse's uniforms or airline schedules. He had put down the book about fur trappers and now thumbed through a well-advertised best seller called *It Was Never Me.* The author, someone who spoke of the sixties as "our" generation, had discovered with great surprise that "our" generation no longer made the six o'clock news; but, undaunted, he turned to a compelling and in-depth exploration of "our" generation's inner space. It was the kind of naïve and childish self-centeredness that tightened Wager's jaws, but he forced himself through the book, knowing that his disgust would keep away the closer anger of waiting through this day, through tomorrow, through next week, perhaps through a lifetime, before moving closer to Dominick Scorvelli. But wait he did, until just after sunset, when the telephone rang.

"That you?" It was Jesus's voice, and Wager answered that yes, it was him.

"I been following Tony-O like you wanted me to. That *viejo*'s a hell of a lot tougher than he looks, man. He about walked my feet off at the knees."

"Did he meet Bernie Chavez?"

"Not that I saw. He talked with—I don't know—twenty, maybe thirty, people. A lot of them were *viejos* like him and I knew some of them. The ones I didn't know I'd ask around about, and none of them was named Chavez. None of them knew any Chavezes like that, either."

"You asked for him by name?"

"Oh, I was cool about it—no sweat. I'd ask around about somebody Tony-O talked to, and then I'd say, 'Oh, I thought that might be old Bernie Chavez. You know old Bernie?' And they'd say, 'No.' If that Chavez dude is around, he's using a different name, *hombre.*"

That, like too many other things, was also a possibility. But if Chavez was afraid, it made a lot of sense. And it would not be likely that Tony-O would go to him openly, either, if he was hiding somewhere. "Did Tony go any place in particular or did he just wander around?"

"Mostly, he seems to have a regular path—the grocery store, two or three bars, a pawnshop, liquor store, a couple hotel lobbies. It's like he goes around once a day to shoot the shit with whoever's there. He went down to Union Station, too, and messed around down there with some more old guys. I always thought that place was empty; that's a real nice old building, you know? I'll have to take the wife and kids to see it before somebody tears it down."

It sounded like any other old man of the village filling his days with visits and gossip. "Did he talk to anybody important?"

"Important? Like a Scorvelli?"

"Or anyone else like that."

"No. But just before lunch he had a meet with a couple dudes maybe in their twenties. That was different—that looked like business. I recognized one; he's got a little action going here and there, but nothing worth making headlines over. He always thinks it is, though. He always has this guess-what-I-know look on his face. But maybe that's because he's a faggot."

"Name?"

"The one I know's Tom Nihisi. Claims to be an Indian, but he's got more Afro-American in him than anything. You ever see an Indian with curly hair?"

"What's he do?"

"Just about anything for a buck. Ha—that's pretty good. You get it?"

"I got it. What's the other one look like?"

"Anglo with long blond hair and a big gold ring on his hand, a college ring or something. He looked like a salesman or a TV broadcaster—one of them 'personalities' with a limp wrist. Tony-O was laying something down and Tom and this Anglo didn't say much. They just nodded and asked a few questions and then the old man split without even finishing his beer. Like I say, it was business, not pleasure."

"Where'd they meet?"

"The Foxtail. Know the place?"

It was a gay bar near the post office terminal building, not too far off lower Larimer. There were a lot of jokes about the bar's service to the mail carriers.

"Man, I tell you I did not feel comfortable sitting there by myself. All them *cangrejos!* I just hope nobody in the place knew my name is all."

"Where's Tony-O now?"

"Home. And there's where I got to go—I promised the wife and kids I'd take them to the drive-in. They're just starting for the summer. There's one about this little girl who can make animals attack their masters; even the worms start chewing on people."

"One thing more, Jesus. Do you know anybody who wears a beret and a long overcoat?"

"Beret? That's one of them little round hats?"

"Yes."

"No. But if you sit at the Foxtail long enough, I'll bet something like that comes in. *Hombre,* what a place. I even saw two guys in the parking lot kissing!"

It was dark enough now so that Wager could keep an eye on Tony-O without the old man recognizing him. He found a corner doorway just beyond the glare of Larimer Street traffic and settled in to watch the small frame house with its two empty chairs on the porch. If Chavez was hiding in Denver, and if Tony-O was in touch with him, the visit would probably be made at night. Leaning against the cool wood of the doorframe, Wager kept a practiced eye on the house and the occasional figure that walked past it. Half heard was the flat honk of a switch engine along the tracks lining the river bottom, and Wager felt himself glide into the state of mind that seemed to dominate most surveillances: alert to the target area, aware of the surroundings, yet his mind floating here and there to touch on distant, unrelated points.

Tilting a page of his little green notebook to the street

glow, he wrote a few words to remind him to request another fifty for Jesus. It wouldn't be enough to spoil his new snitch, but it would make him feel like one of the family. And just maybe he'd buy something for his wife out of it.

The previous half hour Wager had spent in Records reading the jacket on Tom Nihisi, and as he thought back over the file, not a thing important remained from it. It held a couple of arrests for theft and receiving, but no major convictions. Nihisi was one of those smart enough or lucky enough not to be caught yet, but dumb enough to believe they never would be. There was absolutely no reason at all for him to be mixed up in the Covino thing, but his name had come up and Wager was nosy, and cops followed their noses when there was nothing else to follow. Besides, all day the feeling had grown stronger that Tony-O hadn't told everything he knew about the elusive Bernie Chavez, and as Wager had scanned the book that laid bare the very soul of "our" generation, his attention kept swinging back to Tony-O as much as to Scorvelli. He remembered telling the Bulldog that everything that pointed anywhere pointed at Dominick Scorvelli; but he had begun to realize that a lot of those things pointed that way because of Tony-O. Not that it made any sense; just that it was so. But the more he thought about that, the more curious Wager grew. Until, tonight, he found himself consciously ignoring time's passing, waiting for whatever it was he awaited.

Shortly after eight-thirty, a stiffly erect silhouette showed briefly in the glow of the opening front door, then came down the three narrow porch steps to the sidewalk. Tony-O paused to light a cigarette, the flare of the match bright on his seamed face for a moment, then, shaking the flame into a tiny spark, he turned left toward the clustered bars of Little Juarez. Wager drifted behind him on the opposite side of the

216

street, holding to the shadows or turning away as Tony-O paused to say a few words or was stopped by one person after another. Wager watched a bent, white-haired figure in splitting shoes shuffle up to him and hold out a hand; Tony-O dropped a coin into gnarled fingers and the white head bobbed thanks. One of the darting kids who hawked the Spanish newspapers trotted up to him with a paper ready folded and Tony-O felt in his pockets for another coin. Then he turned into La Taverna and, through a scrape in the bright-blue poster paint across the inside of the window, could be seen sitting at a bar stool, the paper flattened to catch the yellow light while the sweating bartender quickly set a beer in front of him and hustled off to serve the thirsty Saturday-night crowd. Tony-O sat there for an hour, nursing two small beers, occasionally answering someone's greeting; when he went—often, as old men do—to the men's room, the busy bartender kept the seat vacant despite the growing crowd and the occasional customer who reached for the stool. It was, Wager knew, a sign that Tony-O was thought to be *muy gente*—a real gentleman. As it neared ten, he finished the last page of the paper and folded it, placed a bill between it and the empty glass, and lifted a hand good night through the room's din of loud voices and the quick thump-thump-thump of a bass fiddle from the jukebox. Out on the slightly quieter street, Tony-O paused again, eyes swinging over the surging crowds of men, some of whom howled out the long, broken ay-yi-yi's of a song, while others argued loudly over which bar was next and who had the right to buy this time. Then he strolled slowly down the second block to the sudden blank end where Little Juarez washed up against the windowless concrete of a new office building's ground floor; crossing the street to Wager's side, he moved with dignity back through the swirl of laughing groups or word-less, restless individuals. He recrossed the street toward his front porch, where George now sat bouncing gently. And then stopped. Wager saw him turn around to stare his way; then his arm made a quick beckoning gesture. Wager did not move, and the arm jerked again, commandingly. There was no one else Tony-O was looking at; Wager, trying not to feel as if his hand was still in the cookie jar, went forward.

"You've been following me all night, Wager."

"That's right."

"Did you put that guy on me this afternoon? The short, fat one?"

That would be Jesus, and it meant that at least Tony-O hadn't noticed him this morning. "Yes."

"Why?"

"Because I'm still looking for this Bernie Chavez. Because I have the feeling you didn't tell me everything about him. I want like hell to talk to him, Tony-O."

In the sliding glow of moving headlights, the old man's face seemed to double its wrinkles, and the gliding shadows masked his eyes. He glanced over his shoulder at the silent, bouncing George, and then said in a resigned voice, "All right. Let's go someplace quiet."

He led Wager around the corner and down a dark block to Twenty-eighth Avenue and a tiny brick building with a single white Budweiser sign lit over the door. Inside, the bar was a small L in one corner, and the floor was crowded with round tables and chairs; all but three were empty, and even the air smelled empty of the odor of stale beer. The middle-aged woman tending bar was glad to see someone come through the door.

"Quiet place," said Wager when they had their beers.

"Like a coffin. I don't know how they keep going."

Wager sipped.

"It sure ain't the Frontier," continued Tony-O. "I'm sorry they closed that place."

218

"Me, too."

"A lot of changes I've seen. Lately, more and more. Most of them's no good."

Wager sipped again.

"You've changed, Wager. I never thought you'd tail me. Not the old *jefe.*"

"How else do I get to Bernie Chavez?"

"You go to L.A., where he's at, goddamn it!"

"We tried that, Tony-O. We tried the L.A. police and they couldn't help us."

"So that's my fault? So you let somebody like Scorvelli go and you give me the heat?"

Wager placed his glass on the table and spoke to it as much as to the old man. "Tony-O, here's what I've got so far: I'm sure Marco was killed by Gerald Covino, not by Frank. And I'm sure that Gerald was killed because Dominick got worried about his reliability. It looks like Gerald called Dominick to ask about his brother's death, or maybe even to make a threat, and Dominick—thinking Gerald might blow up—sent somebody down to talk to him, to tell him that Dominick had nothing to do with killing Frank, to tell Gerald that they were going to get him out soon. And just incidentally to arrange for Gerald's death." He glanced at the old man. "You still with me?"

"I am. I'm not as dumb as you think, Wager."

Wager tried to push the weariness from his tone. "I know you're not, Tony-O. But I think that Gerald believed Scorvelli about not killing Frank. And I do, too—because Dominick had nothing to gain from it. In fact, until Frank was killed, things were going fine for the organization. And even afterwards, things might have stayed cool except for one thing—you told me about a link between Covino and Scorvelli. You were the one who aimed me at him, Tony-O. And the one who told you was this Bernie Chavez. Maybe Chavez

219

didn't have the whole story, and maybe he didn't have it all straight, but he had a part of it—some of what he told you fits, Tony. Now I want to find out where he got that part, and I have the feeling you haven't told me everything about him. Come on, Tony-O—the man's important."

"So important you think I'd lie to you?"

"Too important to take that chance."

"I don't lie, Wager," he said quickly. "I was a *jefe*—I don't lie." The old man drank deeply, attacking the beer, then his stiff back bent a shade and he set the glass down, to watch the bubbles rise through the pale-yellow liquid; he, too, spoke more to the glass than to his companion, and in the sepulchral stillness of the bar, it sounded like a murmured prayer. "You ever notice how the bubbles come up from one spot like there's a little hole in the glass? Out of nowhere. They just keep coming—same distance apart, same size. The string just keeps coming and you can lean your glass this way or that, and they still keep coming from that same spot like nothing's ever going to stop them. Until the glass is empty." He stared in silence, then spoke again. "Things get that way, Gabe. And you twist and turn and wiggle and it makes no difference—they just keep coming."

"What things, Tony-O?"

"You, for one thing. You just don't let up." He sipped at the foam. "You know I got a granddaughter?"

"Oh?" This was new. The man's eyes remained fixed on the tall glass; beneath the folds of thin flesh at the corners, which made them look both sleepy and sad, they were worried. "Is this Ray's daughter?" asked Wager.

"Yeah. Right."

Some time back, Tony-O's son had been given the choice between being sent to Buena Vista or joining the Marine Corps; Wager had talked to the D.A. about it, and the D.A.

had agreed. Two years after that, Ray was one of the first American advisers killed in Vietnam. Tony-O had shown Wager the medal, a Purple Heart.

"Ray got married to a real nice girl, and there was a kid six months, a year old when he was killed. That was in sixty-two."

"I remember. Anita? Was that his wife's name? She remarried a year or so later?"

"That's right. Her and her husband moved out to San Diego." Tony-O groped at a hip pocket. "Kay's the girl's name. She graduated from high school out in San Diego. Got a diploma and everything. Here's her picture."

A yearbook photograph: smooth oval face, straight black hair held back by a headband, Indian style, large black eyes. Carefully inked across one corner was "To Grampa with love, Jeannette."

"She's pretty," said Wager. "It's hard to think of Ray having a daughter that old." Tony-O's son had been three years younger than Wager.

"Yeah. It just don't seem that long ago, does it? She looks a little like Ray's mother did—my woman." He folded the wallet gently and put it back. "Anyway, about nine or ten months ago Jeannette came here and got a job. A secretary at some kind of office supply company."

"Is the name important?"

Tony-O shrugged. "Call it Smith . . . Jones. . . . Hell, I'm not sure. It's over on Eleventh, I think. It's supposed to be a big outfit. But say, Wager, don't go poking around over there—for her sake. Jeannette's."

"What harm would a few questions do?"

"I'm telling you—I'm getting there! Just give me a chance to tell you!"

Wager nodded and sipped and waited.

"I used to go over there every now and then—meet her

for lunch once or twice a week to see how she was doing."

"And?"

"I said I'm getting there! *Estoy un viejo*—have a little patience." Tony-O stretched the pause with a large mouthful of beer and a disgusted wag of his head at Wager's lack of respect for the aged. "O.K. You want to know so much. One day I go by to pick her up and who do I see but Mr. Dominick Scorvelli walking around and looking the place over like he's going to buy it."

"When was this?"

"A couple months ago. Sometime in February. So I got curious—worried—and I started asking around. I can still get some information when I want it, Wager. A lot of people still remember the old *jefe*."

"*Ya lo creo.* What'd you find out?"

"I found out I didn't want Jeannette working there. I ran into Bernie Chavez and I asked him what he'd heard about Dominick. He didn't like mouthing it around, but finally he told me about Dominick having his own brother killed and that Frank Covino pulled the trigger, and that now, with his brother out of the way, Dominick was expanding his organization."

"Weren't you curious about how Chavez knew?"

"Hell, no. Didn't I see Scorvelli going around that place? Don't I know what him and his people are like?"

"And you lost Chavez? He's not hiding somewhere here in Denver?"

"Is that what you think? I swear to the Holy Mother, Wager, he's in L.A. He went back to L.A. That is all I know about him!"

It was Wager's turn to drink slowly and to ponder. "Why didn't you tell me this to start with?"

"Because of my granddaughter! I don't want her or her name anywheres near Scorvelli's. You think he wouldn't

222

check out everybody in that place before he moved in? You think he wouldn't find out whose granddaughter she was? Suppose you let something slip—suppose you got into court and had to say where you got your information about Frank Covino. You think Scorvelli wouldn't go after her to get at me? He can do what he wants to, Wager, and not all the cops in the goddamned world can stop him."

It seemed that way. Maybe that was the thing Wager hated most about the Scorvellis: their insulation. Anything they wanted, they could take; and it seemed that the law never quite reached them. "Then why did you tell me at all?"

Tony-O's voice rose with bitterness. "I shouldn't have! I should have kept my goddamned mouth shut and played it safe. But I know how you feel about the Scorvellis, and I figured I owed you, Wager—for the way you helped Ray that time. I figured it was a debt of honor." His breath hissed in his nose for a moment or two until he was calm again. "Like those goddam bubbles . . . one thing after another, they just keep right on coming, and I'm not so young as I used to be."

"Where's your granddaughter now?"

"Back in San Diego. I gave her this crap about how I heard the business was going to fold and that's why they were thinking of selling. I made her think she'd be a lot better off in computer work in San Diego."

"Do you have her address?"

The eyes in their net of wrinkles turned to Wager. "Don't do that, Gabe. Don't go near her—don't make Scorvelli even think of her. *Por favor.* I'm asking you, Gabe. Tony-O is asking, as a favor!"

He gazed back into the old man's worried eyes at the plea he saw there. In the old days, the *jefe* did not beg; he ordered. But even if those days were gone, Wager did not feel good at hearing the note of pleading in Tony-O's voice, because his loss was Wager's, too. And what more could the girl tell him? Whatever it might be, it wouldn't be as much as this old man was worth to Wager.

"All right, Jefe."

"Gracias, hijo mio."

But Wager still didn't have Bernie Chavez, and he still did not have a killer for Frank Covino.

He dreamed of a man in a beret and a long coat. Wager stood in a line of people waiting for something and this figure came looking for him. Even among a thousand other people, Wager knew that the faceless shape in the beret and coat was looking for him and no matter who Wager hid behind or how he twisted, he would have to hold his spot in line until sooner or later the figure would see him. And it did and came straight toward him, a towering shadow that leaned forward and beckoned and opened the coat slowly to show a skull where the groin should be. The back of the skull had a hole shattered through the bone and as Wager strained away yet stared, the skull gained color and became the back of Frank Covino's head and the swarm of flies began to swirl and pull him forward into the suffocating stickiness of exploded brains until Wager heaved himself out of tangled, binding sleep with a hoarse shout.

Below his partly open bedroom window, the city was quiet with Sunday morning. From somewhere near downtown rang the wind-tossed notes of electronic chimes, and across his still-sweating skin the morning breeze brushed like a light, cool feather. It would be nice if every day were a Sunday morning. It would be nice if there were no such things as nightmares—either in the world of sleep or in the world of wake. But then it wouldn't be this world, Wager knew. Father Shannon—the short, sandy-haired priest who didn't like Hispanos or blacks—used to tell them what the world was like. Wager could remember sitting during mass

224

as a little boy, suffering through the endless Hail Marys and Creeds and Affirmations and then the even longer sermon, when the stubby priest would talk about the virtues of affliction visited on the dark corners of the soul, of the world, of humanity's skin. So the darker people had to try harder, pray harder, suffer more. Their faith would receive the stronger test, but their reward would be just as great. Which, to Wager, didn't seem quite fair. But so secretly that he didn't say it aloud even to himself, Wager was glad he was half Anglo and so would suffer only half as much. Less than the Hispanos, who teased him and called him a coyote; maybe even as little as the Anglos, who called him half-breed.

Father Shannon had told them to accept, and they did—or said they did—going to mass, observing the sacraments, confessing, and doing the penances handed out by Father Shannon or the more popular Father Richter, whose nice deep voice spoke an impressively pure Castillano that his parishioners could only half follow. But more popular or not, Father Richter, like Father Shannon, saw this world as nothing more than a mild form of Purgatory shot through, here and there, with the miraculous light of God's Love, which hinted at the glories of Heaven awaiting the faithful.

Wager had long since lost any hope of those glories, but the priests' vision of this world stayed with him.

He padded into the bathroom and woke up under a cool shower, washing away sleep, trying to wash away the chill of that nightmare but only succeeding in pushing it off toward the distant edge of consciousness. Carefully, he shaved his chin and around the thick mustache, and in the kitchen, began chopping vegetables and cheese for his favorite Marine Corps omelet. Perhaps the priests had been right, and this was a world where humanity was punished for sins unremembered and committed in some previous

225

life or on some other planet. Wager had seen enough people who tortured themselves and others as well, enough people who ripped into each other for things they did not really want and for reasons they never understood. Perhaps that perception lay at the bottom of his disgust with those who wrote or believed things like *It Was Never Me:* they expected to be born into heaven, and when they found that they weren't, they neither served what little good there was, nor offered sympathy to anyone but themselves. Parents had betrayed them or politics had betrayed them, even civilization or life itself had betrayed them, and the only thing left was to blame and whine and write books for other whiners.

Rinsing his dish and stacking it in the small washer, he poured another cup of twice-boiled coffee and, before remembering, started planning on an afternoon of Sunday eating and drinking in the expanse of the Frontier's half-empty dining room. But there would be no more of those. And he remembered something else: he had promised to have supper with Max and his wife. That really was not what he wanted to do; he could barely stomach the occasional family meals at his mother's, with their echoes of old conflict and their tangles of promises assumed, and unvoiced accusations for failures to heed those promises. No one ever said "I told you so"—except his sister, of course—but the phrase lay just behind their conversations, and the more they realized that it no longer made a difference to Wager, the closer it came to expression. But Max's dinner would be different. Max's dinner would have to be different because he wasn't family, and besides, it was too late for Wager to call and back out. Wager told himself that there would be none of those threads of feeling and implication that defined a family meal, and he told himself there was a good possibility he could go there and enjoy it. As he gazed at the clean morning light bringing the mountains sharp and close to Denver's western edge, Wager could really believe in the possibility of enjoying that dinner.

The telephone pulled him in from the balcony and the book on fur trappers, which he had picked up again. It was Jesus.

"Holy shit, Gabe. Why didn't you tell me that Tony-O had me spotted? I thought that old man was going to kick the crap out of me!"

"What happened?"

"Well, I got the wife and kids off to mass this morning and figured I'd go by his place and sit there awhile. Out he comes, and I follow him maybe half a block and then he turns right around and marches up to me like he's in a parade or something, and says if I don't quit stepping on his shadow he's going to fix it so I don't step anywhere any more. He meant it, too, *hombre!* He didn't have much good to say about you, either."

Wager sighed. "I don't guess he did." He had done it now. Another screw-up, and as far as Tony-O was concerned, Wager's name belonged on urinal walls—low, near the floor, where it would get splashed on. "I should have called you last night, Jesus. He picked you up yesterday afternoon and he spotted me last night. I should have called you." Now there would be more apologies—if the old man would even let Wager get close enough to mouth them. Because he would think that Wager, by keeping Jesus on him, had called him a liar; and the chances were good that the *jefe* would take no apologies at all.

"Well, I sure left him alone. I mean, there was no sense me hanging on after that, right?"

"That's so, Jesus. It was my fault, not yours."

"Yeah, well, I guess everybody screws the goose sometime. I know I do once in a while. But not too often. Say, you remember Nihisi—the guy Tony-O met at the Foxtail?"

"Yes."

"His address is 950 East Fourteenth. It was in the phone book and I went over and asked around, and it's the same dude I know, all right. And the other guy—this Anglo—his name's Arnie Alquist. I don't know where he lives, but I got where he works."

Life's little surprises! "Where's that?"

"Let's see. . . . I got it written down here. . . . Information Resources Corporation. The Columbine Building on Seventeenth. Room 1008."

"Who told you this, Jesus?"

"Well, after Tony-O landed on me with both feet like that, I got to thinking about it and it made me pissed, you know? I mean, it's a free country; I got a right to walk down the street just like he does, right? Anyway, I went back to the Foxtail and asked the bartender about those guys. He had a business card that this Alquist guy gave him."

"Why'd he give the bartender a card?"

"I told you, *hombre.* That place is for queers, but they got strict rules—no feelies, one at a time in the crapper, things like that. They don't want to get busted, so everything's kept real polite, you know? Anyway, people are always asking the bartender, 'Who's this guy?' 'Who's that guy?' and he kind of runs a dating service. He thought I was—you know—one of them. But guess what that son of a bitch said? He said I shouldn't bother; I'm not Alquist's type, he said. Hell, I don't want to be his type, but the son of a bitch didn't have to say something like that, did he?"

In the early afternoon, the glare of the sun drove Wager from his small balcony, and he once more gave up on the fur trappers, who by now had moved into the Columbia River

228

system and were dueling with the British. But the sun wasn't the real cause. It was as if he had not fully wakened from that nightmare of a skull flasher, with its lingering unease. An unease amplified by the thought of Tony-O's anger, by the feeling of loose threads that he had not yet tugged. Finally, he made up his mind and went to the telephone to call Records and ask for vital statistics—the name of the man who married Anita Ojala sometime between 1962 and 1964. After leaving Jesus for Tony-O to find this morning, he wouldn't get in any worse with the old man for talking to his granddaughter.

The police person said it would take a while because it was Sunday, and she was right. Almost two hours passed before she called back. "An Anita Rodriguez Ojala married Llewellyn D. Rogers on September 11, 1963. We've only got two other Ojalas being married during those years, Detective Wager. And none of them an Anita. It's not a very common name, is it?"

Wager agreed that it wasn't and then asked her to find out if the San Diego police could provide a telephone number or address for Llewellyn and Anita Rogers. That request took less time, but when the police person called back, she apologized anyway. "They didn't live right in San Diego, Detective Wager. It's near Chula Vista, and the number's area 714-792-2528."

The number rang three times and a girl answered; Wager asked for Jeannette.

"This is she." The puzzled tone said she did not recognize the caller's voice.

"I'm Detective Wager of the Denver Police Department, miss. Are you the granddaughter of Antonio Ojala?"

"Yes! Has something happened to him?"

"No, ma'am. He's fine. Did you work in Denver not too long ago?"

"Yes."

"We're trying to find an acquaintance of your grandfather, a Bernie Chavez. Did he ever mention that name to you?"

"Chavez? Gee, not that I remember. I didn't see Gramps too often, though."

"Didn't he visit you regularly at the office supply place?"

"Office supply? I didn't work at an office supply place. Boy, Gramps sure gets things mixed up!"

"Where did you work?"

"At Information Resources Corporation. The same people I work for now. They had a computer operator's job here, so I moved back."

Wager yanked his notebook from his shirt pocket and turned to the last entry to verify what he already knew. "Was that in the Columbine Building?"

"Yes. Right downtown, smog and all."

"Didn't your grandfather visit you there?"

"Once or twice. But that's all, because the boss didn't like people coming to the office. We have a lot of regulations like that."

"What kind of business does the corporation do?"

A tinge of caution came into her voice. "It's a big company —kind of new. We store and retrieve information from companies and agencies all over the world. A lot of it's general, but it's never been centralized before, and we have these special indexes designed for quick retrieval. Anybody anywhere in the world can call up and get what they want to know."

"Does the company handle confidential stuff?"

"Sure. But you have to have a coded clearance to call for that. That's the Special Section, and I don't know much about that. I think it's mostly research and development information, financial information, that kind of material. I'm sure the

230

sales staff could tell you a lot more about that than I can."

And where there was a need for secrecy and codes, there was an opportunity for someone to make money. Possibly very much money. "I guess some of the companies using the service are pretty big."

"Oh, sure! But we have a lot of smaller companies, too, that don't want to spend the money on equipment and programming. If they get big enough and want to set up their own retrieval system, they can buy their tapes from us, but most don't."

"Have you heard any talk of the company changing ownership?"

"Well, Gramps mentioned something once—he asked me about it, anyway. And I've heard some talk out here. But I'm sure that's all it is."

"I think I know somebody who works for I.R.C.—Arnie Alquist. Did you know him?"

"Mr. Alquist? He was in the Special Section. I don't know him very well, but he seemed like a nice man."

Wager took a soft, deep breath like a man slipping into ice water. "How about somebody else: Dominick Scorvelli? Did your grandfather ever mention his name?"

"No. All we really talked about was my job and how I was doing and so on. Gramps was real interested in me and my work, and that's what we talked about. He's a swell old man, and I'm glad I got to know him."

"Yes, ma'am."

After he hung up, Wager spent a long time sitting and thinking. Gradually, the hot sunshine moved across his carpet to sweep toward the apartment's door. Wager noted it, and knew what it meant, but he was still reluctantly fitting together what bits and pieces were left, turning his facts from one side to another, linking possibilities into categories of most and least likely. And the picture that he kept building was the one he least wanted to see. But it was the only one that explained a lot of things.

The sunlight burned fully through the balcony doors against his legs and finally nudged him to his feet. But the heat was not strong enough to thaw the chill that had started to spread through his chest when Jeannette told him that she worked for Information Resources Corporation.

sixteen

Under the weight of the midafternoon sun, upper Larimer Street was empty. The only other time of day when fewer people dotted the sidewalks was just before dawn, as night's clamor of music and voices thinned to an occasional cry or the scuff of a weary shoe searching out a hole for sleeping. Even the automobile traffic was light and unhurried as Wager steered his Trans Am against the curb a block above Tony-O's small house. He walked through the familiar litter of the narrow alley that ran past private parking lots, shuttered delivery doors, and the occasional sagging garage that marked the surviving homes. Halfway down the alley, he found the one belonging to Tony-O's house; like the others, it seemed too narrow for cars built after 1945, but he cupped his hand to shield the glare from a small pane in the web-hung window of the padlocked door. The bulk of an automobile was jammed into the gloom of the shed, but it was too dim to make out the model. Glancing up and down the sun-filled alley, Wager quickly fitted the rippled blade of his pick into the old padlock and nudged the tumblers into place. A moment later it sprang loose with a tiny squeak. He swung one of the heavy wooden doors partially open, its rusty hinges chattering, to let the sunlight glint off the old-fashioned angles and chrome of a 1959 Buick Le Sabre. The wide fins of the rear deck spread out over the wheels like a billowing cape or the half-lifted wings of a beetle; leaning his weight on the tip of one, he pressed gently, and a raw groan came from some greaseless joint beneath the heavy car. So Whistles had been right after all, it was a car that squeaked, a car with "wings." And Wager, too, had been right: it was a car that Tony-O had access to. Noting the license number, he relocked the wooden doors and walked slowly up the alley to his Trans Am. He radioed for a license check, and the answer came back quickly: "Registered to George Foster, 2263 Larimer Street, City-County Denver."

"Ten-four."

He cruised past the front of the house, debating; but instead of stopping, he first went another two blocks to an empty telephone booth and called Chief Doyle. His wife answered and said, "He'll be right here," and then the Bulldog, voice guarding his Sunday afternoon, was on the line. "What is it, Wager?"

"I need to know what kind of new business Dominick is setting up."

"I told you to drop that."

"It's important, Chief. It has a direct bearing on the Frank Covino shooting."

"You got a suspect?"

"I'm pretty sure," said Wager cautiously. "But I don't have anything yet that will justify a warrant."

" 'Pretty sure' doesn't buy it, Wager. You bring me something definite and I might rethink my position. As it stands now, things are the same—you will stay the hell away from sensitive areas. You understand that?"

"Yessir."

"Then, by God, do it!"

But Wager didn't. When you were this close, you wanted it all. You wanted every possibility checked and accounted for. You wanted to dig your fingers down into the muck as far as you could reach and work out every root of the thing, pulling it into the light until the whole tangled wad lay exposed and drying in the sun. He slid two dimes into the slot and called Sonnenberg. The inspector himself answered, in his crisp manner, and did not seem overjoyed to hear Wager's name or what he wanted.

"I went over that with you and with Doyle, Wager. I had hoped we'd reached a very clear understanding. I had also hoped Chief Doyle told you to back off."

"He did," said Wager. "I'm doing this on my own, and I'm not going near Dominick. What I need is verification for the suspect's motive." He added something else before Sonnenberg could say no. "And I'm willing to trade."

"Trade what?"

"The name of the man with Dominick when we busted him at the Lake Como last week."

"A man? You should have told me about that before, Wager. It was your duty to tell me then."

"I was ordered to keep my mouth shut about the whole case, Inspector. So I did." Besides, Wager hadn't wanted anything at the time.

"Wager . . ."

He spoke slowly and clearly. "Is Dominick planning to take over the Information Resources Corporation?"

"Where in hell did you hear that!" Sonnenberg used one of his rare swear words, and Wager had his verification. "You will tell me, you hear? Just exactly where did you get that information, Wager?"

"While chasing down a suspect on the Covino case."

"That better not be Dominick Scorvelli!"

"It's not. It's somebody who's trying to set up his own network in the company. It's somebody who got wind of Dominick's idea, and liked it, and decided to move in first. I think he killed Frank Covino and tried to lead us to Dominick, so the Scorvelli organization would be under too much pressure to raise the capital it needs to buy into Information Resources."

"My God . . ." Sonnenberg's voice dropped to a tense and level note. "Exactly what have you run across, Wager?"

"Nothing to go into court with. But I know what I'm talking about."

"Yes. You would. I have a lot of respect for your work." The voice died away, and Wager, glancing at his watch, dropped another coin into the telephone. Sonnenberg's voice came back with a weight of weariness. "How much do you think Dominick knows of this?"

"I don't think he knows too much yet. Maybe nothing."

"Oh?"

"The suspect is trying to penetrate the company, not buy it out; he can't afford anything like that right now. He just sees a way to make a lot of money with very little invested —provided he can push Dominick out of the picture somehow. If Dominick stays in, the suspect is going to have real problems; he doesn't have the muscle to protect his people at all. If Dominick ever gets a hint of what's going on, he'll pick the suspect's people out of that company like raisins out of a pudding."

"I see." A pause. "This suspect is still pursuing that plan of action?"

"Well . . . he's still alive."

"Ah. Of course." The silence at the other end of the line meant that Sonnenberg's operation, too, was still alive. "If Scorvelli does get frightened away from that company, it could mean months—even years—before he again tried anything as ambitious."

"Yessir."

"Our man could lose his opportunity. Our whole operation would be wiped out. But if Dominick *doesn't* find out about the activities of your suspect . . ." Sonnenberg shifted from thought to action. "How soon are you going to arrest Covino's murderer? Can you keep the suspect's motive out of it? Let me know immediately the name of the prosecutor on the case!"

"It's not that easy, Inspector." Wager didn't want to sound antagonistic; just factual. "All the evidence I have is circumstantial. And weak."

"You mean that if you go to court, you will need a strong argument on his motive?"

"Yessir, that's it."

"We can't do that, Gabe." Sonnenberg's voice rose with urgency. "I know it's asking a lot, but we can't have that. If you can get the evidence without opening up the question of motive, for God's sake do it. If you can't, you'll just have to sit tight. We'll have to hold our breath and hope that your suspect doesn't scare off Dominick before he makes his move and puts our man in. I know it sounds rotten, Gabe, but there's too much at stake. There's much more at stake than one unsolved murder."

And for Wager himself, more than Sonnenberg knew. "I'll do what I can."

"I knew you'd see it that way, Gabe! Thanks. Say, who was the man at the Lake Como when you arrested Dominick?"

"Vittorio Galente."

Sonnenberg half laughed with relief. "That we already knew!"

"I figure he's the bankroller from Chicago, right?"

"Thanks for calling, Gabe; and thanks again for your cooperation." The line clicked dead.

Wager had a quiet beer and then another in a cool and almost empty tavern near the lower edge of Little Juarez. Slowly turning one page after another of his green notebook, he reshuffled the thoughts associated with the entries, and then he redealt them, and they still came out the same. While he read and thought, customers began to mosey in one by one, rubbing sleep from crusted lids or eying the bartender hopefully for a free one to get them started for the day. Siesta time was ending; Wager drained his glass and set a bill beside it and nodded good-bye to the bartender, who tried to yawn and smile thanks at the same time. Out on the open sidewalk, the heat seemed worse, and Wager felt a film of beer sweat spring out across his back before the hot breeze evaporated it with a single gust. He walked up to Tony-O's house and found him and George in the dark shade of the porch, each holding a glass of iced tea.

"Buenas tardes, Jefe."

The old man's head bobbed curtly. "Here's the man who calls me Jefe, but who sets dogs at my heels."

Wager sat on the edge of the porch and leaned against the cracked paint of the wooden roof post. "A good liar keeps as close to the truth as possible, Jefe. And you are very, very good. But you gave me more truth than you should have."

Tony-O's reaction was not anger but sudden caution. He

238

held his tongue and waited, and so did Wager, listening to the rhythmic squeak of George's metal chair.

"I called your granddaughter."

At last he said, "I asked you not to do that. You promised me you wouldn't drag my granddaughter into this, Wager."

"I was looking for Bernie Chavez, Tony-O. But I didn't find him. I don't think I ever will. I did find out where your granddaughter worked, though."

"Meaning?"

"Meaning that I began to wonder why you put me on Scorvelli. Meaning that I found out. Meaning that I know how you did it. You had a beer with me, and you told me about Frank Covino; then you went looking for that kid." He tried to keep his voice calm; he tried and almost prevented the anger from quivering his words. "You gave him some story—a friend in trouble, maybe something about his brother—to get him over to that warehouse. Then you wasted him. As easy as that, you wasted him." Wager cleared the cramped feeling in his chest with a deep breath. "You used the both of us, Jefe. You used that boy for bait. And you used me for a hound."

Tony-O squinted against the hot glare at Wager, the wrinkles of his face a net of lines that seemed on the verge of smiling or frowning, of looking stern, or kindly, or calm. But no definite expression came through. "You going to serve a warrant?"

Wager said nothing.

Tony-O's mouth stretched into a tight smile. "You can't do that, can you, Wager? If you had any evidence, you wouldn't be sitting here talking about it. You got nothing but guesses—and they're all wrong. Every goddamned one of them I deny, and you just try to prove any different! I know you, Wager; I know you inside and out, and like they say, it's not the size of your tool, it's how you use it. *Buenas tardes, hijo mio*—you're trespassing on my porch!"

In the near distance over the awakening rush of late-afternoon traffic, a fire siren wailed into a high note. George stopped bouncing and cocked his head. "Station Five!" he said. "There goes Station Five."

seventeen

Polly Axton's nice dinner was a disaster. The four of them sat at a small, candlelit table, Max and his wife, Wager, and —across from him—a girl named Kathy. In her late twenties, she was, as Polly had whispered to Wager when he arrived, a very sweet girl. And, Wager had to admit, she was. A bit smaller in the chest than he liked them, though she had a nicely proportioned body and, as if measured to fit, was an inch or so shorter than Wager himself. Her face had regular features that, with a smile, were almost pretty. If she was looking for a husband, she didn't seem anxious about it; in those moments when a repeated question or remark from Polly pulled Wager from one of his long silences, he found Kathy half smiling at him as if he were another person caught in a summer shower without an umbrella.

As the candles grew shorter and the dinner grew longer, Polly's conversation went through three stages; and the casserole, something she was very proud of, cooled on the plate

241

in front of a brooding Wager. First she spoke with quick excitement and eagerness about Kathy's fascinating job as a trade journal editor and about Wager's fascinating career in the organized crime unit. Then she began asking questions concerning the things Wager and Kathy might talk together about—hiking, music, books, sports. Neither was interested in a comparison of classical versus popular bagpipe music, and for some perverse reason Max didn't want to pursue that topic, either. Finally, she lapsed into an apologetic and forced chatter with Kathy and her husband, which was ended only when Kathy said, "I'll help you clear the table," and the two of them disappeared into the kitchen with the relief of nervous laughter.

Max, completely unaware of his wife's anxiety, stretched and pushed back from the table as he stifled a yawn and led Wager into the living room for an after-dinner drink. From some far corner of the house, a television set murmured, and Axton's daughter, hands full of dirty paper plates, peeked shyly into the living room on her way to the kitchen. Axton handed Wager a small glass of Drambuie and poured one for himself. "Nice girl, Kathy—a cousin of one of Polly's friends at church."

"Things have fallen into place on the Frank Covino murder," said Wager.

Axton stopped pouring. "You found Bernie Chavez?"

"There is no Bernie Chavez."

Max turned back to the bar and slowly plinked ice cubes into a glass for his wife. "Then where did Tony-O get the information he gave you?"

Wager didn't reply immediately; instead, he touched his lips to the liqueur. Then, as if repeating something he had recently read and still could not quite believe, he placed each word precisely, like chips of glass in a mosaic, and told Max all about it.

Max considered for a long time before he finally spoke. "This Arnie Alquist—the one who worked for Information Resources. He was going to be Tony-O's plant in the confidential section?"

"Yes. I figure he and Tom Nihisi came up with the idea. But they needed someone with marketing contacts, so Nihisi went to Tony-O. Or else Tony-O ran across Nihisi God-knows-where and found out about Alquist at about the same time that he learned about Dominick and Information Resources; the old man knows a lot of different people, and they all talk to him. Either way, things fell together for him, and Tony-O saw a chance to get back on top."

Axton whistled in a quiet, ragged way between his teeth. "And that's why Tony-O told you about Frank—he'd heard just enough somewhere to link Covino to the Marco Scorvelli killing. But Gerald was in jail and he couldn't get to him, so he had to settle for that poor son of a bitch Frank."

"Maybe he thought Frank really did it. Whichever, his purpose was to aim me at Dominick."

"He sure did it. We ran after him." Axton's large head wagged slowly from side to side. "Lord God, did we run after him!"

Wager gazed through the half-pulled drapes of the living room's picture window toward the night beyond. From the kitchen, Polly's high-pitched voice had gradually dropped to a calmer murmur and there were occasional giggles of woman laughter as she and Kathy talked and cleaned dishes. Tony-O had told Wager he could read him like a book, and the old man was right; he gave Wager just enough to start him off, then sat back to watch a real professional go to work. A cop who took a lot of pride in doing things the right way —who spent his life tracing out leads that other cops would ignore. Which is what made a few other cops only almost as good as Wager—and what made Wager think it was all worth the effort. Tony-O had used that. That, and the old times. Remember the old days, a little sympathy for the old *jefe;* how about a beer at the old Frontier and a stroll down memory lane. Used. No better than one of his own goddamned snitches; no better than Fat Willy or fawning Jesus.

The window glass threw back Wager's dark outline against the bright reflection of the living room, and at the same time, his shadow let in the dim outside lights, revealed the dark behind the mirrored room. A paradox of light where there should be darkness, dark where there should be light. And the paradox that he had done his best work for the wrong reason—and only through accident had discovered it. If that was fate, then it was far more malignant than he had imagined, going beyond the distortion of external values—his marriage, his family, his history—which he had already given up on, to attack the only value that remained, the internal one that structured his relation with himself: his sense of serving well.

Axton had been whistling again, the tiny wavering tune noticeable only when he stopped. "Let's go get that bastard, Gabe. Let's go get him right now."

"Fine. What do you use for evidence?"

"The kid at the movie theater—he saw Tony pick up Frank."

"He saw a coat and hat. Not a face."

Max poured straight soda water into a glass of ice and gulped at it, cracking a cube between his teeth so that its muffled splintering was loud in the room. "How about the bum, Whistles? He saw the car." Then he answered his own question. "No—from what you told me, he'd never make it through cross-examination." Snapping his fingers, Axton grinned, his heavy jaw pushing out like a sliding drawer. "Laboratory tests! Fred Baird said that if we found a suspect, he could match the clothing to the environment!"

244

"Tony-O lives about eight blocks from the crime scene, and he wanders all over that area. Any trace material would be easy to explain."

Axton splintered another ice cube. "So every bit of it's circumstantial."

Which was the worst kind of evidence, especially in a murder trial, where jurors tended to be cautious. And there was something else, too: "Don't forget Sonnenberg's operation."

"Yeah. There is that. And Tony-O won't have trouble coming up with an alibi, either."

Wager couldn't stifle all the bitterness. "That's right—he was a *jefe;* people will help him out."

Polly and Kathy came in from the kitchen, Axton's wife ready to try again with an eager, "Well, now! I hope you two haven't been talking police business!"

Neither Wager nor Axton answered, their thoughts still chipping and prying on the rough fact of Tony-O.

"Would you boys like to challenge the girls in bridge?" Polly looked hard at her husband, who seemed to be gazing somewhere beyond his nose. "Scrabble?"

After a pause that seemed a lot longer than it was, Kathy patted Polly's hand and said she had a very early conference in the morning and really had to go, that she enjoyed meeting Detective Wager and hoped they saw each other again sometime. Wager answered something, and a few minutes after Kathy left, Polly said an extravagantly polite good night to Wager and went to bed with a headache.

Axton poured himself another drink; Wager shook his head no to the lifted bottle. "You really are sure you want to do this?" the big man asked.

"I'm sure."

"It's a wrong move, partner."

Wager didn't bother to answer. There were a lot of rights and wrongs that traded places back and forth, and then there were a few that never changed. But not everyone held to the same few. What Wager chose, Max didn't, and it wasn't open to argument any more.

"You realize what can happen if anyone gets a whisper of this?"

"Yes." Though that wasn't something he worried about; that was simply a part of the landscape now.

"Both Marco and Frank will go on the statistics as unsolved cases, Gabe. Doyle won't like that a bit."

Wager's silence told him where Doyle could shove his statistics.

Axton's restraint finally cracked. "Wager, God damn it, how can you do it?"

It was a nasty, smelly little job, like scraping shit from a shoe, but he would do it. "Easy."

Axton lapsed into silence and pulled at his drink, the bare ice cubes making a high-pitched rattle as he set the glass down. "Gabe—partner—there's no statute of limitations on homicide. Let the law work the way it should. Don't do it this way."

"Sonnenberg's operation could take years to complete. This is the right way."

"It is not, goddamn it. You're a cop, and a good one. Good cops don't create violence; they prevent it!"

"I'm not asking for help, Max."

"Ah, shit." Axton's thick fingers wriggled as if the table he leaned on were burning to the touch. "You're my partner, Gabe, and a good one. We work well together, and we both know how seldom that happens. But after this, I don't know. I just don't know if I can call somebody 'partner' who goes outside the law."

Wager had not counted on losing that; but if that's what

246

it cost, then that, too, would be paid. The sooner the better. "I ought to be going. He'll be there by now."

"I said I'd back you up with Scorvelli."

"I'll go by myself. If something does leak out, you won't know a thing about it."

"I said I'd go."

"Max, I don't want you to. I don't want you going with me any further."

Axton looked at him for a long time and finally spoke without heat. "It's the wrong move, Gabe. And you know Scorvelli won't go for it; you'll just be wasting your time."

"Tell your wife the dinner was good and that I enjoyed meeting Kathy."

"Sure."

Wager parked across Federal Avenue from the Lake Como restaurant and walked toward the parking apron that surrounded the dumpy building. The curtained front door was open to the cool night, and as he pushed through, he smelled the warm odor of freshly brewed coffee.

The quiet talk and laughter faded, the lounging figures on bar stools and around the booths stiffened. Henry, wearing another denim leisure suit and a broad collar open at the neck, rose out of a booth, his glance checking the mirror behind the bar, which showed the empty doorway and its black curtain undisturbed. "What the hell you want, cop?"

Dominick was at his usual rear booth, cigar halfway to his mouth; Wet Dick stretched his head around the seat back and muttered "Shitbird" as Wager pressed the fingertips of both hands gently against Henry's chest.

"Hey—"

"My business is with Dominick."

Henry's angry face started to say something.

"Don't fuck up, Henry—better see what Dominick says."

247

The young man glanced over his shoulder and Wager saw Scorvelli half nod. He shoved Henry's awkwardly twisted body aside and went to the rear booth.

Scorvelli asked flatly, "What are you here for, Wager?"

"I've got some questions for you. Let's go outside."

"I want to see your warrant."

"If I get a warrant, I'll have to book you. That means hauling Counselor Freiberg out of bed and wasting a lot of time with paper work down at headquarters. You know how slow things can move on Sunday nights."

"You got something to say, you can say it here."

Wager shook his head. "What I have to say you might not want on your tape recorder."

Scorvelli's brown eyes, alert beneath his bushy eyebrows, blinked to hide surprise and a wary interest. "You got some kind of proposition for me?"

"Just a few questions that only you might want to hear."

The bright eyes studied Wager's, then Scorvelli scraped a feather of ash from his cigar and slid out of the booth. "Henry," he said to the bodyguard, "you come along."

"Yessir, Mr. Scorvelli."

Dominick led Wager through the kitchen to the back door, pausing to let Henry go out first. After the bodyguard looked around briefly, Dominick ushered Wager into the dimmest corner of the parking lot. "You carrying a body plug, Wager?"

Without answering, Wager raised his arms. Henry roughly patted him down, searching for a transmitter, and then shook his head. "He's got his piece is all, Mr. Scorvelli. You want me to take that?"

Scorvelli shook his head and Wager said, "Your turn."

"What?"

"You want privacy—so do I, Scorvelli." He quickly ran his hands over the older man's body and legs. "Stand over there," he told Henry. "This is grown-up talk."

Henry did not move until Scorvelli nodded again. "All right, Wager. What's these questions?"

"Suppose someone laid a murder at your door?"

"What murder?"

"Just a kid—just somebody who was wasted in order to frame you."

"The law would protect the innocent, right? And justice would triumph."

"Suppose it didn't? Suppose the guy who arranged all this was smarter than the cop working on the case?"

"If that cop was you, I'd say it's a good possibility, Wager."

"Where does that leave you?"

Scorvelli puffed on the cigar and shot a stream of smoke into the chill night air. "It leaves me wondering just what the hell you're after. It leaves me wondering just what the hell you mean, because I don't know of any murders laid against me."

"Tony Ojala—Tony-O—told me you were behind the Frank Covino killing."

"That so?" Another deep puff. "Well, it's plain you didn't believe him. People say a lot of things about me, and most of them's lies."

"Why would Ojala do this?"

A shrug. "I don't know. Ask him."

"I did. But I don't have the leverage to make him talk yet. Like I said, Scorvelli, he's a very smart man. Maybe smarter than you, and he knows something. Right now, I don't have a thing I can take him into court on. But I found out that he's the one who killed Frank. What I don't know is why he wanted me to think you did it."

"Maybe he needed an alibi, Wager. People who commit murder generally need an alibi."

"I get the feeling it's something more. Something bigger. I was hoping you could tell me."

Scorvelli flipped the long cigar butt across the gravel in a bounce of scattered sparks, then pulled another from his vest pocket and slipped it out of its metal tube and cedar wrap. Deliberately, he fitted a cigar snipper over the end. The blade of the snipper clicked sharply. "I don't know."

"If Tony-O gets away with it, it'll be all over the street that he did a number and a half on Count Dominick Scorvelli."

Scorvelli's eyes laughed coldly. "You're trying to get me to handle your work for you, right, Wager?"

"I'm trying to find out why he'd want to do that to you. If you won't tell me, I'll keep working on him. Sooner or later, he's going to let something slip. Sooner or later, I'm going to find out, and then I'll have him."

"The world is full of sooner or later, Wager. And a lot of things people sweat over never happen. You've had your questions, cop, and my heart bleeds that I can't help you. Now take off." He strode into the kitchen door, Henry close behind him.

Wager turned, his shoes crackling dryly in the gravel of the parking apron. When, earlier, he had told Max what he was planning, one of Axton's first questions had been, "Do you think Scorvelli would do it?"

"What choice will he have?" Wager asked.

Max, upset at the idea, said, "It's almost like lynch law. It's like going back to lynch law."

And Wager asked, "What choice do I have?"

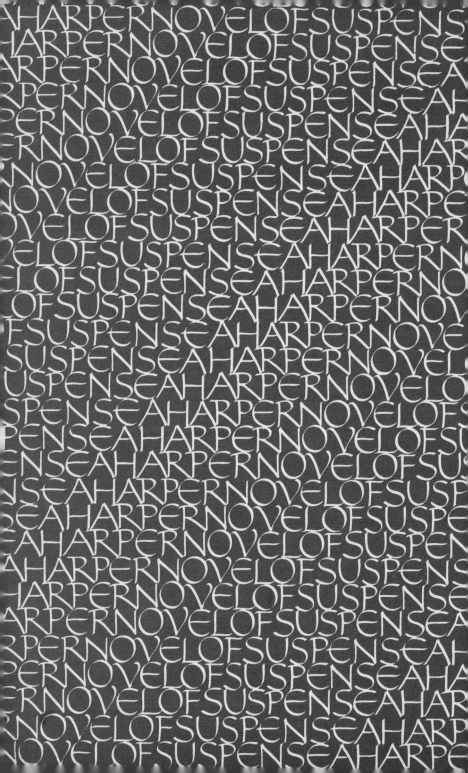